P9-DFY-412

Hungry Death

In the middle of the white nimbus, as if in a robe of white fox fur, was the piquant, sanguine form of Roxane, Death's Queen.

Randal wanted to rush forward, to put himself between the Nisibisi witch and his archmage, but his limbs wouldn't obey him.

Before his eyes, the archmage's robes caught fire. Beyond the smoke, only the witch's smile was visible—her red lips, her white teeth, her darting tongue.

The smoke from the archmage, whose moans were horrible and whose flesh was beginning to stink, was drawn into that smiling mouth, which worked as if chewing a delectable delight.

The tongue licked up the last wisps of smoke; the velvet voice said, "Thank you, Randal, for the snack. Next time, bring me a younger offering . . ."

Don't miss these other exciting tales of Sanctuary: the meanest, seediest, most dangerous town in all the worlds of fantasy. . . .

THIEVES' WORLD
(Stories by Asprin, Abbey, Anderson, Bradley, Brunner, DeWees, Haldeman, and Offutt)

TALES FROM THE VULGAR UNICORN
(Stories by Asprin, Abbey, Drake, Farmer, Morris, Offutt, and van Vogt)

SHADOWS OF SANCTUARY
(Stories by Asprin, Abbey, Cherryh, McIntyre, Morris, Offutt, and Paxson)

STORM SEASON
(Stories by Asprin, Abbey, Cherryh, Morris, Offutt, and Paxson)

THE FACE OF CHAOS
(Stories by Asprin, Abbey, Cherryh, Drake, Morris, and Paxson)

WINGS OF OMEN
(Stories by Asprin, Abbey, Bailey, Cherryh, Duane, Chris and Janet Morris, Offutt, and Paxson)

THE DEAD OF WINTER
(Stories by Asprin, Abbey, Bailey, Cherryh, Duane, Morris, Offutt, and Paxson)

SOUL OF THE CITY
(Stories by Abbey, Cherryh, and Morris)

BLOOD TIES
(Stories by Asprin, Abbey, Bailey, Cherryh, Duane, Chris and Janet Morris, Andrew and Jodie Offutt, and Paxson)

BEYOND WIZARDWALL

JANET MORRIS

ACE FANTASY BOOKS
NEW YORK

This is a work of fiction. All the characters and events portrayed in this book are fictional, and any resemblance to real people or incidents is purely coincidental.

This Ace Fantasy Book contains the complete text of the original hardcover edition. It has been completely reset in a typeface designed for easy reading and was printed from new film.

BEYOND WIZARDWALL

An Ace Fantasy Book / published by arrangement with the author

PRINTING HISTORY
Baen Books edition / June 1986
Ace Fantasy edition / May 1987

All rights reserved.
Copyright © 1986 by Paradise Productions.
Cover art by Gary Ruddell.
This book may not be reproduced in whole or in part,
by mimeograph or any other means, without permission.
For information address: The Berkley Publishing Group,
200 Madison Avenue, New York, New York 10016.

ISBN: 0-441-05722-5

''THIEVES' WORLD'' and ''SANCTUARY'' are trademarks belonging to Robert Lynn Asprin and Lynn Abbey.

Ace Fantasy Books are published by The Berkley Publishing Group,
200 Madison Avenue, New York, New York 10016.

PRINTED IN THE UNITED STATES OF AMERICA

Book One:

TOKEN OF THE GOD

The young officer's face was shiny with sweat, his eyes closed, his back against the stallboards. In his lap lay the head of his pregnant sorrel mare, exhausted and blowing hard from her long labor.

The straw around them was fouled from her water and scattered from her struggles, but the Trôs foal she carried remained unborn.

Niko's mare wouldn't let anyone else in the stall with her and Niko was no closer to grabbing the unborn foal's hooves and pulling it from her womb than he'd been before nightfall.

Outside a snowstorm raged but, in the stall, mare and master were hot and thirsty. He'd been drunk when one of the Stepsons from his unit had come to fetch him at Brother Bomba's in Peace Falls—as drunk and drugged as he could manage, keeping his thoughts at bay.

Heavy snows had put the war against Mygdonia and its Nisibisi wizards into hiatus; magic had been employed by Niko's commander, Tempus, to bring his mixed cadre of shock troops (Rankan 3rd Commando rangers, Tysian "specials," guerrilla hillmen of Free Nisibis, and Niko's own unit of Stepsons) back to Tyse for the winter. Though the fighting had ended inconclusively, with the Mygdonian warlord Ajami still at large, Tempus's joint forces had

1

declared themselves victorious—they'd won the battle, if not the war. They'd ridden through a tunnel of cloud and into Tyse triumphant and had settled down to wait for spring, content, all but for Niko, with the season's work.

But then, no other fighter in the Stepsons had Niko's problems: he was the only member of its core group of Sacred Band pairs who had a wizard for a partner, a witch for an enemy, and a dream lord after his very soul.

He hoped his mare's plight wasn't a matter of magical intervention, some reflection of the accursed luck that had dogged him ever since he'd joined Tempus's private army. He couldn't bear it if her suffering turned out to be his fault.

All Niko had left which mattered to him was this mare, who looked up at him from anguished, exhausted eyes that still were trusting: she expected him to be able to save her.

Full of despair, he rubbed her muzzle, then scratched a favorite spot under her jaw. He couldn't do much more than sit with her until she died. He couldn't help her; he couldn't even help himself.

Suddenly she shuddered and started thrashing. He tried to hold her head. She was tearing herself up inside; the foal was in breech. The vet had told him to put her out of her misery, hopeful of saving the foal, which was half Trôs horse and worth more than its mother.

But he couldn't do it. He couldn't walk away and let someone else do it either. The remnants of honorbond within him, reduced to that between man and horse, wouldn't allow him to sacrifice the sorrel mare, all he had left from his life before he'd joined the Stepsons.

And he couldn't hold her, couldn't even keep her from hurting herself. He watched helplessly, his eyes filled with tears, as she groaned and bit herself, then sank back, exhausted, blowing hard through distended nostrils.

He could save her, if he went crawling to the mageguild and begged his estranged partner, Randal the Tysian wizard, to help him. He could probably make it there in time.

The storm outside was winter's last; he could take one of his commander's uncannily powerful Askelonian horses and ride down across the Nisibisi border into Tyse, find Randal, and trade the last bit of his self-esteem for the sorrel mare's life.

Even if it didn't work, if he couldn't reach the mageguild in time, he'd be out of here—he wouldn't have to watch her die.

The mare twitched weakly, gave a long, sighing snort, and rolled her eyes at him pleadingly. She was soaked in sweat and so was he.

"It'll be all right," he lied to her. Her ears pricked at the sound of his voice.

Digging with trembling fingers in his beltpouch, he found his drugs and sniffed the last of his krrf. It wasn't going to make him feel any better, he knew, but it would give him the energy to do the cowardly thing and get the hell out of here before he broke down in tears.

As the drug seeped from his nose into his brain, he got his legs under him and pushed himself up. The mare was watching him as he sidled toward the door, so he said, "You just rest. I'm going to get help. I'll be right back . . ."

Outside the stall, he closed its door and leaned his forehead on it, swearing softly in gutter-Nisi.

He was still standing like that when he heard low voices and the rustle of winter uniforms coming toward him in the quiet stable's gloom.

"We've got to do something about him," one voice said. "It's bad for morale, discipline . . . we can't just sit back and let him go on this way. It makes the whole unit look bad."

A deeper voice responded, "What would you suggest, Crit?"

"Either shape him up or shed him. If it were anybody else, you'd have done it long ago. He's just not that special—and if he is, that's worse. You can't have one set of rules for Niko and another for everybody else. Even the

Sacred Banders don't try to make excuses for him anymore. You've got to talk to him.''

The other sighed rattlingly and said something so low
that Niko couldn't hear the words as he turned to watch
Tempus and his second-in-command, Critias, come down
the line.

By the time they reached him, the words he'd heard and
the drugs in his system had combined to make Niko's
greeting abrupt: ''If you're here to kill my mare to save the
foal, you'll have to kill me first.'' He crossed his arms and
stood his ground.

Crit was about Niko's size. Tempus was taller and
heavier and insurmountable: the Stepsons' commander was
undying, a quasi-immortal as strong as a bull whose flesh
regenerated itself and whose fighting skills had been honed
through centuries on a multitude of battlefields.

It might be an acceptable way to die, picking a fight
with the commander of the allied Tysian militias; it wasn't
a fight that Niko, despite his western training, could hope
to win, and both his superiors knew it.

Crit said, ''See what I mean, Commander? The bas-
tard's addled—dangerous to himself and the rest of us.
Suicide's not an honorable—''

''Crit, go tell Randal he can come now,'' Tempus ordered flatly.

Crit ran a hand through his short feathery hair and said,
''Yes sir, Commander. Niko, when you're done here, I
want to see you in my quarters.'' Then, with a wry
grimace, he headed for the barn door.

The young officer and his commander looked at each
other in silence until Niko judged that Crit was out of
earshot: ''Randal's not touching my mare. She's better off
dying a natural death than living on, beholden to wizardry.''

''And you, Stepson,'' Tempus said gently, ''is that
what you want?'' The man who was called the Riddler
stared sorrowfully at the young soldier.

''Maybe. What if it is? It's my choice—the only one

I've got left. I never wanted to pair with Randal—a mage, an accursed sorcerer." Niko tried to stop himself, but the words came pouring out: "I can't take it any longer—the other fighters avoid me like a plague-carrier; the Sacred Band pairs say I've violated the spirit of my oath; the Free Nisibisi—even my blood brother Bashir—shun me. I'm a pariah, an outcast in all but name. So let's call it like it is: I quit. I'm out of it, officially resigning my commission. As of this moment, my mare and I are beyond your jurisdiction."

From inside the stall, a grunt of pain and frustration reached them.

Tempus watched the young fighter who had once been so promising but now, haggard, haunted, and hunted by supernatural forces he wouldn't try to understand, teetered on the brink of madness.

"That might be best for all concerned," Tempus said slowly. "But let's end it properly: you and I should be able to save both mare and foal, if you'll take direction from me this one more time. Then we'll keep the foal and you can take the mare with you when it's weaned."

Niko squeezed his eyes shut, his mouth suddenly dry, feeling as if he'd been disemboweled. At least he'd saved Tempus the painful duty of discharging him. It had to come to this, he told himself. It was just a matter of time.

Yet the shock of being separated from his unit officially was devastating. Numbly he said, "Fine. Let's try it, Tempus," using his civilian prerogative to be impolite to the man he respected above all others.

In the stall, the mare's ears barely twitched; her breathing was too loud, too deep. Her distended belly shivered.

Tempus knelt down beside her hindquarters and took out a dagger.

"No!" Niko protested.

"I'm just going to make her a little wider, Niko. She'll hardly feel it, the state she's in. Sit on her neck and hold her head."

Automatically, the ex-Stepson did as he was bid, one more time. He couldn't see what Tempus was doing behind his back, but he could feel the mare shudder and twitch.

Then she uttered one piercing scream and her forelegs jerked madly as she struggled to roll over, to rise up. Niko had all he could do to obey the order he'd been given.

"Good, good. Hold firm. That's it, Niko," said Tempus, and then added: "Here it comes . . . that's got it." And: "You can get off her neck. Get me some hot water, cat gut, a hot needle, clean cloths. And . . . take a look, on your way out."

The straw was full of blood and placenta, but in its midst an iron-black foal kicked shakily. Tempus was wiping the mucus from its nostrils with his tunic's edge and Niko's sorrel mare was trying to help him.

When he left the stall, Niko saw his mare nuzzling her newborn and Tempus, covered with mucus and blood, grinning after him fondly.

Coming back with a bucket of water and an armful of cloths, he met Randal the wizard, slogging through snow up to his bony knees.

"Stealth," Randal called Niko by his war name, "I got your message. Whatever's wrong with her, we'll—"

"Randal, I didn't send for you, but I'm glad you're here."

The scrawny wizard struggled to keep up. "You are?"

"That's right. Not because of the mare—Tempus and I took care of that without any magical incantation or soul-rotting spells."

Randal tried not to show his disappointment, the depth of his hurt. Randal idolized Nikodemos, but since coming back from the front, Niko had been treating him very shabbily. Fighters were moody and Niko had been under terrible strain—possessed by a witch, sought after as an earthly avatar by the very entelechy of dreams, banned from the western Bandaran isles for consorting with magicians.

So Randal only said, "I'm glad. The mare's out of danger? And the foal? Then perhaps I should be getting back—"

"No. You'll have to stay awhile. We have to dissolve our pairbond formally. You can do what you want, wizard, but I've quit the Stepsons. There are plenty of fools who'll pair with you for status and mundane advantage—or Tempus will keep you on as a single, I'm—"

"You *what*?" Niko was a son of the armies; his unit, with its stringent and convoluted code of honor and its lust for glory, was his entire life. Niko without his rank as squadron leader of the finest special forces unit in the north was like Randal without his guild-standing, or Tempus without his curse: unthinkable.

"You heard me," Niko said. "I'm quit of you and all my former allegiances, after tonight. We'll go see Crit and say the words, sign the papers. Then it's done."

"Done? Don't *I* have anything to say about—"

Niko glanced at Randal sidelong; in the moonlight reflected from the snow, Niko's stare was so eloquently threatening and so full of distaste that Randal broke off in mid-sentence.

If Stealth, called Nikodemos, had truly lost his taste for honor and glory, if the debauches Randal had heard about from scandalized 3rd Commando regulars had taken its place, then there was nothing Randal could do about it. He was part of Niko's problems, not his solutions.

But he was terribly sad, hurrying after his onetime left-side leader into the Stepson's Hidden Valley barn.

Randal had given up a lot to be able to say "Life to you, Riddler, and everlasting glory." He saw in Tempus's sad little smile when he spoke those words that he was expected to rise to this occasion, to stay on as Tempus's staff adept, to ask no questions and trust his commander to turn things aright.

But without Niko, it wouldn't be easy.

* 2 *

Randal would never forget the way Critias looked past Niko, as if he didn't exist, when the Stepson submitted his resignation.

Critias, Tempus's intelligence officer, had no right to judge Niko: he didn't understand Niko's problems, didn't care about anything but himself. The Stepsons were a cold lot, clinging to their barbaric honor code in lieu of anything more stringent.

Sour-eyed, Crit had scrawled out release forms for Niko and slapped them down upon his desk: "Come on, hurry up, citizen. I've got better things to do than waste my time with you."

Stealth hadn't batted an eye, just signed what Crit put before him. Randal wanted to give Crit a piece of his mind, but his *kris*—a magical sword given to the mage by Askelon, lord of dreams—rattled in its scabbard on Randal's hip as if it were ready to jump out and skewer Critias of its own accord.

And since the kris was capable of doing just that, Randal had to hold it firmly and keep his temper well in check: his kris couldn't distinguish between real enemies and perceived ones; it was probably just reacting to Randal's confused emotions.

As they were leaving, Straton, Critias's right-side partner and the Stepsons' chief interrogator, came in. Strat, a man as large as Tempus, gave Niko an offhanded salute, disregarding Randal as Strat always did when he could.

Niko just nodded to Straton, who frowned and said, "When are you going to quit fuddling your wits with krrf, Stealth? You can't even manage a civil—"

"*Civil*ians don't salute Stepsons. They're polite and they know their place—somewhere else," Crit said.

"What's this? Another covert operation? Last time Niko played 'civilian,' his partner died of the game. I—"

"No game this time, Strat." Niko's voice was soft and slurred from drugs or distress. "My mare stays here till the foal is weaned. I'd like your word that you'll see to her—I'll make it worth your while."

Strat's wide forehead furrowed; he looked from Crit, to Niko, to Randal. Then his big hands lashed out, catching Randal by the tunic and lifting him off the ground: "This is *your* doing, you droolbucket, you slimy prestidigitator. Couldn't stand it that Stealth was—"

"Strat!" Crit said. "It's too late for that."

"Put him down, Straton," Niko warned, "or you won't be able to lift your skirts hereafter." Niko's tone, flat and promissory without a hint of feeling, made Straton turn his head.

Then Randal's feet touched the floor and he could speak. "And don't you forget it, you lumbering—"

"*Randal!* I don't need any help from you with this." Niko's sunken eyes swept over him and Randal flushed.

Regarding Crit steadily, Niko said, "Let's be polite, ex-task force leader, now and in the future. Someone might get hurt, otherwise."

"Stealth," Straton said, "this is madness. What are you going to do? Deal drugs from Brother Bomba's? Play martyr with Bashir's guerrillas when the snow melts and the Mygdonians attack again?"

Niko, still looking at Crit, said, "Something like that. It doesn't matter. Randal, get out of here. Go back to your mageguild and spin your globe. I'll be in touch."

There was more said, Randal was sure, but he didn't hear it. Straton, with an ugly grin, opened the door wide for him and bowed sweepingly. "Out you go, witchy-ears, and I can't say I'm sorry about it."

So he left, his neck hot with embarrassment and his eyes swimming with tears. Stealth wasn't like this; something was wrong—even more than he'd thought.

All the camaraderie and much-vaunted brotherhood of the Sacred Band was meaningless, the whole thing a sham, an excuse for violence and viciousness.

Randal was crunching through the Hidden Valley snow, wondering if he could ever convince his archmage that he'd seen the error of his ways and regain his former standing among the Tysian wizards, when a long shadow fell in his path: Tempus, a dark lord in the moonlight.

"Life to you, Randal," the Stepsons' commander said.

"Don't 'life' me, Riddler," Randal flared, drawing himself up to his full height. "You may think I'm still a member in good standing, but your task force leader has made it clear that I'm not welcome."

"Crit's got problems of his own—my daughter Kama, for one; relations between the Stepsons and the 3rd Commando, for another."

"That's no excuse." Randal wanted to push by Tempus, find a cozy place to change his shape, and wing homeward: an interval as a hawk would ease him, dull the pain of rejection.

But before he could, Tempus said, "Whatever you said or did in there, as far as I'm concerned, you're still my right-hand mage. And I've a task for you no lesser could accomplish."

"You *do*? That is, oh no, you don't. Niko quit, so I'm out of it, too."

"An oath means so little to a mage? I doubt it."

Randal's feet were getting cold and, in the moonlight, Tempus seemed some faceless hulk, even more daunting than usual.

"Well . . . yes and no," the Hazard temporized. "I mean, if you really *need* me, then of course I'll do my best but . . . how? I can't make another liaison; Niko's still my partner, to the death with honor, no matter what *he* says. It's like a marriage, isn't it? You can disavow it before men but not before . . . well, you know."

"I know," said the avatar of rape and pillage kindly.

"As for how you can help, you can keep Niko safe while this fever in him burns out."

"How? I don't know what's wrong, what I've done, why he doesn't want me anymore . . ." Randal trailed off miserably, then sniffled, then turned his head to blow his nose: "It's cold out here, Riddler. Could we go inside if we've got to talk much longer?"

When he got no answer, he looked up again, and Tempus was gone.

* **3** *

Niko was on his way out of the free zone, his purse nearly empty and his heart heavy, when two mounted 3rd Commando rangers took it into their heads to roust him.

He'd been everyone's favorite target of harassment since he'd quit the band a week before; he'd had about enough of it. He was tired of talking and unwilling to explain—it sounded too much like complaining when he did.

There was only one way to stop it: when the two horsemen came up on either side of him, he grabbed the booted foot of the ranger on his right and wrenched it around and upward, pushing the man from his saddle, while with his left hand, he dug into the tender nerves above the other rider's knee, simultaneously unhorsing the temporarily paralyzed second commando also.

The two men, cursing, scrabbled in the dirt while all about, the free zone crowd thinned out: none of the refugees wanted to be a witness, be too close, be involved.

Before their horses shied away, Niko grabbed a crossbow from one saddle.

By this time, one ranger had gained his knees, his dirk out; the other, his leg still useless, was trying to draw his sword, telling Niko, "You'll pay for this, Whoreson, and wish you'd—"

Niko nocked an arrow and levered the crossbow to ready, stepping in between the two, the bow pointed now at one, now at the other. "Drop your blades, hilts first."

"Can't you western women count?" the one with the palmed dirk retorted. "There's two of us; you'll bleed your life out among these Maggots if you don't put down that bow."

Niko took another step, toward the one whose leg he'd numbed, bending as he did so: "Open wide, princess," he told the soldier, whose eyes crossed, looking at the business end of the crossbow bolt. "Now!"

As the prostrate ranger opened his mouth to argue, Niko shoved the crossbow in it up to its flare. The man froze, eyes wide; Niko looked at the other. "You want to kill your friend, here? Say one more word."

The fighter with the dirk met Niko's eyes; seconds passed. Stealth's training in the western isles had taught him to read auras—not minds, just the colors a living being gives off in joy or war or treachery.

So he knew the first commando was going to rush him, even as the man lurched to his feet, his dirk cast Niko's way.

Reflexively, his finger squeezed the trigger and the bolt shot from the bow, through the mouth and skull of the commando on the ground, as Niko ducked the thrown dirk and prepared to meet the first ranger's assault.

The man barreled into him with concussive force. It was one-to-one, hand-to-hand, the kind of combat Niko liked. The ranger went for Stealth's throat with both hands, their faces so close it was clear that the ranger had had onions with his lunch.

Bringing up his arms, Niko snapped the hold, kicked up with his knee, and slammed down with his open hand on the commando's neck as the fellow doubled over.

His assailant went to his knees.

"More?" Niko asked, standing over him as the soldier, in fetal position, groaned upon the ground. "I'll wait."

But the soldier only gritted that Niko had started something he couldn't finish.

He knew that. He picked up the crossbow, nocked another bolt, and backed away, looking right and left, hoping to melt into the free zone shadows, lose himself among the Maggots—refugees from the war-torn north who had the freedom of the camps.

There were tunnels underneath the free zone, and he headed for them, crouched low, wishing he'd let the rangers rough him up. It was a private war now, declared—Niko against the growing contingent of Rankan elite shock troopers wintering here.

He was breathing hard when he squeezed into a tunnel entrance beneath a fall of rock. He didn't understand why he'd let things escalate, why he'd shot the first ranger and wrestled with the second. Niko was a master of Death Touch. He could have marked each man for death with a finger's jab or an elbowed bruise during a scuffle they would have thought was real, let them take the few coppers and the bit of pulcis he had on him, endured their slurs and insults, and walked away free and clear, comfortable in the knowledge that both men would die of unexplained causes within a day: that was the way of Death Touch.

He could have, but he hadn't. In the tunnel, alone with his raspy breathing and his shaking hands, he tried to understand. He'd needed to lash out, to fight a living, breathing enemy, wrestle with those unlucky fighters because he couldn't wrestle with his fate.

Niko was what they were calling him—a Maggot, a Tysian refugee, a child of the streets grown cold and hard over years of mercenary war. But he was also a western-trained adept, a specialist in silent kill, a Bandaran initiate of the mystery called *maat*—balance and equilibrium and the intuitive edge that meditation brings.

Maat, in Bandara, was peaceful. Maat, in the world,

was an expression of nature's search for balance, of chaos devouring itself, of the flux called war.

Because of his maat and his past, Niko had become sought after by the Nisibisi witch, Roxane, known as Death's Queen, who fought the Rankan empire as an ally of Mygdon; and by Askelon, regent of the seventh sphere, lord of shadow and of dream.

An initiate of maat acquires a purity of soul, a serenity of spirit that no worldly strife can despoil. It was this that the dream lord Askelon wanted from Niko, and this that made Roxane come to him repeatedly in all manner of women's forms.

Between the two of them, the lord of dreams and the queen of depredatious magic, Niko was like a contested haunch of meat. They tugged on him and pulled at him so that meditation was a torture, sleep was fraught with danger, and even the comfort of his fellows was denied him.

Niko, who needed touch and love and human contact, who was never happier than when he could do a favor for a friend or end the suffering of an unfortunate, was afraid to seek a woman's arms—she might be Roxane in disguise. Barred from the peace of his mystery by Askelon's dominion over his mental rest-place, Niko was unwilling to bring his curse upon his unit or his friends.

All that was left in him now was anger. He wanted to hit back, to shake off these supernatural beings who coveted his soul.

Slinking through the free zone tunnels with no destination in mind, he admitted finally, in words, what he'd decided: the drugs and drink he used to keep sleep and misery at bay might be the cure for all that ailed him. If he could degrade his mystery, despoil his soul, become less than he was, neither Roxane nor Askelon would want him. He'd no longer be a talisman of power craved by beings who sought to use him like a pawn.

He had to win this fight, even if it cost him all he'd

once struggled to obtain. Rejection by the Sacred Band
had convinced him that he had no other choice.

But he was so lonely and so tired, so angry and so at
war within himself, that when he came up out of the
tunnels at a randomly chosen exit, his mood was blacker
than the warrens he'd just left.

It was night by then, and that suited him. Above the
alleyways leading to Peace Falls, he could see the mountain range called Wizardwall gleaming in winter's pale
moonlight.

He could climb its peaks and ask Bashir to help him.
Bashir and he still had a bond of sorts, and Bashir was
Father Enlil's priest, a man of devout character who had
the northern Storm God's ear.

But that was trading one master for another.

In the alley, Niko shook his head and paused to lean
against a closed door, shivering and sweating all at once.
There was no answer but to continue what he'd begun.
Running to Bashir was just running, as staying with Tempus was hiding behind the Riddler's skirts.

A born warrior and son of the armies, he was going to
become a criminal, a drug dealer, a man free of scruple, if
it killed him, for the sake of owning his own soul in
whatever afterlife he'd earn.

But it hurt. It hurt to hate the world and to know it hated
him back. It hurt to hurt his friends and make them hurt
him. Whenever he wasn't drugged or drunk, it hurt so that
he could hardly stand it.

There was a cure for that: he pushed away from the
alley doorway, headed for Brother Bomba's inn. Madame
Bomba and he had an arrangement, a profitable trade in
drugs between the Bombas and Niko's uncle in Caronne.

He'd have to sneak around now, not walk up Commerce
Avenue as if he weren't a hunted man. He slid through
byways and under eaves until he crossed the town line
separating Tyse from Peace Falls, then slipped into Brother
Bomba's through the kitchen.

One of the cook's helpers, a free zone boy Niko had recommended to the Madame, dropped a pot of stew when he spied him: "Niko, my lord! The specials were here looking for you. They said you killed a man . . . a 3rd Commando." The youth's pale eyes were wide.

"That's right. What of it? I killed him in the free zone, where Tyse's laws don't apply. And don't call me 'my lord.' If you've a lord, he's up in heaven, not stumbling around with blood on his clothes and dirt on his face."

He pushed by the boy. "Clean that up before the Madame finds you incompetent to serve."

"But . . ."

"What *is* it, pud? I don't have to explain myself to you."

The boy's eyes sparkled. "But they *left* someone here, in case you showed up. The Madame told me, if I saw you, to be sure and let you know."

"I'll go up the kitchen stairs. Tell her I'm here and waiting."

He didn't blame the Madame for wanting to avoid trouble in her bar.

Up the back stairs and three doors down the hall he had a room. In it, he broke the ice on a water basin and splashed the slush on his face, stripped off everything but his breech and washed the free zone grime from his skin.

Then, shivering, he knelt to build a fire in the sooty hearth, lighting a broadleaf soaked in pulcis from it as soon as the sparks began to catch.

Pulcis was slightly hallucinogenic, an aphrodisiac and stimulant only the wealthy or corrupt could afford.

By the time Madame Bomba came knocking, Niko was lying stretched out on the sheepskin rug before the hearth watching colors waft across the plastered ceiling, so forgetful of reality he merely called out, "Come," without thought to safety or security.

Madame Bomba came in first, leaving someone Niko didn't recognize waiting in the hall.

She frowned down at him, gigantic from his vantage on the floor. "Get up, Stealth. Put on some clothes. Wipe that silly grin off your face. I've brought someone to see you . . ." The Madame knelt in a rustle of skirts that sounded like Bandaran windchimes to Niko's drug-sharpened ears.

Then she had his face in her hands, turning it slightly, squinting. "Stealth, boy, try to listen to me. This is important—dangerous. Here drink this."

She pushed a faience vial against his lips, uptilted it. Bitter liquid flowed onto his tongue, spilled out and down his chin.

She let his head fall back; seconds later, his euphoria fell away, leaving him nearly sober and resentful.

"What is it? Who's there? Someone from these specials?"

"Get dressed and listen closely." She stood up and paced back and forth as Niko dressed, explaining: "The specials left a Rankan here, some muckety-muck from the capital who wants to talk to you. He won't tell me what he wants, but he's up to no good, that's certain from the way the specials were acting. This is a secret meeting, just you and him, and I've already been threatened with mayhem should I reveal it even happened."

Niko, pulling on hillman's trousers, said: "Rankans killed my parents; I served Tempus, not the empire. Now that's done, I want nothing to do with them." He struggled into a woolen chiton and buckled his workbelt over it; on it were strung what weapons he might need to convince a Rankan to let him be.

The Madame's hand closed heavily on his shoulder, spinning him around. "Niko, boy, this is serious—you're in no position to snub an overture from the empire, and we've our business to think of. See the man. Be polite. If there's no commission or pardon in the offer, don't worry—I've arranged for you to spend a week or two with friends of mine north of town . . . until the 3rd calms down or Tempus can be prevailed upon to help you."

"I don't want his help . . . I don't want any help."

"That's all too clear," the Madame said, her face showing all its lines. "But you've other folk to think of . . . we
who love thee."

When Madame Bomba lapsed into "thee's and thou's,"
things were serious indeed.

"How do you know this Rankan isn't going to arrest
me—free zone or not? It was a Rankan ranger I—"

"Hush, child. This man couldn't arrest a sneeze. You'll
see. Trust me. Now, ready?"

He shrugged and she showed her yellowing teeth, then
opened up the door and ushered in a short plump man with
a beard only on his chin.

"I'll leave ye now," the Madame offered, and when the
little Rankan only nodded, she left and closed the door.

The Rankan wore a fur-lined robe and boots which, in
the capital, a man would buy for hunting tigers with the
emperor. His cheeks were pink and his eyes cold. He said,
"Stealth, called Nikodemos?"

"The same." Niko crossed his arms.

"I'm Brachis, priest of the Storm God, Conservator of
Heaven, Sole Confidant of the—"

"Spare me a recitation of your titles. If you've come to
save my soul or claim it for an affront against the armies,
priest, you're wasting your time either way. The Madame
said I had to listen to your proposal. If you've got one,
make it. Now."

The priest unlatched his cloak and let it fall; the gar-
ments underneath substantiated his claim: Niko hadn't seen
such high-caste priestly raiment of the hierarchy—worked
in golden thread with the bulls and lightning of the Storm
God and the mountain—since he'd fought with Abarsis,
the southern Storm God's dead warrior-priest.

"As you wish, Stepson . . . ex-Stepson, that is." Though
his flush was spreading and priestly anger lit his eyes,
Brachis signed a blessing Niko almost fended off, and
minced close: "We have a proposition for you, your Ma-

dame Bomba is right. What is said hereafter cannot be repeated on pain of becoming anathema to the gods and losing your place in heaven." Brachis's eyes met Niko's solemnly.

"Fine. I understand. Get on with it, priest."

"May I sit?"

"Go ahead," Niko said, exasperated. Priests were a different matter than Rankan henchmen of the secular sort. This one had true power to damn, even though the Rankan Storm God was missing, some said dead.

The priest said: "We're here because Abarsis came to us in a dream and singled you out for glory."

"We? Glory? I've given up glory. I'll settle for survival." A superstitious chill ran up Niko's spine: Abarsis had been called the Slaughter Priest; no man who'd served the god in his Sacred Band could forget what it was like to be an instrument of heaven.

" 'We' in the sense that I'm the temple's representative. As for survival, we're offering you no obvious exoneration in the world of men—you'll have to take your chances with the 3rd Commando. We do, however, offer expiation in the world of gods. Abarsis's ghost came down from heaven and laid your name upon our altar when we asked how to go about making an end to accursed Abakithis, that travesty of an emperor who has caused the Storm God to turn his face away from the Rankan people—"

"Hold, priest. Let's not get theological . . . I'm not as pious as I used to be. You want me to *what*?"

"To assassinate the emperor, for the good of Ranke, the Storm God's temple, and your own soul."

Niko, who'd been leaning against the wall, slid slowly down it into a squat. "And for the good of the next faction that comes to power. Whose man are you, priest?"

"Brachis, my son; call me Brachis." The priest, having said what he'd come to say, was now paling visibly, so that his pink cheeks seemed like disfiguring birthmarks. "Abarsis chose you, and the death of that commando tonight is a sign that he was right: you're free of allegiances and pure as—''

"Ghosts don't benefit from coups; men do. Is it Theron's faction? Tempus has worked for him off and on.''

"You don't want to know, my son. Will you accept this commission that the gods have laid upon you? Joyously labor to release the Rankan people from this bondage of ineptitude and return our missing Storm God to us? We shall be very grateful—all the funds and covert aid you ask for shall be yours. The only thing we cannot do is associate ourselves with you openly.''

"I know,'' Niko muttered. "And when it's done? Will you then pack me off to heaven to let Abarsis thank me personally? I won't die for your cause; I won't hang or endure the Endless Deaths traitors earn without mentioning your names. You'll have to grant me some kind of immunity, and do it publicly.''

The priest scowled. "We shall find a way. Are we agreed? You'll do the deed?''

"I want something for it, something more.'' Niko's mind raced: Abakithis had been the Rankan emperor when Tyse was sacked and made a Rankan satellite; his family—mother, father, sister—would be avenged. And Abarsis, up in heaven, the holy spirit who looked after all the living members of his Sacred Band and even personally appeared on earth to escort the fallen heavenward, had chosen him. "I want your word and the word of whomever you're grooming to sit on the Lion Throne of empire that Free Nisibis will remain free—an independent nation, with Bashir its recognized ruler.''

"We . . . will consider it.''

"You do that. I'll consider it, too.''

"Nikodemos,'' the priest shifted, "your immortal soul is at stake here.''

Niko chuckled harshly: "You're right about that. And my physical person, too, I'd wager. You can't very well let me walk away if I refuse you, is that it?''

"The gods say you will not refuse."

Niko's hands were cold, and his heart also. No matter what he did, he was always being pressed into service by nonphysical beings for reasons he didn't understand. "Then the gods are on the side of the Nisibisi free men. Yes or no, priest?"

Brachis sighed and made a spirit-invoking sign with his plump fingers. "Yes. We agree. And you must agree not to say anything about our arrangement, not to tell even the Riddler what has transpired. You must accomplish your task at the Festival of Man, in the third week on the third day, during the evening's celebration. The emperor will be among the winners then—you must be one."

"Festival of Man? A winner? I'm not even among the contestants. I don't have a sponsor—I'm not a Stepson, not a member of Tyse's garrison. I certainly can't go as a Rankan entrant, after I've just slain a Rankan ranger!"

"Perhaps Bashir will sponsor you. Free Nisibis has a right to send a contingent to the games, as does any other buffer-state of empire, city-state, or powerful lord. If Nisibis refuses, you'll have to make your peace with Tempus or go as a Tysian entrant." The priest waved his hand. "These are political matters, and politics are only one weapon of the gods. A way will be shown to you; you have only to do what the gods desire."

So saying, Brachis held out his hand. In it was a small figure, that of the Storm God on his bulls, worked in silver. "A token, to identify you to the priesthood as our agent. Show it, if you're in need of help."

Niko looked at the outstretched hand, at the little amulet on its leather thong, then up at the pasty-faced priest.

Then slowly he reached out to take the token of the Storm God.

* 4 *

Brother Bomba's ground-floor bar looked as if it had been struck by the wrath of the gods when Tempus arrived there the next evening.

The pecan bar was in splinters, the copper mirror behind it eaten through with acid; fire had charred the beams above and no table had four legs under it.

In the wreckage, Madame Bomba wandered, dazed and bruised; by the archway leading up to rooms rented by the hour and down to her drug den of renown, Critias leaned against a smoke-damaged tapestry, a wistful smile on his lips and a faraway look in his eyes.

Beside Crit, scrawled in blood three cubits high, the 3rd Commando had left its calling card: a rearing horse with lightning bolts clenched between its teeth.

A half-dozen Stepsons labored amid the shambles. Madame Bomba was their self-proclaimed den-mother; she'd taken the band under her wing when they'd first come upcountry to Tyse. Her ''boys'' hadn't waited to be asked when the Madame needed help: they'd volunteered.

Tempus headed straight for Madame Bomba without a word to those who greeted him. Crit intercepted him: ''Commander, let's get the bastards. No matter where Niko's gone or what he's done, Sync's 3rd Commando needs a lesson and a dozen of my men are ready to teach it.''

The 3rd had gutted Madame Bomba's the night before, looking for Niko. They'd blockaded themselves inside and terrorized the Madame all night long, hoping to force her to reveal Stealth's whereabouts.

''Revenge, is it, Crit? Vengeance is what started this,'' Tempus rasped. ''We hurt them; they hurt us. Where will it end? Fight each other all winter, and we won't be fit to fight Mygdonians by spring, let alone win our events at the Festival. Tell your task force," Tempus's voice lowered, "that accidents may befall the 3rd, but none we'll be blamed for." Then, louder: "Niko's forsworn his oath to us; we won't shed a drop of blood for him. As for the Madame, if she wants to count on our protection, she'll cease harboring fugitives and murderers. Clean this place up, post a guard, and let it go at that."

"Yes, sir," Crit said equably, his cynical smile under wraps. "I'll do that. Now, if you're ready to interview the Madame . . ."

Just then Straton, Critias's right-side partner, came in, swearing copiously at what he saw.

"Bring Strat when you come upstairs," Tempus whispered as he left Crit and took the unresisting Madame Bomba by the arm.

Up a flight of stairs in Bomba's office was a small room which overlooked the bar. Tempus seated the puffy-faced woman in her favorite chair and went to stand before the alchemically-crafted one-way glass, staring down upon his men at work, trying to think of something to say to this woman, who was suffering on his account as all who loved him did.

It was Tempus's curse that those who loved him died of it, and those he loved were bound to spurn him. Once, the god Vashanka had mitigated his curse and the pain it brought; now, like the Rankan empire which faltered without its war god, Tempus staggered under the malediction's weight.

As if reading his mind, Madame Bomba said: "It's not your fault. I should have known better. But who would have thought that Niko would kill a—"

"Tell me about Brachis," Tempus interrupted. "What did he want with Niko?"

"You know, then," the Madame sighed. "I can't say." The Madame's voice was dull and hopeless: caught between the Stepsons and the 3rd Commando, she saw no safe course to take.

"You *can't* say?" Tempus turned, incredulity in his voice. The Madame and he had been through the wizard war together; she'd not turned a hair when magic had collapsed her wine cellar, or mistrusted him when death squads had wreaked havoc in the bar below and left the Stepsons' calling card.

But the 3rd was another matter: he'd trained them, formed them, written the manual they plundered from and the oaths they swore. He'd been younger then, and angrier; they were the most vicious and brutal strike force his three centuries of expertise could concoct.

They must have raped her, he decided; her face was too pale under its bruises, and her spirit, for the first time in his memory, too low.

"That's right—Niko didn't confide in me. As for his whereabouts, Riddler—save your breath. I didn't tell that monster Sync, despite everything. I'll not tell you." A trace of the fire he remembered sparkled in her eyes. "Whatever's wrong with Niko is your doing—he loves you like a father. Whatever he did, he had good reason. Before you destroy that boy, the best you've got, think of this: it's your curse which brings harm to those who love thee." She blinked away tears and her hands went to her face.

Tempus could count the women he respected on the fingers of one hand; the Madame was the foremost of these. And she was right: all Niko's troubles sprang from him.

But before he could answer, Crit appeared in the open doorway, Straton beside him.

Strat was saying, "What? Why didn't you tell me?"

And Crit replied, easing in and shutting the door behind them, "I couldn't. It had to look right. Niko doesn't know, himself. We can't be sure the witch isn't spying on us through him; we need somebody out there to draw fire.

And we need to know what Brachis is doing here . . . it had to be done this way.''

Madame Bomba looked from Crit, to Strat, who was shaking his head in disgust, to Tempus, who was wishing Crit didn't trust Madame Bomba quite so much.

Then she said, her face so suffused with rage that the purpling bruises on her cheeks seemed to pale: "You did that to Niko purposely? Maneuvered him into the state he's in for some unholy operation to test the empire?'' She spat Tempus's way. ''I'm appalled.''

Strat grunted in agreement, his huge arms crossed.

Crit started to make excuses, raking a hand through his short feathery hair: ''Who'd have guessed he'd kill a ranger? He seems so calm, you forget about his temper. Brachis isn't just any priest, Madame—he's here on business for Theron's faction, and that's serious. We have to know what, why, maybe even how and when, if it's the sort of business we think—''

''That's no excuse for turning a fighter into a renegade,'' the Madame retorted. ''And driving him to drugs and drink. The way you Stepsons treated him—''

''*We* drove him to drugs and drink?'' Crit took a step toward the Madame and balled his fists. ''If you weren't—''

''Crit. Madame. Cease,'' Tempus thundered, not as angry as he sounded: this was the Madame Bomba he knew and loved; concern for another had roused her from her shock.

''I didn't want to involve you, Madame, but now you know what only a few task force members suspect. We'll retrieve Nikodemos when the time is right; I've got Randal looking out for his welfare, body and soul.''

''Soul?'' Straton snorted. Crit shot him a withering look which Strat ignored.

''Straton, we're counting on you to get to Niko and tell him—'' Tempus began.

''That the whole thing's a fix?'' Strat interrupted. ''I hope he takes it well.''

"No," Crit said. "That we need to know what Brachis is planning. He asked you to take care of his mare; you're the only one who can get to him without arousing suspicion."

"And if the witch *is* possessing him again?" Straton asked. "What then?"

"Forget the witch." Crit turned to Madame Bomba, his face grim. "You see, Madame, you've got to help us. We need to know where he is before the 3rd finds out. Otherwise, we can't protect him."

Madame Bomba sighed and shook her head, then reached into her skirts and pulled out a pouch from which she took broadleaves, pulcis, and a little box of krrf. "Soldier, if you were a belly-son of mine, I'd spank you. But since you're not, I'll make it clear another way: if any ill befalls Niko because of this plan of yours, Crit, I'll take it out on you in ways you haven't dreamed could hurt."

Strat, out of her sight, smirked: Madame Bomba continually tried to reform Crit, treated him like an errant child. And Crit, with whom no man but Strat dared argue, took from Madame Bomba chastisement and lectures not even Tempus would have offered.

"But you'll tell us where he is?" Crit pressed.

Then she turned to Tempus: "And if I do this," her eyes glinted mischievously, "and one or two Rangers die, there is no blame?"

"None," he said, giving her permission to take revenge as she chose—the Madame was not without resources.

"Good." She nodded, stretched, and began rolling broadleaves. "It's a long time since I've worked so intimately with the armies. Come, soldiers, let's seal our bargain with a bit of smoke."

* 5 *

In the Tysian mageguild, Randal stood at his chamber's high window, staring out upon Mageway and the traffic far below.

He had sweat on his brow and his kris in his hand; behind him, in the center of the mosaic floor, the globe of power he'd won in the raffle for Wizardwall gleamed, its inset stones catching torchlight as it spun lazily on its stand.

The globe and its stand might be the problem, Randal thought, running the kris Askelon had given him through his fingers. His kris had been forged by the dream lord's own hand and no mage had a weapon so powerful.

But today, when he must use his powers to their fullest and every magical attribute he had, the kris was not behaving. Randal had said the words and stroked the blade as Askelon had taught him, but as yet, not a single hornet had issued forth from the kris's tip.

The magic of the kris and the magic of the power globe were of different planes, different sources. Randal had been using both the whitest and the blackest of magics, and now, when Tempus had decreed that Randal must protect his partner—when he most needed all the magic a seventh-level Hazard could command—neither tool was working right.

The globe's stand must hold the key, he'd thought; he spent the morning sequestered, trying to determine what that key must be. But the globe was very old, and of Nisibisi manufacture, and the glyphs incised in its base gave only single commands, no explanation of how or why they worked or when to use them.

So he'd set the globe to spinning with the command to

"summon power" invoked. It had spun the morning long, and nothing had happened.

It had to be that the globe's magic and the kris's magic were canceling each other out. So he departed the circle of invocation and, at the window, spoke words in an ancient tongue, stroked the blade as Askelon had taught him, and envisioned a stream of hornets issuing forth, his eyes tightly closed and his brow furrowed.

In his mind's eye, clearly pictured, a veritable plume of hornets swarmed. But when he peeked, there was nothing but the kris's blade glinting in the sunlight.

"By the Writ," he cursed, morose and angry, "Askelon, who art . . . wherever Thou art, get off Thy butt and hear this supplicant's plea—it's for Niko, after all!"

Eyes closed again, he stood there, every muscle tensed, willing the magic into being. And finally, when he was about to give up, he heard a "Bzzzzzzz."

His eyes popped open. He held out an arm to direct the mighty hornet swarm, the proper words upon his tongue.

But he saw no great swarm. It seemed that there was nothing there, and yet, the "Bzzzz" continued.

He looked again, holding the kris up to the light, turning it to squint down at the point.

And there, hanging from its tip, was one hornet—a single large wasp, stinging the kris's tip with all its might.

"*One* hornet? One measly hornet!" he muttered querulously, and shook the kris in disgust, as if he could shake the others out.

The single hornet stopped its manic stabbing of the blade and held on tight, its wings fluttering as it tried to keep its balance. Then, dislodged, it plummeted through the air and landed on the floor, where it crawled toward his foot.

Furious with himself and disappointed with the kris, Randal flung the weapon; it clattered to the floor. Then he raised his foot to squash the bug.

The buzzing he'd heard before came louder: the hornet took wing and flew right at his face.

"You want a swarm of hornets, witchy-breath? Squash me, and you'll die the death of a thousand stings."

"Who said that?" Hands up to protect his face, Randal retreated from the window.

"I did," said the hornet, hovering before him. "Don't you know it's winter? Whatever you want, it better be important."

Amazed, Randal lowered his hands. The hornet landed on his nose, stinger poised. "Don't move," it suggested.

Randal's eyes crossed, looking at the tiny antennae, the vicious little head.

"That's better. Step on me, will you—not likely. Name your enemy. I haven't much time—the cold is making me sleepy."

"Enemy? I have no enemy . . . that is, I do, but . . . I want you hornets to go protect Nikodemos." Randal gathered his courage. "I want you to watch him and I want daily reports."

"You do." The hornet bore down just a bit with its stinger. "That's right, sweat. It'll warm me up. We don't do that sort of thing. We just sting your enemies. What about the Nisibisi witch-queen, Roxane? Isn't she your enemy?"

"Roxane? She's routed . . . isn't she?"

Waspish laughter buzzed in Randal's ears. "She's Roxane, isn't she? If you want us to protect your Nikodemos from Roxane, that's one thing. But don't disturb our sleep for something an ant could do."

"Yes, yes, that's what I want. Protect him from Roxane. And let me know how he's doing." More than anything, Randal wanted the hornet off his nose. He didn't want to be stung. Randal was allergic to many things. Hornets were just big wasps and Randal was allergic to wasps. "Get going, wasp. There's no time to lose."

"*King Hornet*. That's what you call me. Don't you

black artists have any respect? Askelon's apprentice or
not, you've got a lot to learn." The hornet lifted off, its
wings beating.

Randal rubbed his nose, relief flooding him.

"Have fresh flowers waiting—or some fat caterpillars,
if you can manage it. And don't bother saying thank
you—" The hornet spiraled upward, toward the open window, and dwindled rapidly against the pale winter sky.

"Wait, Ki—" But the hornet was gone before Randal
had a chance to ask it about Roxane the Nisibisi witch or
anything else.

As he picked up the kris he'd thrown and headed toward
the globe, still spinning in the middle of the room, there
was a knock at his chamber's door.

"Oh drat," he muttered, looking between the spinning
globe, which now had a pale nimbus around it, and the
door.

The knock came again.

Carefully sidestepping the mosaic spiral-within-the-circle
in the middle of which the globe spun, Randal hurried to
open the door: it could only be one personage.

And it was, indeed, Randal's First Hazard, the nameless
archmage who ruled the Tysian mageguild. And the ancient one did not look happy.

Parchment lips pursed and a nearly translucent hand
reached out to touch his forehead: "My son, what are you
doing? To whom are you talking? The wards are disturbed.
Are you . . . have you . . ." Looking beyond him, the
First Hazard saw the spinning globe of power, the nimbus
around it now milky and filled with sparks.

"Come in, Master." Randal scurried out of the old
man's path. "I was just trying the "Summon Power"
command; nothing much is happen—"

Then he turned around and saw what the First Hazard
was looking at: in the middle of the white nimbus, as if in
a robe of white fox fur, was the piquant, sanguine form of
Roxane, Death's Queen.

The old First Hazard seemed to float past Randal toward the power globe; the witch seemed to grow more substantial. Every hair on Randal's body stood on end.

"Ah, Randal, my inept little friend. I see that you're busy now; I'll come back another time," came the witch's velvet voice from the middle of the nimbus.

And as she began to fade, beside Randal the ancient adept quivered; his breathing became labored and his vestments started to smoke.

Randal wanted to rush forward, to put himself between the Nisibisi witch and his archmage, but his limbs wouldn't obey him.

Before his eyes, the archmage's robes caught fire. Beyond the smoke, only the witch's smile was visible—her red lips, her white teeth, her darting tongue.

The smoke from the archmage, whose moans were horrible and whose flesh was beginning to stink, was drawn into that smiling mouth, which worked as if chewing a delectable delight.

As the archmage crumbled in upon himself and what was left of his person crumpled to the floor, the witch laughed again and Randal's kris lifted itself from its scabbard and levitated toward the smiling mouth.

The tongue licked up the last wisps of smoke; the velvet voice said: "Thank you, Randal, for the snack. Next time, bring me a younger offering."

Then the kris stabbed the place where the mouth was, just an instant too late: Roxane was gone.

His paralysis lifted, Randal stumbled forward, grabbing his kris from midair.

Trembling like a leaf, he went to his knees before the archmage, now just a pile of charred flesh and clothing—all but for the skull, which was untouched by flame. The face there was contorted into a silent scream and black eyes stared sightlessly from yellowed whites at a horror so terrible that Randal hugged himself and nearly cried.

There was no way to disguise what had happened here:

fooling around with his Nisibisi power globe, Randal had somehow made it possible for Roxane to breach the mageguild's wards and murder the First Hazard.

With his kris clattering in its scabbard and his teeth chattering in his head, Randal ventured into the mosaic circle and took the globe from its stand, thinking to throw it from the window.

But if he smashed the globe on the street below, then he'd be helpless before the witch.

So he didn't; he decided to tell the truth about what happened and pay the consequences. Even if he was expelled from the guild, he'd survive it.

Somehow.

After all, it wasn't really his fault. He was doing what he'd been told to do—protecting Niko. And now he knew he had to do more. Though it frightened him, he was going to pay a call on Askelon, lord of dreams.

*   **6**   *

Madame Bomba's friends, those who sheltered Niko-demos, lived right above the cataract for which Peace Falls was named. The estate was walled and whitewashed; its red-tiled roofs sparkled in the winter sun. Plump retainers scurried here and there about their business; children laughed and fat stallions paced Straton's mare as he rode up the fenced-in path beside their paddocks toward the great house.

This was the third time Strat had been here, seeking Niko; it seemed as if he rode into another world whenever he rode between the gargoyle-headed gates: no sign of wizard wars or sack, no hint that a siege spanning seasons was under way marred the pastoral beauty of this walled estate.

Children had made a snow goddess the last time he'd been here. Then she was graceful and imposing; now she'd melted and refrozen, smaller, distorted into a misshapen crone whose paper crown sat askew. As before, though, presents for the goddess and her consort, Father Enlil, lay at her feet: winter wheat, a haunch of meat wrapped in sheep's fat which would have fed three families in the free zone; amphorae of wine which would have brought the price of a healthy slave if auctioned in the souk.

The place gave Straton the creeps: these were more than pious folk—they were inordinately lucky; you could almost feel the god breathing down your neck.

Straton didn't like coming here—he didn't like his mission, he didn't like these folk who served the northern god, Lord Storm, and called Him Father Enlil with fond familiarity. You didn't tell lies in a temple or try to fool an oracle, and this place had the feel of the altar or the sybil's cave.

Every time he came here, Niko wasn't in; he never saw the noble family, just retainers. He was always treated impeccably—given "guest rights" of food, drink, gifts, and hospitality—but he never met his hosts.

He'd told Crit that this was the last time; either he found Niko today, or admitted that he'd never find him here without a search team.

He slid off his horse at the great house, looking wistfully at the crossbow on his saddle—levering a bolt to ready might change a tune or two. But these folk were kin to the ancient Tysian nobility and Tempus had forbidden any show of force here.

So Strat could only knock, and smile, and ask once more: "Is Nikodemos in?"

This time, to his surprise, the little chipmunk-faced retainer who opened the door nodded, his hands in his sleeves, and said, "Yes, my lord, come right this way."

Inside, the house was warm and fragrant with cedar; the long corridors niched with alcoves hosted statues of the gods. Strat kept track of every turn they took, in case Tempus ever changed his mind and led a sack in here:

since giving the Outbridge station to the 3rd Commando,
the Stepsons were in need of a barracks closer to town than
Hidden Valley.

But the god-feel was everywhere inside; the place was
eerily quiet and overly calm, like Niko just before he
exploded into violence. Strat wished that Crit would come
up here and see for himself how strange the place was, but
Crit had his hands full restoring amity between the Stepsons and the 3rd Commando in the wake of Niko's kill.

Six corridors from the front door, the waddling retainer
before him stepped out into an atrium court, walked by a
pool free of ice in which fat gold fish swam just below the
surface, then went through a door leading into darkness.

Caressing his swordhilt, Straton followed. He always
got these jobs: Crit was too headstrong, too impulsive; if it
had to be done secretly and without repercussions, the
Riddler and Crit always turned to him.

As Strat's eyes accustomed themselves to the semidark,
he could make out racks of weapons against the walls,
crates of crossbow bolts, man-high jars which, from the
smell, contained incendiaries.

Then, finally, Straton understood what kind of place this
was: the old-guard nobles who lived here were a part, if
not the head, of the Tysian faction which craved auton-
omy. There were enough weapons here to supply an entire
militia, field death squads, start a revolutionary war. No
wonder Madame Bomba had been hesitant to reveal where
she'd hidden Niko. No wonder she'd insisted he was safe
here from the 3rd Commando. A man could be safe here
from anything.

He noticed other things now, as his guide led him down
a narrow hall: arrowloops in walls thick enough to stop a
Rankan battering ram; water casks; smoked carcasses high
up in the rafters.

Then the fat retainer stopped: ''Through here, m'lord.''

Light split the gloom—a line, an oblong, a portal, as his
guide pulled open a door and waved him through.

On the far side, as the door closed behind him and he blinked to adjust his eyes to the light, he saw three men silhouetted before a low-burning fire which had the look and smell of a sacrificial altar.

One man turned, turned back, nudged another.

The second man was Niko, who came his way. The first, who watched covertly as he poured drops of oil onto some burning offering, was Bashir, the warrior-priest who ruled on Wizardwall.

"Strat," Niko said, "my mare? Is she sick?" Niko's angular face was striped with priestly soot—some Nisibisi ritual marking. He wore hillman's garb, mottled and loose; around his neck was a thong from which an amulet dangled.

"She's colicky; I've come to consult with you about her feed. The colt's fine, though, if bad-tempered. No one told me you were praying. Is that Bashir?"

Niko nodded. "Come this way."

Following Niko into a side room, he said, when Stealth had shot the bolt: "Tempus sent me."

"So I surmised." Niko squatted down before a low table and poured two cups of wine from a lion-headed rhyton there. "Drink? It'll warm you."

Niko's hands were shaking as he held a goblet out. "Don't mind that; I get nervous around the gods these days, and here it's hard to avoid them."

Straton had a feeling he'd better take the goblet; when he did, the tension in Stealth's posture eased. The former Stepson's infectious grin came and went: "Good, you're not going to lecture me." He drank deeply and sat on his haunches. "Tell me about the band. Does Tempus hate me?"

"He's concerned. We all are."

"Don't worry; the 3rd won't take me alive." He grimaced to make a joke of it, then frowned. "Bashir's going to save me, whether I want to be saved or not—take me up to Wizardwall and rehabilitate me." He stopped, his brow

furrowed, and emptied his goblet, setting it down with a
thud. "More?"

When Straton shook his head, Niko refilled his cup and
glowered: "Don't judge me, Straton. I know what I need."
Then, as quickly as it had come, his hostility faded: "I
wish I could make them understand—the Band—that it's
all right. It had to be this way."

"Come home with me, then, Niko." Strat hadn't meant
to say it. "Wizardwall's no place for you. You'll never be
content among the guerrillas. You were a boy when you
were happy there before. You're a man now. Running
away does nothing but—"

"Strat," Niko's voice was thick; his eyes blinked rapidly, as if trying to focus through unshed tears. "How's
Crit? Did he make peace with the 3rd?"

"After a fashion. We've warned them off. They gave
Madame Bomba a bad night, but—"

"Because of me. Yes. They would." He uptipped his
cup, then said, wiping his lips, "Strat, it's really good to
see you. My mare's not sick—it's just a sham?"

"We want to know what Brachis said to you," Strat
said flatly. "The Riddler needs all the intelligence he can
get. We need your help."

"He said that?" asked the young fighter eagerly, then
sat back, scowling darkly: "I can't help wondering what
all my Sacred Band brothers would say if they knew that
what I'm doing is exactly and completely what my oath
demands." He peered at Strat earnestly. "You understand,
Strat. You're the only one who does."

"Understand what, Niko?" Strat probed gently.

"That I can't bring my troubles home to roost. Bashir
loves me; if he doesn't kill me with solicitude, it won't be
from lack of trying. It's the strictures of the oath I took
before the god—not the way men interpret my behavior—
that matters. Isn't it?" Rage and frustration flashed over
the ex-Stepson's stubbled face.

"Sure it is; you've got to please yourself. But we'd like to help. You let Bashir help, why not us?"

"Help? I don't need help. I need to get drunk." Once more he filled his cup and waggled a finger at Strat: "I'm two ahead of you, man. Drink up."

Wondering if he could get anything out of Niko with the fighter in this state, Straton drained his goblet and held it out: "Niko, if we're going to get drunk, then we've got to have a good reason. I'll tell you a secret worth drinking to, and you tell me one. Agreed?"

"Agreed," Niko grinned boyishly. "I knew you wouldn't hold all this—" he waved his hand aimlessly, "—against me."

"Witchy-ears disappeared from the mageguild the same night that the First Hazard, bless his departed soul, died of unrevealed causes so weird that the mageguild's been locked up tight in midpurification ever since it happened, three days ago."

"Randal's gone? The archmage is dead?" Niko rubbed his stubbled jaw. Above his head, a single wasp on a rafter buzzed softly. "Poor Randal; poor, poor little fellow . . . he took all this personally." Niko peered earnestly at Strat once more. "It's just that I'm sick of war, you know. Tired of fighting something that won't fight fairly. You've seen the witch, had your brushes with her. What am I to do?" Niko spread his hands.

"I don't know, but I know you can't do it alone."

"Is that the Stepsons' consensus, or your opinion? They still think she's after me—if not right here, right now . . ." Niko looked around and Straton, too, glanced behind him, so that Niko added: "See, so do you. There's no hope for me, not for a normal life as a normal man, not until I've shed her taint." He wiped the back of his hand over his eyes. "Everyone's afraid of me but you . . . even Crit doesn't trust me."

"Tempus isn't afraid."

"That's true," Niko said judiciously. "He probably still

loves me. But look what happens to those who get too close to the Riddler . . ."

"Niko, what did Brachis talk to you about?"

"About?" Niko looked sly. "About a way out, a worthy cause in which to labor. An end to this war . . ." He put his elbows on the table and his chin on his fists. "Do you know how long this war's been going on in Tyse? I was born here, and it was raging then. You should have seen this place. The gods brought me back here for a purpose. With Abakithis dead, at least we'll have a chance—Bashir's Nisibis, Tyse, all of us. Empires fall, Strat . . ."

So that was it. It was all Strat could do not to get up and say he had to leave. Instead, he sipped his wine. "If you're involved in some plot with Brachis, you're in trouble. We've worked for him before. He's a double dealer and a welsher—"

"Me? Involved? It's not me, Straton—it's the dream lord and the Nisibisi witch. I don't want to talk about it anymore." He stood abruptly. "I've got to get back to the sacrifice. Bashir doesn't like it when I don't take the gods seriously."

"Since when do you care what—"

"Bashir has made me a brother, once again," Niko said lightly. "I'm a citizen of Free Nisibis, even one of their team for the Festival of Man." He looked down at Straton and held out his hand, weaving slightly on his feet.

Strat took the hand and got up; Niko's palm was cold and moist with perspiration. "Then we'll see you there, if not before . . ."

"On contesting teams, I suppose. It's sad," Niko said thickly, and Straton wanted to knock him senseless with a blow, hoist him on his shoulders, and drag him out of here, where someone could talk some sense into Niko before he killed himself.

But then the boy smiled ingenuously and added, "When you and I contest, don't be angry when I beat you . . . I have to be a winner."

"Stealth," Strat said through gritted teeth, "the day you beat me to the outhouse, the shape you're in, I'll hang up my armor and put on an apron. Do you understand anything I've said? About the band? About the 3rd? About Randal, your blasted partner? By Vashanka's third and mightiest ball, if you didn't have yourself in so ticklish a spot, I'd beat some sense into you and drag you home."

"You would?" Niko said mildly, as if considering the thought. "I believe you would. Well, too bad it won't work—for both our sakes. Tell Tempus that if Randal's not about, he's with the dream lord. As for the 3rd Commando— all but the Riddler's daughter, Kama, of course—if they come near me, it's at their own risk. Tell them that."

"I will," said Strat dully, wishing he hadn't come, hadn't found Niko, hadn't learned what he'd come to learn. "You know, Stealth, none of us can protect you from yourself."

"Quite right, Straton. But it may be that I can protect you from the witch. Think about it. Askelon's got an altar in the free zone—I built it. It's not imposing, but it does the job. Any Stepson who chooses is welcome to worship there. All you have to do is listen to your dreams, step beyond the veil, and take heed to what's in your heart."

So saying, Niko bent down, scooped up the lion-headed rhyton, and gave it to Straton: "Take this to the Riddler; token of my affection."

Then, swaying slightly as he walked, Niko showed him to the door.

* **7** *

Chasing a riderless, runaway sable stallion through Tyse's streets under a waning moon one night soon after, Tempus caught up to the horse in the free zone at the altar pits, where refugee Maggots supplicated a dozen gods to ease their fates.

Before an inconspicuous pile of stones, the wild-eyed Askelonian stallion plunged and reared, blowing hard through distended nostrils, froth-covered flanks phosphorescent in the moonlight so that superstitious worshippers muttered wards against the "devil horse" and hid behind votive statues of their favorite gods.

As Tempus dismounted, rope in hand, he realized that someone else was closer to the maddened horse than he.

A dark-clad youth approached the horse, hand out, murmuring softly, from the beast's far side.

"Stay back! He'll break you in two!" Tempus called in his best battlefield bellow, but the slim tall figure didn't seem to hear.

And Niko's Askelonian stud—who'd kicked down his stall door and run roughshod over two men who had tried to stop him as he bolted out of Hidden Valley—came down on all four legs, his ears pricked forward, and whickered softly, then put his muzzle into the youth's outstretched hand.

By the time Tempus reached the pair, the great stallion was rubbing his head against Niko's shoulder, his blazing eyes half-closed, content under his master's hand.

Tempus almost turned and left when he realized it was Nikodemos—the last thing he wanted was a confrontation with the youth.

But Niko said conversationally, in the same croon he was using to calm the horse, "Just give me the rope, Commander, and I'll halter him for you. Then you can take him home."

Tempus found himself replying: "Not unless I can take you with him. It's clear where he wants to be. You should have taken him before this—he's made a shambles of my stable. And you must learn to take what you deserve."

The horse was Niko's, given him by the entelechy of dreams; Tempus had his sister, but the stud was invaluable.

Niko replied, when the rope was not forthcoming, "I gave him up. He belongs to the Hidden Valley stud farm."

"Tell him that. He's more trouble than he's worth, like you. And I owe you a gift, fair exchange for the rhyton—a token." Tempus tossed the rope and Niko caught it as the horse, seeing it, tossed his head and danced backward.

"Token of the god," Tempus heard the Stepson say under his breath as, rope in hand and speaking softly, he approached the horse, fashioning a hackamore as he went.

When he held out the makeshift bridle, the ill-tempered Askelonian meekly lowered its head and snuffled the boy's clothing as Niko slipped it over the tiny, pointed ears.

Then Niko turned to him: "Take a ride with me, Commander?"

But Tempus was looking at the altar, plain but plainly functional, with offerings scattered at its foot: an altar to Askelon, the horse's breeder, the boy's patron, an archmage with delusions of godhead, the entelechy of dreams. "You built this travesty?" Tempus couldn't help but say. "And invited men to worship here? You're worse off than I'd thought." He headed for his horse and swung up on it.

Niko, already mounted, reined the Askelonian along-side. "Perhaps. Bashir thinks I must ask Father Enlil for help. It worked for you . . . invoking a god's aid against an archmage . . ." In the moonlight, Niko's ashen hair seemed silver, his eyes just deep black holes.

"And look where it got me. I'm in thrall to both, curse and god." Tempus felt a chill come over him: hanging from Niko's neck was an amulet of the southern Storm God, Vashanka. Without thought, his hand lashed out, caught the talisman by its thong, and ripped it from Niko's throat.

Examining it, an awful foreboding overcame the Rid-dler, who'd labored for centuries in behalf of the god of rape and pillage: "Don't do this, Niko. Don't follow in my footsteps; don't let the priests use you." He leaned so close to Niko he could smell the youth's winy breath. "If you're so anxious to destroy yourself, I'll offer an alterna-tive: become my right-side partner—if you dare."

And before the youth could answer, Tempus spurred the
Trôs horse toward the altar. It snorted disapprovingly as
his knees told it what to do, but obeyed him: its hooves
came down repeatedly upon the altar of piled stones,
scattering them until none lay upon another.

When Tempus's horse stood again on four feet amid the
ruined altar, Niko and the Askelonian were nowhere to be
seen.

Tempus didn't mind losing the sable stallion, but he
minded terribly about the boy: Tempus's own evil history
seemed to be repeating itself in Nikodemos's life, and
there was little he could do.

Tempus had sought a god's aid to deflect a curse, and
been doubly damned for his trouble. Now the god had
deserted him and the curse remained. He doubted that
Niko would fare much better.

Riding through the free zone gates, his yellow-lined
mantle whipping around him in a sudden wind, he remembered the amulet he'd ripped from Niko's neck and found
it still clenched in his right hand. Although syncretism was
accepted by mortals, gods knew who they were: the southern Storm God, Vashanka, was not the same deity as the
north's Father Enlil, though treaties equating them were
signed routinely throughout the Rankan empire.

The little silver Storm God, his feet upon his twin bulls
of potency, held lightning bolts in each upraised hand. If
only the pillager would return to Tempus, whisper in his
ear once more, he'd be able to finish what he'd started: the
war against Mygdonia, the war for Niko's soul, and even
the war within himself.

But until the god was found, chaos would reign and
every prayer go awry as every plan miscarried.

It wasn't Tempus's fault that this was so, but it was his
misfortune to know the truth of it.

So as he walked his mount through Tyse's curfewed streets,
late for a meeting with the military governor to discuss the
coming New Year's fete week and his band's departure as
Tyse's entrants for the Festival of Man, he wasn't optimistic.

Book Two:

FETE WEEK

The First Hazard of the Tysian mageguild went nameless—a protection common to his kind. His predecessor had died mysteriously in the summoning cell of Randal, a seventh-level Hazard whose career had stalled for numerous reasons, not the least of those being his congress with god-loving mercenaries.

Since that night, Randal had been absent from the mageguild, from all of Tyse, so far as the First Hazard could tell. And he could tell many things. He'd been waiting for the old master to die; he'd even helped that time along—there were many ways to skin a cat and send a soul to its deserved unrest.

This affair, the first of Fete Week, was the one at which he'd make his mark; he'd invited all the proper people. The noble caste of once-mighty Tyse would be here in abundance; the militia leaders would attend; even the priesthood had accepted his invitation—no less than the Rankan high priest of Vashanka, Brachis, would be among the celebrants.

Some mages are benign, some not. Some magics are pure, some sullied. The nameless lord of Tyse's coven hadn't gotten where he was by being fastidious, but he'd done his best to keep his compromises unknown, his fail-

ures hidden, his pacts with mighty demons off the mageguild
record.

The mageguild he now headed worked within the laws
of Ranke; if he did not, it just proved how little the laws of
men could really mean, where the laws of plane and
sphere and hell obtained.

He had three goals this evening: to wrest from Randal, a
minion of his by the Writ, the Nisibisi globe of power the
poor fool didn't know how to use; to lay a curse on
Brachis to take with him back to the capital, the final blow
which would shatter the empire totally, leaving Tyse an
independent state; and to make a pact with whatever power
had destroyed his predecessor, be it the outlawed adepts of
Black Nisibis, or the Lords of Hell themselves.

He'd been saving the greater portion of his soul for just
such an opportunity, waiting for the chance to trade it for
immortality and unbridled power. His sybils told him the
time was nigh.

In his bronze mirror, man-high on an electrum stand, he
examined himself: his robe, oversewn with diamonds; his
staff, capped with a sapphire frog found in the free zone;
his amulet of fiends' tooth—all of these were but a setting
for his fine-boned aristocratic face, his limpid eyes, his
auburn hair. It wasn't the face he'd been born with, but
one he'd chosen—one to earn respect from the Tysian
nobility who respected only their own bloodline, one to
make the pious quake and bring the superstitious to their
knees.

On his bedspread of quilted Maggotskin was his jewel
of office: a pinwheel-bright blue diamond as sparkling as
his eyes. He picked it up and slipped its chain around his
neck, then donned his slippers and, prepared to go downstairs, turned once more to survey the effect.

And there, in the mirror, was not one form reflected,
but two: a woman stood off to one side, a bit behind
him, where no woman had ever stood or could possibly *be*
standing.

"How—? Who—?" he blurted, astounded. The wards he'd spun here should have been impregnable: a weakness he'd helped instill in his predecessor's had ended a century of life.

"So?" said a husky voice from a ripe, wide mouth. "You do not know me?" She chuckled richly and his mind raced: her hair was piled high, thick and black, shot with silver; her eyes were gray and wide as the Nisibisi wizard-caste's were. She wore claret velvet—not a dress, but a curve-hugging shirt and leggings; beneath the laces of her shirt, her breasts were white as driven snow.

"Know you?" he repeated. "I'd like to know, my lady, how you got in here . . ."

As he spoke, she came up behind him and brazenly put her arms around his waist.

"In the usual manner," she said lightly, her fingers stroking along his girdle, her loins against his hips.

He turned his head and found himself fascinated by her long dark lashes. She raised her face to his and, as her hands went lower, finding the vent in his robe, they kissed.

It must be a Nisibisi witch, he told himself; only Death's Queen, or another of such power, would break in here and not want to give her name.

Then her tongue parted his lips and her fingers parted his undergarments and her breasts seemed to burn into his back and he found himself in lust's own grasp: his mouth was too busy to ask questions; his hands went around to cup her buttocks, to pull her in front of him where he could undo the laces of her shirt.

He felt her chuckle more than heard it; his face was between her breasts.

All magical considerations abandoned, he let her strip him below the waist. His hands forced her legs apart and he realized she had nothing on between her tunic and her leggings.

As he lifted her by the buttocks and sat her upon his manhood, she took down her long black and silver hair and arched back in his embrace, her legs wrapped about his waist.

Then, as she twirled wands of sparkling diamond in her fingers and he found he could neither move nor look away, she whispered, "It's for old times' sake, you see; come now, you'll still enjoy it." And as the diamond wands came closer and closer to his open eyes, she closed herself upon him and the fear and anguish and pleasure together took his breath away.

He'd never draw another, he knew. He tried to fight, in that last moment, as the wands took his soul through his eyes and Cime, the sorcerer-slayer, sang a song which damned him to a hell from which no adept could ever escape. Not a single demon could aid him; no awful power could save him. He was dying without even enough left of his brain to safeguard his immortal soul.

When his body stopped jerking under her, when he was spent from his loins and spent from his eyes, Cime released the spell that had held his body upright and let him fall.

Standing with legs spread over him, she crooned a while. Then she went to his bedspread made from the skin of refugees and wiped first her body clean, then her wands.

Then she stripped the dead Hazard naked and, putting on his robe, his slippers, and his jewel of office, stood before the mirror. "Let my form be his," she told the bronze reflection. "Let his manhood and his adepthood be mine in every way, so that I am he to any eye, no matter what spell or magic is invoked."

And, secreting her wands in a scabbard on her thigh, she ran her hands over her own form from head to toe, then laughed delightedly, like a happy child.

In the mirror, the First Hazard of the Tysian mageguild stood, manly and auburn-haired. Her laugh became a deep and wizardly chuckle, and from her lips came certain forgotten words. Then she said in Nisi: "Hazard I am,

Hazard I seem. This one more time, Lords of the Twelfth Plane, bless my scheme.''

Then the First Hazard, sapphire-headed staff in hand, went downstairs to greet his guests, none of whom would ever guess that in his stead Tempus's sister, Cime, had arrived.

None, that is, but Tempus, who was tempting the gods in the person of Brachis, the politicking Rankan priest.

As she descended the bone-and-lava staircase, prestidigitators salaamed and probationers bowed low and her brother's long, slitted eyes met hers—and held; his mouth twitched in a defensive little smile which promised havoc.

He knew her, she had no doubt. He knew her despite spells and incantations, as brothers always know their sisters. Among these lycanthropes and misanthropes, palm-readers and politicians, warlocks and war-mongers, only his eyes saw her clearly. And since this was as it had always been, she wasn't overly surprised.

When she reached him, he was dangling something before Brachis's face: an amulet, a charm, some little silver object that seemed to have the Rankan priest enthralled.

Brachis was hissing like a sulphurous spring: ''Give it here, blasphemer. Fete Week brings the gods to earth: thwart me and you'll feel Their wrath.'' The fat-fingered priest snatched for the amulet dangling on its thong.

''Now, now,'' her brother said, with a twist of wrist catching the amulet in his fist before the priest could grab it, ''not yet. You should have come to me about this matter. As it is, you're lucky I don't accuse you publicly of treachery.''

''You? We can't afford you—we can't afford to pay your price.'' The priest flushed red. ''Now give me that!''

''This?'' Tempus unfolded his fist and in his palm a shapeless lump of silver, bent beyond recognition, sat. ''Here.'' He tossed it and, as the priest lurched to catch it, Cime heard her brother warn Brachis: ''Niko's mine, not

yours. And no Stepson—current or former—will play assassin for an impotent god or an arrogant fool.''

The priest, the lump of silver in his hand, spied Cime
but spoke to Tempus: "No wonder the god has spurned
you. No wonder the very mention of the Stepsons inspires
fits of laughter in the capital. You've lost your touch,
sleepless one, as your men have lost their honor and
besmirched their repute. The tales from Sanctuary of their
ineptitude do not do the matter justice. As for your precious Stealth—if I'd known he was a drunkard and a dope
fiend, I'd not have bothered: it's clear he'll be no better
finishing what he starts than you.''

Furious, Brachis turned to Cime, his eunuch-cheeks flaming red: "And you, nameless one: beware the wrath of
Vashanka!'' He reached out with the distorted amulet and
tapped the sapphire frog atop the First Hazard's staff.

There was a spark of light, a puff of smoke, and the
frog turned from sapphire to swamp-green, croaked twice,
its pale throat palpitating, jumped off the staff, and hopped
away toward the mageguild garden.

Murmurs filled the air from those guests close at hand,
who'd seen the god undo magic in its citadel. Folk drew
back as the high priest flounced away.

For a moment, all eyes were on Cime in her mageform.

Her brother said, so low only she could hear, "Well, go
on; avenge the slight. Either you're a Hazard or you're
not.'' And on his lips his killsmile played.

Cime turned and with her staff pointed at the Rankan
priest's retreating back, said gruffly: "Get thee hence,
foul god-licker, back to the Rankan capital with the other
swine of empire!'' And, surreptitiously fingering her diamond rods with one hand while with the other she shook
the staff, she cast a spell she'd learned once, long ago: to
fight magicians, to rid the world of heinous sorcery, she'd
just about become one.

And her studies had borne fruit: the pink-cheeked eunuch of empire shuddered; his red robes seemed to grow

too large. He snorted and squealed as, velvet fouling his pig's feet, he fell down on all fours.

Silence rippled through the room. The military governor's wife fainted in his arms; a Tysian noble covered his son's eyes and held him close; three Hazards whispered, heads together; merchants fingered favorite charms as in their midst, a pink-snouted, red-eyed pig struggled in velvet robes.

Certain folk moved aside as the pig began to squeal hysterically. Three in the black leathers of the 3rd Commando came forward, hands upon their hilts, their eyes on Tempus steady, awaiting orders. Across from them two warlocks rubbed amulets of power; Bashir of Free Nisibis and a plain-clothed Stepson in the crowd eased right and leftward toward Tysian militiamen as factions sorted themselves out. But before any man could draw a blade in error, Cime decreed: "Begone, Rankan pig. To the emperor's seraglio, go!" She tapped her wands and shook her staff and the pig, with another ear-rending squeal, was wholly gone, leaving only a pile of damp red velvet on the floor.

"Great," her brother whispered, his arms crossed. "Now what? Are you ready to be arrested, Cime? Content to die for a crime against the empire? We're under Rankan law here, sister . . . I can't save you this time."

He crooked a finger and his men moved in a pace; wizards followed, as if to protect their archmage.

Cime smiled what would have been a winning smile, had she still worn a woman's face. "No problem, brother mine. Only say loudly that you'll escort me personally to my jail cell and give me leave to gather my effects upstairs before you do."

Shrugging, his long eyes masked, her brother did that: "First Hazard, I arrest you in the name of Imperial Ranke. Go pack your things—and don't think you can escape. The rest of you, keep in mind that bloodshed's an evil omen in Fete Week and go about your business."

The unlucky wizards and Rankan soldiers who escorted the Tysian First Hazard upstairs found, when at last they broke down the door she'd barred, a dead adept upon the floor.

The woman in his bedroom went unnoticed as the suicide of the archmage was announced.

She slipped downstairs in the confusion, dressed as she'd been when she arrived, and out into the garden where her brother stared out upon the hedge-maze.

Coming up behind him, she said, "You haven't said you're glad to see me." Her hand slipped around his waist.

He turned to face her: "Because I'm not." He brushed her hand away. "Haven't I enough trouble without you here?"

"You've too much trouble to solve without me," she said softly, and pressed forward, until he stood with his back against the garden wall.

"Why don't you stay where you're supposed to be— with the entelechy of dreams . . . buy your way out of purgatory?"

And she replied, "Dear brother, don't you see? My year is up; my curse is lifted. For the first time in three hundred years, I'm free."

* 2 *

To quell unrest among his factions and heal the rift resulting from Niko's kill, the Riddler had decreed war games spanning Fete Week—3rd Commando against Stepsons, no holds barred but murder.

Kama, the Riddler's daughter, was on Sync's team the morning the 3rd Commando colonel took the bladder-tipped dummy bolts from his crossbow and nocked armor-piercing ones instead.

Levering a bolt into place, Sync said: "Today you make your choice, Kama—it's them or us."

Kama knew Sync—the 3rd's first officer wasn't bluffing. Marking a man with red dye as a kill was one thing, serious mayhem among the militia's ranks was another.

She should have realized, when they'd ridden so far out of town, up past the cataract and across Peace River, that Sync had more than gaming on his mind. But Kama had given up too much to earn her 3rd Commando rating to lose it now. Sync might be simply testing her—Kama was Tempus's daughter and Critias's not-so-secret lover; it had taken all her skill to fend off questions of her loyalty so far.

So she had to say, "You know where I stand, Sync. It's the 3rd I'll represent at the Festival of Man, as it's been the 3rd I've represented all along. Didn't I even manage to reunite us with my—with our founder?"

Sync had wanted very much to join with Tempus; if he didn't like it now, that was only natural: the 3rd was a harder, bolder unit than the Stepsons, less constrained by gods and honor and not inclined to love one another in the way the Stepsons did.

Sync grunted an affirmative and pushed up the visor on his helmet; beyond him, eleven of the 3rd's first contingent lurked like shadows in the dawn. "We'll trust you then—if you trust us." His eyes flickered over her coldly. "Our objective is to get into that estate, steal what we can, and get out."

"There?" Kama looked where Sync was pointing: the red-roofed estate due west was squat, high-walled, unfamiliar. "Steal? Steal what? From whom? No Stepsons billet out this far—"

"Steal Niko's magic armor." Sync grinned wolfishly, "And maybe a horse or two."

"Sync, Niko's not a Stepson any longer. And those aren't gaming arrows." Kama's gut rolled; she couldn't be a party to this, yet she'd given her word.

"I didn't *think* you had it in you. Stay here, then—we need a rear guard. It's a good place for a woman."

Without waiting for her reply, the commando leader scuttled forward, waving his men on and down the hill.

She was still sitting there, mentally composing her resignation from the 3rd, watching the fighters approaching the estate, their helmets laced with brush, when she heard a noise behind her and something thudded against her leather jerkin with enough force to take her breath away.

Before she could turn around, someone grabbed her; a hand muffled her scream, and she was dragged bodily, kicking and writhing, into the piney woods.

"That's one," she heard. "Let's truss her and call it a kill."

A Stepson team had caught her; face in the dirt, she stopped struggling against the knee on her back and the hand on her head.

A second voice said: "We ought to interrogate her. This is getting porking nasty—the Riddler's declared that estate off-limits. Get Crit or Strat."

Someone moved away; the weight on top of her didn't ease; a man's hand moved impertinently on her backside. "If this weren't a game, Commando, you'd learn a thing or two today," her captor said.

She tried to kick him, but he grabbed her ankle; she tried to curse him, but her mouth was pressed against the mulching leaves.

Then she heard Crit's low, clipped voice: "Let her go."

She sat up, rubbing dirt from her lips.

Around her were six grinning Stepsons. She reached behind her back and touched the place where she'd been struck; her hand came away stained with red dye.

Crit squatted down before her: "What's going on out here, Commando?" Crit's keen eyes were grave. Straton came up beside him and hunkered down, a truncheon in his hand. War play among Tempus's factions was rough-and-tumble; neither her off-and-on relationship with Crit nor her propinquity to Tempus would save her from a very realistic interrogation, if Crit thought it would help his team.

"I'm dead." She held out her dye-stained hands. "I can't tell you anything."

Strat craned his neck and looked at the dye on her back: "You're dying, maybe, not dead—yet. And this game may have gone too far. Talk and save us all apologies tomorrow when it's over," Strat suggested, slapping his sand-filled, canvas truncheon against his palm.

Beyond them, Stepsons on their bellies worked their way to the pine grove's edge. Someone called back: "They're definitely going over the wall: they've got grappling hooks and ropes . . . maybe business quarrels."

"Kama," Crit said very softly, "we don't have time—if this is real, you'd better tell us. Nobody wants to hurt you."

Strat just watched her like a hungry wolf.

She thought about honor, about surrendering without a fight while all these Stepsons watched. And then she thought about the coming coup, about an end to Abakithis, and about Brachis's mission here, which she'd been called upon to abet: Niko was inside those walls.

"You're right, Crit . . . it's too serious to wait. Those are real arrows; the assault's not play. Sync wants a piece of Niko—his charmed Askelonian panoply, a horse, whatever he can get. As far as he's concerned, once a Stepson, always one."

Crit was up before she'd finished, calling out orders in a jargon she'd only half-mastered: "Truss her, Strat; we'll pick her up later."

She couldn't even argue that it wasn't fair, but Strat, sensitive in his way, said, "Come on, soldier," and bound her to a tree where she could see the estate and the men before it. With a final jerk on her wrists, he said, "Don't go way, now, will you?" and jogged down the hill to find his partner.

So Kama had long agonizing moments to consider what it meant to be trysting with a Stepson who already had a partner: Strat was to Critias what she could never be. The Sacred Band pairs who formed the Stepsons' core were teamed for life. Strat wasn't jealous of her; there was no reason for him to be.

Though she understood the 3rd Commando, she despaired of ever understanding the motivations of the Stepsons. And she must . . . it was the Stepsons, not the 3rd, who'd be her subject for the heroic saga she'd tell in the bard's contest at the Festival of Man.

Immersed in her own thoughts, tied ignominiously to a tree, it took Kama a while to realize that something odd was happening at the walled estate: the sky was growing dark overhead; thunder rolled in on a winter sky, and the men who climbed the walls on ropes seemed to move too slowly, as if time itself had slowed.

Kama, the 3rd's historian, had seen the heavens do battle in the wizard war; she'd seen a wind of stones suck fighters from a battlefield, and a tunnel of cloud come to take her father's weary contingent home when the war was done.

But you never expected magical intervention; you couldn't, and remain sane. Gods and magicians warred through men, most times; when they warred on them, simple human fighters couldn't win.

As the sky blew black and the clouds dipped down, her heart skipped beats: she couldn't tell what god or witch the storm was serving; she feared for Crit so that she called out his name and only then realized how loud was the rumble coming down from the vault of heaven.

And though she was not pious, Kama prayed: she prayed for Crit and the Stepsons first, and then, feeling guilty, she prayed for Sync's 3rd Commando. But most of all, as the storm winds shook the trees and howled, she prayed for it to stop. If she hadn't been tied securely to the tree, she might have been blown away like the men who tumbled from the walls of the estate.

She heard yells upon the wind, saw men trying to hold ropes steady so those high up could climb down.

Crossbows were useless in the maelstrom; men held onto one another, making human chains.

Then, from above, lightning flashed and speared down like a serpent's forked tongue amid the men who struggled now to save each other, not to fight each other.

Again the lightning flashed and this time, looking at the raging sky, Kama thought she saw a face: eyes like holes in the firmament; an angry mouth from which the lightning spat; and on its head, so bright she had to squint and turn away, was the crown you saw on every statue of Enlil—the crown of heaven.

Her eyes tearing, terrified, Kama watched the lightning which ran along the ramparts of the estate and quested down along its walls, driving back the fighters, herding them together, chasing them up the hill.

And when they reached its crest, as suddenly as it had come, the wind abated, the thunder rolled away, and the sky began to clear.

Men dashed past Kama without stopping, so that she began to fear she'd be left to die here.

Then Crit and Straton crested the hill, looking backward every now and again as they came toward her.

"I told you that place was weird," Strat was saying as they reached her; Crit already had his knife out to slit her bonds.

"You should have told Sync," Crit grunted, cutting Kama loose.

Rubbing her wrists, she blurted: "Sync—the 3rd . . . any casualties?"

"Some broken limbs, nothing major," Crit said. And: "If you want, you can ride home with us—we've horses down in the rift. Someone's got to tell the Riddler . . ."

"Tell him what?" Sync demanded, breathing hard, limping as he came up beside them.

"That's up to Kama . . . that we war-gamed a little too close to some holy place nobody knew about, and the god took a hand," Crit suggested without looking up from his feet, more than a touch of cynicism in his voice.

"That's right, Sync—it's Fete Week," Strat agreed generously. "Everybody expects some manifestation of the gods, this time of year. What would New Years be without some god's prank?"

The question hung in the air while Sync thought the matter over. Then he hawked into the pine needles and said: "Fine with me. If you think that's all it was, that's all it was," and limped away to regroup his men.

"Coming, Kama? I'll need you to back me when we tell this tall tale to your father," Crit told her, while Straton grumbled that Critias always strode right in where even gods feared to tread.

* 3 *

Niko was out in the exercise yard behind the great house belonging to Partha, his host, doing as he'd been asked, giving two of Partha's children pointers on their event training for the coming games, while around his head a pesky hornet buzzed.

The day before, the sky had turned black on the heels of dawn and Niko's stallion had chosen that moment to break out of his stall and mount some hapless mare in the stables.

At that very instant, Niko had been doing the same to Partha's daughter, Sauni. He hadn't meant to do it; he was trying not to do it: any woman might be Roxane in disguise.

But the girl wouldn't leave him alone. She found excuses to brush against him in the halls and developed cramps during training only he could seem to ease.

It had gotten to the point where Partha himself had interceded on Sauni's behalf: at dinner the night before, Partha had belched good-naturedly and sent his teenage son and daughter off to bed, then turned to Niko, asking:

"Is there something wrong with my daughter?"

"Not at all," Niko demurred. "She's coming along fine. She's fast as the wind and strong as a deer. She'll place in the footrace, certainly."

"Nikodemos, you know what I mean."

"I wouldn't abuse your hospitality, my lord," Niko had replied, taking a drink of Machadi wine and brushing at a buzzing insect circling above his head. The estate, commodious otherwise, had a hornet problem; Randal could have solved it, no doubt, but Niko had no intention of asking for the wizard's help.

"Then it's settled," said the father contentedly.

"What? What's settled?"

"It's Fete Week. Sauni's fifteen and a virgin. You wouldn't have me send her down to a public temple to sit in the dirt until some fat merchant deigns to do a favor for the goddess?"

Niko looked into his wine cup. "I'm not . . ."

"Even if you prefer boys—and I've heard the Stepsons do—as you've said, you shouldn't abuse my hospitality. The gods love you; I'm not asking you to marry her, just give her a good start on life."

"I—did Bashir have anything to do with this?"

"Bashir?" the father said with exaggerated surprise. "He's had his eye on Sauni for years; we need a priestess of the Lady down here in the lowlands. But Bashir had nothing to do with it . . . it's the girl herself."

"How's that?" Niko emptied his wine cup and his host eagerly refilled it.

"She's in love with you, Stealth. Any fool could see it; she moons around after you—'Stealth did this, Stealth said that.' If it weren't so propitious, I'd be jealous."

"But, under the circumstances, you're in favor?" Niko

said doubtfully. He didn't even know if he was capable of doing his host this service. He didn't like the idea of being contracted like a stud, and he *knew* Bashir was involved: Bashir was bound and determined to make Niko a productive citizen of Free Nisibis, a permanent adjunct to his staff.

"Not only in favor, I'm about to shower you with gifts as soon as you make my lucky house the proud repository of Our Lady's new priestess. Thus it's decided, as the gods foretold. Drink up, my friend." And with a bearlike paw, he clapped Niko on the back.

So in the dawn, the girl had come creeping into his bed, dressed in nothing but a Fete Week virgin's silks, and Niko did what the god intended, while in the stables his horse had done the same and, outside, the heavens had roared and bellowed like the stallion as he climbed the mare.

Niko couldn't remember how it had been with the girl— he'd been too drunk. But she was happy and trying to please him, so it must have gone well enough for her.

He kept telling himself that this girl couldn't possibly be a representative of the Nisibisi witch, that Bashir wouldn't have done that to him, and that he'd get out of here in the next few days, before he became any more entangled in the Partha family's affairs.

But the next day he found himself sitting on his horse with a wineskin in his hand and the pestilential hornets plaguing him, watching Partha's children train with javelin and bow and mumbling pointers whenever he remembered what he was there for, whiling away the time.

When the sun was settling and the three of them went to the stone house to steam the soreness from their muscles, Sauni was boasting to her brother about having become a woman of the god.

Naked, she rubbed her flat belly and stretched out, her head on Niko's knee, regaling them both with a tale of Niko's performance which must have been apocryphal: if the gods had attended their tryst, Niko surely would have remembered it; and if he'd been as much the stallion as she claimed, he would have had some recollection.

But then Grippa, Partha's tow-headed son, started telling them how men had come scaling the walls at the very instant that Sauni became a woman, and that Father Enlil had appeared in the sky above with his lightning and his thunder to drive the men away.

"What? You mean figuratively, of course." Niko sat bolt upright.

The boy pouted: "I *saw* it, didn't I? Rangers, then Stepsons. Then the god . . ."

Niko got up and left the two children there, grabbing his clothing as he strode through the anteroom with its water buckets and sponges, suddenly sober and not liking it one bit.

Sauni came racing after him, wide-eyed and shivering, half-naked: "Niko! Niko! Don't mind Grippa, it's . . ."

"It's what?" he snapped unkindly. "I never should have gotten involved with—here."

She shivered as if he'd struck her: "You're going to leave, aren't you? Bashir said I shouldn't expect it to last long, but . . ." Tears welled in her eyes; she bit her lip. "I've just found you; please don't go."

"Gods, girl, don't you understand what's happening? They're using you like they're using me. And mortals always get hurt when the gods play games."

She was shaking her head: "But I . . . love . . . you."

"You don't even *know* me. I'm just the first acceptable candidate who came your way. Look at me."

Chin high, she stared at him soulfully, a perfect Tysian beauty with a heart-shaped face and a body like a nymph.

"If the gods," he said slowly, hopeful of making her understand, "have got you with child, then that's one thing. If I did, then that's another. Only you will know the truth of it. If you're pregnant and you come to me at the games and ask me to, I'll make good on what's happened

here. Do you understand? I'll marry you. But if you're
some daft little priestess with Father Enlil for a husband,
then you don't need me anymore.''

"Niko . . . I . . .'' She came into his arms.

He felt reprehensible and foul, holding her, her sweet
hair brushing his nose. But he had to get out of here; he
couldn't sink any deeper into the morass of his own fear.

If the god really had staved off an attack on the estate,
then the omen spoke clearly: he couldn't run, he couldn't
hide. Others were being hurt because of him.

He was tired of drinking and nearly immune to drugs; he
was making errors his conscience couldn't support. Still
holding the girl by her quaking shoulders, he said softly,
"Come, Sauni; help me pack."

An hour later, armed and armored, he was riding out of
the estate on the big sable stallion, who danced with joy
when Niko turned him toward Wizardwall and gave him
his head.

*   **4**   *

Rumors of Enlil's sanction upon the militia and of
mage-killers abroad in Tyse sent Randal hurrying to Crit's
safe haven in the Lanes as soon as he got into town. For
once, Critias seemed glad to see him.

Even Straton was polite: "Where have you been, Randal?" Strat greeted him. "We've been looking all over for
our favorite mage."

Not "Witchy-ears," not "mageling," but pleasant words
accompanied by what, for Strat, was a civil smile.

"I've been to see the archmage, Askelon," Randal said
proudly. "I've been to Meridian and back."

"Well, it can't be him, then," Crit sighed. "We've
been looking all over for you, Randal. Strat's right. I
suppose you know that the mageguild's shut tight, Fete

Week or not; that the latest First Hazard expired—this time by suicide?''

"Suicide?" Randal repeated dumbly, all his joy at having come home triumphant from Meridian bleeding away. "Impossible. Mages don't commit suicide—we don't consider death a refuge. Especially not an archmage . . . not *that* archmage! You don't know what death means to one such as he . . .'' Randal shivered; he wasn't looking forward to his own dying day, and he'd been very careful—he'd only bargained away pieces of his soul and pacted with one demon, and that once it had been for Niko, not himself. Before pairing with the Stepson, Randal had been content to be a low-level adept, and sleep at night.

"The Second and Third Hazard have been here, telling us all about what it means, and how it couldn't have happened that way, and why no new First Hazard will be appointed until the magekiller is apprehended," Crit said in his sardonic way. Taking his feet off his littered desk, he leaned his head back against the safe haven's iron shutters, staring at Randal pensively.

"That's why we've been looking for you," his partner said. "You're just the man to help us identify and apprehend the culprit who's killed two guildmasters of yours." Strat put an arm on Randal's shoulders. "Sit right down here and tell us about Meridian. You went to see the mightiest wizard of all. Could *he* be persuaded to help us find—''

Randal shook Strat's arm away. "We don't need Askelon for that. I know who it was; I know how it happened. I—''

"Who, then?" Crit sat forward.

Randal took a deep breath: "Roxane." The mages knew; he'd told them. He didn't understand why they hadn't told Crit until Strat said, "Crap, no wonder they dropped this in our laps." Straddling a chair, the big Stepson took out his beltknife and began digging at the wood of Crit's desk.

Randal, too, sat down on a ragged hassock: "Our laps?"

"That's right, Randal," Crit sighed, getting up and

beginning to pace. "The mageguild is a necessary evil, you know: the mageguild network transfers intelligence north and south. The sorcerers are useless to us now, sequestered like that. They won't come out until we find the murderer, they say. We 'owe' them that, they say. The wizard war may well be hotting up again, Tempus thinks, and this whole thing a ploy by the Nisibisi renegades to lay our underbelly open for a sorcerous incursion."

Crit stopped pacing: "Get the point, Randal? Damned inconvenient time you picked to disappear. The Riddler's been here looking for you every day."

Strat said dourly: "Better tell him, Crit—he'll find out soon enough."

Randal looked between the two Stepsons; both men were almost trembling, and not with eagerness.

Crit said, "Right," went back to his seat, forsook it, and sat on the desk instead. "Randal, Cime's back. *Don't* panic, we've got her word she'll leave you be."

"But she's sworn to kill me!" Randal was up on his feet but Strat was faster: Strat got between him and the door.

"I told you he wouldn't have the belly for it, Crit," Strat rumbled. "Let's give him to the mageguild—say it's him that's been slaying their . . ."

"They'd never believe it," Crit said nastily. "Randal, you don't have any choice in this. Let's get busy, before it's too late. I need a signed affidavit from you that it was Roxane, something we can slip under the mageguild's door." He tapped a stylus.

Randal knew that look. He went to sign the paper, not really understanding what Crit had in mind. "Then what?" he asked, stylus in hand.

"Then we set a trap for Roxane, Randal, with Niko as the bait. And by then you'd better have figured out some way to deal with her. We've got to deliver her to the mageguild—Riddler's orders. And by the end of Fete Week."

Randal, putting ink to paper, said slowly: "But what if they don't believe me? I told them once. What if they think the Riddler's sister did it? By every page and line of the Writ, she's capable enough."

"We don't care," Crit said, enunciating carefully, "if she's Roxane in disguise. Cime's the Riddler's sister, and her name's not to come into this. If you saw Roxane, then we'll assume Roxane's behind the second slaying also. Got that?"

Then Randal realized just why the Stepsons were involved, and what had made the Riddler promise to help the sorcerers, whom he deplored: Tempus, Crit, and Straton were involved in this to protect Cime from whatever retribution she'd doubtless earned.

But since it was a matter of honorbond, and since Stepsons never argued with an order or asked foolish questions, Randal didn't say a word, only signed his name and agreed to take the affidavit to the mageguild: with Niko as the bait, he couldn't refuse to go up against a witch, even if it was Roxane, Death's own queen.

* 5 *

Roxane was hiding in Frog's Marsh, hungry and weak. She'd sucked the life from more than one Tysian adept, but this time it might not be enough. She'd taken wounds in the wizard war that were hard to heal.

She had no snakes here, either, no minions of consequence. Her warlock brethren had cast her out of Mygdon, a punishment for having failed them. All because of the accursed Riddler and his supernormal allies—gods and sprites from the twelfth plane, dream lords and the like.

She was nearly as weak as a mortal, but her spirit was still strong. At night she snuck out of her marshy bower, making undeads, one by one, who'd serve her, or lurking by the mageguild's gates to catch an unlucky apprentice napping, a familiar she could munch.

Most of all, she wanted to change her shape and hide among the throng in Tyse, become beautiful once more. For Roxane had been crippled by the war so that her body was infirm.

She'd come so close to winning, she didn't know how to admit defeat. If she could get the power globe that Randal had, she'd be able to straighten broken limbs, suck souls now far beyond her reach.

As night settled, she donned her foxfur robe and limped slowly down to the river's edge, reduced to eating fish like a mortal tramp.

When she'd supped, she forded, and lurched toward Commerce Avenue where she'd go whoring, her foxfur helping to disguise her crippled gait.

And as she limped along the back streets, she uttered spells between clenched teeth: one to loose her few undeads upon the party-goers uptown; one to bring her luck and bring ill-fortune to her enemies; one to lure young Nikodemos, the soul she longed for above all others, close enough for her to grab him. Should she conquer Niko, she'd stand head to head with heaven once again.

It wasn't Nikodemos who crossed her path, but a towheaded teenaged boy named Grippa. Still, he was fair and whole and he trembled in her hand when, thinking her a whore and comely, he followed her into an alley close by Brother Bomba's. "Come, come, that's it, boy," she said, and as he swooned with ecstasy, she reached into his mind.

And held her hungry self back from devouring him, for she found thoughts of Niko there.

She read the boy's young mind and then she took her pleasure with him, as he'd taken his with her. Trying not to think how low she'd sunk or what sad estate the finest Nisibisi witch had earned, because of Tempus, she de-

voured his soul and then his flesh, discorporating him on
the spot.

She'd never masqueraded as a boy, never been a man,
never thought nor chose to try it. Yet this boy was a friend
of Niko's.

When the tryst was over, only the youth came out again.
Left behind in the alley was a woman's foxfur robe around
a skeleton whose leg had once been broken, then mended
wrong.

And out into the night went Roxane, whole and hale in
an athlete's sweet young form, a boy whom Niko favored,
unless Grippa read the signs wrong, more than any girl—a
boy Niko had sworn to coach and help to win at the
Festival of Man.

* 6 *

Tempus himself went up to Wizardwall to fetch Niko—
he'd have gone anywhere to get away from Cime before he
succumbed and lay with her.

Askelon had made good his word, given Tempus's nemesis eternal youth and beauty, lifted her curse in exchange
for a year of female company.

How anyone could stand a year of Cime's bullwhip
tongue and devious mind, Tempus couldn't understand,
but once he'd said that donkeys would choose rubbish
rather than gold. And Askelon was nothing if not an ass.

The spires of Wizardwall no longer gleamed with
ensorceled light; the gods lived here now. A pinkish tinge
was over everything—the rocks, the chasms, the steep
defiles Bashir's guerrillas called their own.

Tempus's Askelonian mare rumbled a greeting as soon
as the gate came down: if Tempus had doubted that Niko
was here, the mare's reaction to the smell of her brother
eased his mind.

Getting Niko out of Bashir's clutches was not going to be easy, especially when the reason wasn't one with which Bashir would sympathize.

But Niko must draw the witch; no other could be sure to do so. It was cruel, but necessary for everyone concerned: Niko needed to see a witch-corpse to heal his soul; Tempus needed a witch to blame for Cime's mischief; the mageguild needed to be strengthened before the thaw.

And the witch would never venture up the high peaks, not while the god held sway.

As Bashir's guerrillas crowded around him with ribald greetings in sibilant Nisi, Tempus reflected that life was teaching him a lesson he'd never thought he'd need: Tempus, who was afraid to love, admitted to himself how deeply he'd come to care for Niko.

Climbing stairs which had once led to a Nisibisi wizard's aerie, he swore silently to find a way to save Niko from an eternity in thrall: even if the boy died young, it would be a gift if he died with his soul intact.

Bashir greeted Tempus at the stair's head, his godridden eyes concerned: "You bring great peril, Riddler, treachery and pain—the god has shown me." Bashir's arms crossed. He wore only a Nisi tunic, despite the cold. His flat face glowed with sanctity; his flaring cheeks were hollowed; his tightset jaw told Tempus the god had told this priest too much.

"Bashir, you've got to let me help him. He'll end up just like me. Do I look happy? Fulfilled? Transported with joy at the life the god has given me?"

"A different god," Bashir intoned; "a different life."

But the priest stepped aside and let Tempus mount the stairs, then paced him.

"I have to see him. If Enlil is wise, he'll let a mortal make a mortal's choice."

"Sleepless one, Niko cannot sleep these nights, because of you and your magicians. Have you no sympathy? No soul? Let him be; the god and I can save him."

"Soul?" Tempus rubbed his jaw. "Perhaps I don't, Bashir—it's been centuries since I've thought to look. As for Enlil—or any god—saving any man . . . if that's what you think gods do, you're not as wise as you look. Nothing I can do to Niko will hurt him like what you propose. You stare at me, you're staring at the horse's mouth. You ought to listen when I tell you: being god-ridden is as bad as any devil's curse. He told you once himself that he didn't want salvation at the price either one of us has paid."

Bashir looked at his feet, his long braided sidelock swinging as he walked: "Riddler," he said, his voice thick and troubled, "I want the best for Niko. When we were boys together, plying banditry among the high peaks, he was my trusted friend. But now, where is that person? The man who's here loves drugs and drink, fears honest women, goes armed and armored all the time."

"I know, Bashir. Just let me take him if he wishes it—don't stand in his way. Let me see if I can free him from the archmage, the witch, and then let him choose the god—choose freely, and not from fear."

That brought the priest's head up. For a moment, fanatical light blazed in his eyes, then subsided. "I suppose it has to be this way." Bashir stopped, his voice a whisper. "He's in here. But be warned, Riddler: Father Enlil wants Niko's soul enough to fight the very dream lord for it. Don't think what you can do or say will stand in His way."

"Would that I could, my friend. If Niko doesn't mend by the third week of the Festival of Man, I myself will help you with the final godbond rights."

Bashir's forehead wrinkled. "I'll hold you to your word." He reached behind him, pushing open a heavy door. "In here. I'll be in the god's room; seek me when you're done."

And then Tempus stepped inside, closing the door behind him, waiting for his eyes to adjust to the dimness.

"Who's there?" Niko called, his voice strained and nervous.

From the sound of it, the boy must be sitting near the windowsill.

Tempus joined him by the window. "Niko, I've come to take you home. We need you—the witch is loose. Randal can't fight her all alone, and the mageguild seers are all hiding in their closets."

He hadn't meant to be that honest; he didn't want to be so cruel.

The youth beside him turned his head. "I had to leave—the god came down to Partha's. I can't have the Stepsons cursed on my account. If the god wants me, then perhaps it will balance off the greed of the entelechy of dreams."

"Don't talk that way," Tempus nearly snarled. "We've more immediate concerns. The witch . . ."

"The witch. She seems enticing. I *know* what she wants—just my body, a bit of soul. The archmage steals my sleep and wants an avatar; the god wants a representative on earth." Niko coughed, and Tempus realized he'd been drinking. "If the witch can conquer gods and demigods, then she deserves me—she can have me. Maybe then I'll get some sleep."

"You'll sleep forever, sleep a sleep you won't enjoy." Tempus took Niko's face between his hands. "Look at me. Listen well: there's a way out of this, there always is. Even my sister finally earned her freedom, and she's a wanton slut who still kills witches when and where she can."

"A way out? Of this? . . ." The boy spread his hands, then dropped them, unresisting.

"There's always hope. Without it, we'd all kill ourselves as soon as we learned we were born to die. And there's *maat*—you might yet regain it. Even failing that, I'll promise you a hero's death: I'll slay you myself in single combat before I'll let Ash"—he spat the dream lord's nickname, one only he and his sister were old enough and wise enough to know—"take charge of you, or let a god no better than Vashanka twist your soul."

"There's that," Niko agreed tonelessly. "If you'll do it, if you'll promise . . ."

Tempus let go of Niko and the boy leaned his head back against the sill. "Do you ever even nap? I'm so tired, I can't think straight. And even krrf, which used to wake me up, now just makes me sleepy."

"I doze, now and then, after a good love match or a strenuous fight. Randal's waiting, down in Tyse. He'd have come himself, but we didn't want Bashir to have to purify this place all over again. Come on, I'll race you to Hidden Valley. If you can't sleep on your own then, my sister will be more than happy to help tire you out."

Niko got to his feet, wavered there.

Tempus steadied him.

"I can do it. It just takes time," Niko said, and took slow steps while somewhere high above a hornet buzzed softly. "You've squared this with Bashir?"

"I have until the Festival to convince you that the god's way isn't yours. If I can't do that, the sun may refuse to rise."

Niko grunted and felt his way toward the crack of light that showed beneath his chamber's door. As he did so, Tempus heard the rustle of armor and knew that Niko wasn't as far gone as he seemed: whatever its provenance, that enchanted panoply of his could still keep body and soul intact.

* 7 *

On the last night of Fete Week, the Bombas threw a party, opening Brother Bomba's bar to all their friends, inviting Stepsons, Rankan rank and file, Tysian nobles— even 3rd Commando fighters and certain merchants from Commerce Avenue, sellers of flesh and fate and charm.

Among those from the Avenue who came was one

low-caste enchantress, a woman who was responsible for a scaly rash on the face of Sync, the 3rd Commando's colonel, and for the diminishment of his ranks by two: those who'd raped Madame Bomba would never rape another.

But since Sync himself had never laid a hand on the Madame, and since it was Fete Week, when Sync came to her with apologies and hopes that she'd know someone to heal his face, she put him in the hands of the very woman who'd afflicted him, so that she could "set this poor man right."

Thus Madame Bomba showed compassion and forgave a wrong in Fete Week, as the gods prescribed.

Others, though, were not so mindful of the gods: Tempus lounged in the renovated bar's far corner, picking at the snowy linen on his table, dressed in his finest leopardskin and boar's-tooth helm, waiting for the witch to show, his sharkskin-hilted sword well-whetted, his Stepsons at the ready.

Randal was sure the witch would come: he'd spun his globe and uttered phrases to assure it. He waited now, upstairs, his nose pressed to the one-way glass, a spell of "Seeing Through" invoked to pierce any wizardly disguise.

Among the celebrants, Stepsons wandered, alert to any woman who might seem too interested in Niko, to any girl they hadn't seen before, to any unfamiliar courtesan or stately matron they didn't know.

Bomba's was lit with paper lanterns; brightly colored streamers laced the beams. Pipers played and lutes were strummed and bell trees tinkled, carried on staves by Tysian boys approaching manhood, as youngsters who'd trade their wooden swords for iron in the morning said goodbye to childhood in the time-honored way.

The Partha family had come downtown for the occasion. Old man Partha, in his patriarch's orange, matched Niko drink for drink, round for round, while the girl most

Stepsons had wagered was the witch, comely Sauni, hovered near, refusing even Critias a dance to stay by Stealth.

Her brother Grippa, among the youths who'd officially be men by morning, shook his bell tree at a dozen girls, racing up and down the stairs with one and then another, so that Crit remarked: "I don't care *who* he is, no man, let alone a stripling boy, can make that many dreams come true."

Yet well on toward midnight, Grippa still was dragging girls upstairs and bringing them down dazed and smiling dumbly, while Niko sat, befuddled with wine, his chair tipped back against a freshly whitewashed wall, untroubled by any girl but Sauni.

When the midnight chimes were struck and the celebration took the raucous tone of men and women chasing out the evils of the year gone by, Tempus forsook his watch and sought Randal, still alone, upstairs.

"Life, Randal, how goes it?" Tempus had half expected to find his mage asleep, or dead by sorcery, or bewitched where he sat.

But Randal was awake, on duty, and bleary-eyed. "Riddler, by all the Writ's power, there's something wrong here: she's in the room, but I can't tell which girl she is."

"Maybe she didn't come; perhaps she suspects the trap." Tempus had convinced three mages to attend in deep disguise, to back up Randal should a battle of magics ensue. Everyone was briefed, and a concoction Cime guaranteed would subdue the witch if sprinkled on her had been doled out to the fighters as if it were poison for their arrows. Everyone was ready—everyone but the witch, it seemed.

"Not a chance. Look here." Randal indicated his Nisibisi globe of power, spinning slowly on its stand: "See how bright the stones shine? See how it hums? Come close and you'll hear it. By these signs, she's here. I can't imagine why I can't tell where."

Tempus, curious despite himself, approached the globe, which began to spark as he came near.

"Uh . . . Commander, my lord, that's close enough. It doesn't like you . . . that is," Randal tried to be polite, "it remembers the wizard war. Power pieces never forget a—"

Randal broke off and pressed his nose against the glass. "By the Writ, that's it. She's not a *she*. That is, look here, Riddler—quickly! Drat and blast, I hope it's not too late!"

"What's this?" Tempus grabbed the mage and shook him by the shoulder. "Too late? Speak plain, mageling!"

But then he saw Niko, arm in arm with Grippa, Partha's son, headed toward the back door—whether to the drug dens below or the alleyways outside, Tempus couldn't tell.

Even as Randal was gathering up the globe and telling him to: "Hurry! It's that boy! She's a *boy,* not a girl! Oh, hurry, Riddler, before it's too late!" Tempus was taking the stairs two at a time, headed for the rear door.

"Get your mages, Randal, and Crit!" he called out over his shoulder. "Meet me around the back."

As he ran, he drew his sharkskin-hilted sword, a blade that for years had slit the finest spell like silk and glowed pink with Vashanka's blessing. But without the Storm God's blessing, here in the north, it didn't glow at all; he wasn't sure what it could do against a witch.

Pounding down the darkened back stairs, while somewhere out there Niko, drunk and terrorized by gods and magic, reeled right into the clutches of the witch, Tempus considered what had been, till then, unthinkable: with Vashanka gone, hiding or helpless, he had an option. By the Law of Consonance and in behalf of Niko, Tempus might make a bargain with Enlil.

And as soon as he thought those thoughts, a rumbling began in his inner ear such as he hadn't heard since Fete Week last, in Sanctuary, when Vashanka had done battle in the sky, then disappeared.

But it was not his familiar loved and hated Pillager who

rustled in his head: this voice was deeper, the power older, the might of it enough to stop him in his tracks.

"You called, blasphemer? You wish to go down on your bony knees, mortal? In extremis, My power and My glory, My battle and My fury, are not too frightful for thee?"

"Listen, God, I need some help. I'll make a bargain with You—leave the boy untouched by Your Haughtiness, and I'll serve Thee for a year."

Tempus wasn't on his knees yet, he was still standing; he didn't like the feel of this Enlil in his head. There was too much of the four-eyed, blazing Ravager, who'd begotten frightful battle before Vashanka had drawn a baby god's first breath, to make him comfortable. This god was already asking more than Tempus had thought to give.

"Down on thy knees, then, creature; supplicate My Majesty. Then your battle will be terrible once more and your enemies grovel in blood up to their genitals. Wherever they go My ground will open up before them; My rain will blind them; the beasts of My fields and the predators of My mountains will gobble them up! They will know terror of Me and of thee, My servant, as you never dreamed when the boy-god Vashanka was thine—"

"Hold, Enlil! The day I bend my knee to any god, especially one who treats a supplicant as You've treated poor, unknowing Niko, will be the day the moon eats up the sky! I called Thee forth to tell Thee what I think of Thee, who's done evil to Thine own faithful. Thou art a vicious god, and powerless, to let a paltry witch snatch a soul like Niko's from underneath Thy long and awful nose."

He could see the god now, a shining manifestation on the staircase—a face with fanged mouth, a face from time's beginning, a face to swallow empires and make the ignorant bow down.

But this god was canny, wiser than Vashanka, not as easily fooled. *"You're wasting time, man, thou who art an insect in My sight! Your love for another man is not My problem; your love of heaven is what's in question."*

"Help me save the boy—or do it on Your own. You gods ought to take responsibility for what You've wrought."

Now Enlil was closer, god-glowing eyes narrow and filled with craft. *"He's not yet Mine, and you know it. Thou art a deceiver, manling, if man you are. Will you bend your head to Me, and receive the power of My battle unto your shriveled soul and the strength of My blessing unto your sword? Or must you lose against your curse once more?"*

They were always promising to protect him from the curse, yet they seemed a part of it. But Niko, by the moment, drew closer to damnation. "That's right—he's not yet chosen You. And if I choose You in his stead, You must be content with that. I'll even go down on my knees if I have Your promise—by whatever power gods can swear—to leave the boy unblessed by Your horrific love!"

Having made his offer as clearly and as carefully as he could—for gods do take advantage, adhering only to what's explicated in an oath, never what's meant but left unspoken—Tempus waited, ready to go down on his knees for power, one more time.

And to his disgust, the staircase under him began to shake, the walls about to tremble, and a ruddy light surrounded him: the light of the primal god, Enlil, under which all things came out of heaven and in which he'd now have to bow and swear and compound his already awful fate.

He almost changed his mind, but then rethought it: he'd lived three hundred years under deific sway and hadn't liked it; he couldn't stand by while the boy he loved, Niko, who was the son he should have had, if men could only choose their offspring, stepped unknowing down a path from which there was no retreat.

"Bow down, and embrace thy fate, mortal minion! My power and My glory are thine, reflected light. My Word is given—My wish is thy command, as thy bargain is accepted!"

It was hard to bow down to another god, this one worse, if any were, than Vashanka. He hoped he wouldn't live on, regretting it, too long. Before his eyes he saw fierce and awful battles, an eternity of man up to his hips in blood because of godhead and gods' quarrels; he heard martyrs' voices and the death screams of whole peoples, genocidal wars that had, and did, and would take place.

Then something touched him and he shuddered; throughout his person, agony and ecstasy admixed.

When he looked up, he saw great horny feet with clawed toes and golden scales. A hand reached out, as large as his whole trunk, plucked him up, and out among long-tailed stars, set him down again in darkness:

"Fight well, Riddler! And make it interesting—something more than simple slaughter."

Then Tempus felt the familiar emptiness that told him that the god was gone.

Well, he thought, what difference does it make, really? One god or another, what they do and what they want's about the same.

And then he saw, ahead, a group locked in ensorceled combat: he saw Niko, blue shining light like ropes or snakes enveloping him, propped up against an alley wall, his face uncomprehending as before him, witchfire raged.

The witch was in a boy-form, true, but overlaid on that was a crippled, tortured female form and her eyes were fierce and thirsty as, clawlike hands outstretched, she reached for Randal's globe.

The mageling held that globe tight against his chest, both arms wrapped around it, blue snakes of magic fire striking at him, while on each side and right before him, other sorcerers from Tyse fought back, red mongoose-ghosts in see-through battle with Roxane's ectoplasmic snakes.

Meanwhile, about the edges of the fray, Tempus saw his own simple, human fighters: Crit, trying to get to Randal, fighting spiderwebby nets which bound him; Strat, his huge hands on Crit's collar, his muscles bulging, trying to keep his partner from being sucked into a cobalt maelstrom building in midair among the garbage of the alleyway; Sync, frozen in mid-movement, a vial of witch-subduing potion uncapped in his hand, its droplets glistening but unmoving, as if encased in amber.

From the maelstrom, an eery yowling issued, and Tempus realized that his moment was at hand. He'd see if Father Enlil was out to trick him, or just bluffing: if the maelstrom coalesced and demons, fiends, and devils joined the fray, then all was lost—at least his men would be. And he really didn't want to bury Stepsons on New Year's Day. It wasn't the sort of omen he'd accept.

Drawing his sharkskin-hilted sword, he sallied forth, howling battle cries. And the sword turned pink as it encountered magic, and began to warm and quiver in his hand.

That's more like it, he thought, slitting Crit's bonds of magic netting with a slice that sent them up in smoke, so that Crit yelped from the sparks and stumbled back when Strat's hold on him could help.

By then the witch had seen Tempus, and she cast a lightning bolt his way.

But the sword was as good as its god, and his new god as good as His word: he parried the bolt and it split, pink swordmetal glowing red as opposing forces met, sparks flying, thunder roaring.

At the same time, with his other hand, he got his own vial of witchstuff out and threw it. Then, as she howled, hands up, and before she could strike again, he took a chance, turned his back on her, and leaped toward the sucking maelstrom, in which demon heads and fiends' white teeth and devils' horns were beginning to appear.

He had to stop the incursion: this wasn't only Niko; it was the beginning of another wizard war. Back unprotected, trusting Randal and his mages to do their best for him, he thrust his blade deep into that sucking maw, from which the fumes of hell were beginning to escape.

The concussive force of sword striking hell-mouth rocked him to his core: "Well, God," he snarled, "are we out of our league, here?"

And in his head he heard a chuckle: *"Not yet, mortal, not yet."*

He had to trust the god; he couldn't even look away to see how his men were faring: a devil's warty hand had his sword by its pink tip and was pulling him inward with all its might.

He dug in his heels, but it was useless. If he let go the sword, he didn't want to consider the consequences: the sword was linked to him by the god and to the god by him. He had to fight it.

He pulled back with all his strength, but the devil-grip was heating up the sword and it stretched instead of coming loose.

And hand over hand, fiends helping it, the devil pulled him closer to its maw.

Fiendish arms reached out to grab him; warty jaws gaped in horrid laughter. His sword, as soft as clay, glowed so that he had to look away.

Closer and closer, he was drawn. He could smell the roasting flesh of hell and hear the devil's war cry. It grated on his nerves and made his teeth ache.

Then once more he called upon the god, and this time the heavens opened with His answer: a freezing wind began to blow, hail pummeled from a clear night sky, and all about him steam began to rise.

Steam rose from his sword and blinded the closest devil, half out of the maelstrom, who screeched and rubbed its eyes.

His sword released, he thrust and skewered the devil, who right away exploded, spraying ichor everywhere.

The stink was awful. The steam hissed and roared, obscuring everything as the hail and wind reacted with the hellish maelstrom.

But Tempus's sword was hard once more, if bent, and

he hacked away with abandon, humming gleeful curses under his steaming breath.

Before his onslaught, his god-inspired battle, the maelstrom quivered, then it heaved. Then it gave out a human-seeming sigh and caved in on itself with an audible thud, leaving a severed demon trunk and arms of fiend littering the cobbled street.

He stared for a moment at the garbage heap beyond, where the maelstrom had just been.

He realized that his clothes were still steaming, that acid ichor had splattered his face and hands, that his sword-holding palm was burned, and that, amazingly, he was breathing heavily from the fight.

Then he turned and saw his allies: Randal, his globe hugged tight like a baby, directing his mageguild betters in the binding of Roxane, the Nisibisi witch, with magical bonds; Crit, welted with blisters and striped with soot, sitting on a splintered wine cask while Straton fussed over him like a mother over a naughty child; Sync, talking softly to Niko, who still leaned against the wall and favored the 3rd Commando colonel with an uncomprehending stare.

When Tempus was sure that no casualties were serious, he took Niko by the arm.

The boy was coming out of whatever spell he'd been under, asking: "But Grippa, where's Grippa? Is he safe? The witch didn't get him, did she?"

That was a good question, but one for which Tempus had no answer. He said, "Grippa will turn up; the witch took his shape."

Niko shook his head, his brow deeply furrowed. "No, that's not true. He was right with me, a moment ago."

Beyond the dazed Stepson, Tempus saw Randal shake his head. The brave little mage's lower lip was quivering: Niko ignored Randal as if the mage did not exist.

"Wait here, Stealth," Tempus growled, and took Randal aside. "You did well, Hazard. We're all proud of you."

"*He's* not; he won't even speak to me. Commander
. . ." Randal tried not to sniffle; he turned his head away,
then back. "It's really over, isn't it? He despises me.
Despite our oath, and everything. I didn't think it . . ."

"Randal," Tempus said as kindly as he could, "Niko's
just had another brush with witchcraft. You're a part of
what he fears the most right now. Eventually, you'll understand what I'm saying now, but until you do, just take
me on faith: if Niko spends a while as my right-side
partner, I can mend him. Then you'll have your left-side
leader back again. Until then, try not to be offended. The
rest of us value you more highly every day."

But he had to leave the mage alone in the alley: Randal
had a prisoner, the once-mighty Roxane, to escort to her
incarceration in the mageguild.

And Tempus had the Stepson, Niko, to take in hand and
try to heal, a god on his back, and some wholly spooked
fighters to cajole into pretending that all this was a normal,
or at least anticipated consequence of Fete Week in Tyse.

* 8 *

Partha's son, not Roxane, was found next morning in
the mageguild holding cell where the witch had been
incarcerated.

By then, it was clear that Grippa wasn't lying dead
somewhere—a nightlong search had turned up only one
corpse, and it a desiccated pile of bones wrapped in foxfur
in an alley. And since the corpse had bones once broken
which had mended wrong, and Grippa'd never broken any,
the skeleton, all agreed, could not be his.

When Partha heard that his son was safe and sound, if
locked up in the mageguild, he used all his influence to try
to free the boy.

The military governor thus summoned Tempus to the

mageguild dungeon, where Partha and his daughter, as well as Randal, were waiting.

Young Grippa sat inside a cage wound with colored wool, his hair matted with straw and his eyes red from sleeplessness or weeping, holding his sister's hand through the bars when Tempus got there.

Partha, seeing Tempus, thundered: "Riddler, give me one good reason why my boy should have to languish here! The witch possessed him, yes. But that's no crime— Niko's suffered the same way and he's free to come and go! She possessed him, now she's gone, any fool can see!"

The military governor, in shadows, his face impassive, said not one word; Sauni sobbed softly, her brother's hand pressed to her cheek. Randal made a sign all Stepsons learn: he wanted a private word with his commander.

Tempus said: "Possession's nothing to take so lightly, Partha. She might come back. She might be right here, and the boy's shape just an illusion. Randal, come with me. I have to talk to you."

Out in the dank and musty hallway, Tempus said, "Well Randal, what do you think? Let him go, and wander, or keep him here, and make an enemy of the strongest single lord in Tyse?" While in the Riddler's head the god's voice hissed: "*Let my servant go!*"

Randal, clearly agitated, said: "Riddler, they've made me First Hazard of the mageguild! Me, a lowly seventh-grade adept! If you want, I'll decree we free him, but something tells me it's not right."

Tempus wondered if a witch could fool a god, and then reminded himself that neither dark nor light, bad nor good, were different, but one and the same thing, in heaven's sight.

And he was more concerned, right then, with Randal, whom his guildbrothers had chosen not out of respect, but as a sacrifice, mere bait to tempt fate, an expendable lamb to tether where a mage-killer was sure to find him.

So he said: "Forget the boy; it doesn't matter if she's in him now or comes back later. We need Partha's good will in Tyse."

Randal frowned uncertainly. "As you wish, Commander." Then he brightened: "Congratulate me, Riddler; I've come to high estate today."

"Randal," Tempus said carefully, "I'd like you to consult with Cime, if you insist on accepting this appointment—your Brothers of the Writ have put you on the front line in this battle of magics. It's not a safe place for anyone, even a Stepson, to be."

Then Randal looked away, down at his fingers, twining one another. "That's just it, my lord. I'm not sure I can remain a Stepson—conflict of interest, you see."

"Randal, you've sworn an oath. And because of Niko's problems, you can't unswear it. If you have to, pretend to leave the band, but only that: I still need you. I'll feel free to call upon you when and how I must."

"But . . ." Randal's gaze met his and it was deeply shadowed. "All right." He heaved a sigh. "I'll do the best I can."

"And declare the boy a victim of possession, free him on his father's recognizance? At least until we've further proof?"

"Yes, I said we would," Randal snapped, his tone uneasy, then wheedled: "I really don't think I need to see your sister. Me being First Hazard and all, it might be more temptation than she can stand. She'd like nothing better than to kill anoth—" Breaking off before he admitted knowing that Cime had slain his predecessor, Randal smiled weakly, then added: "Let's give Grippa to his father then, and hope we won't regret it—that Niko won't suffer because of what we do today."

But as a Stepson must, Randal followed orders with which he obviously did not agree: first he freed the boy, who stumbled dazed into his sister's arms, while Partha gloated that he should have known that Tempus would "make things right."

Randal accompanied his commander across town, through half-deserted New Year's streets, to a First Day reception being held on Embassy Row, where Cime feasted with foreign dignitaries in the Rankan embassy wherein Tempus had found her lodging.

At the embassy's portico, half hidden among the evergreens, they saw Crit and Kama, arms around each other.

Tempus touched Randal's arm and cleared his throat.

"Ah . . . Commander, we didn't see you." Crit disengaged, his blistered face embarrassed.

Kama smoothed her fete clothes and raised her chin high: "You didn't let the witch go, did you? Aunt Cime said you would, that you never learn, but I told her that where Niko is concerned, you'd not risk . . ." She trailed off, looking at Randal's face, then shuddered and whispered, "Men!" disgustedly, turned and went inside.

"I'm sorry, Riddler," Crit apologized for Kama. "You know she's just upset. Cime's been giving her lectures on comportment as befits a—"

"Don't apologize for my daughter," Tempus rumbled. "I told you before, no good will come from her. She knows too much and she's a born dissembler. She and my sister are two of a kind." Then, to Randal: "Go on in, find Cime, tell her what's transpired and that she's to help protect you. Crit and I will be along presently."

When Randal, his courage obviously failing, had hesitantly mounted the chocolate granite steps and gone inside, Crit said, "What's this? What happened?"

"Randal's the new First Hazard. The witch—if she's that boy—is loose again: I can't risk trouble with Bashir, or a war with Partha's faction."

"Wonderful," Crit said, and fell in beside him as Tempus headed through the hedgerows to enter the embassy from the rear. "Commander, can I ask a question? That is,

I've heard something that, if it's true, the task force ought to know . . ."

Crit was taciturn, often secretive, the most perceptive and efficient of his men. "What is it, Crit?"

"Niko's in there . . . he came with Cime. He's drunk as a lord and he told Strat that he's rejoined us—as *your* rightman. Can that be true?"

"It can. It is. What of it?"

Crit opened his mouth, said, "But the witch . . . Brachis and the planned coup at the Festival. You must realize that if a Stepson's involved in that, we're doomed—outlaws, sacrificial sheep . . ." then shut it and shook his head, eyes slitted.

"The Festival's a long time off, Crit. When there's something to worry about, I'll give you plenty of notice. Right now, worry about keeping my sister and Kama at arm's length."

Crit grinned mirthlessly and allowed that, with the god's help, he'd do his best.

Book Three:

BEYOND THE VEIL

When Niko rode out to Partha's to bid Sauni and Grippa fond farewells, the Nisibisi witch was ready for him.

Roxane, in the form of Grippa, had been lying low and gaining strength, learning what it was like to be a boy. She'd never unequivocally quit her body, not in all the years she'd lived, and taken up another as a permanent abode.

But desperation had mothered invention, and Roxane was now a boy, her crippled woman form discarded, its bones parched to ashes in some Tysian crematorium. Whenever she saw Niko, urges arose in her much more forcefully than when she'd been a woman. It was lucky, she told herself, that Niko was by nature a Sacred Band boy-lover, not ill-disposed to loving men.

If he'd been that way, she might have risked another change, invaded Sauni's nymphlike form, even though it would have taxed her strength. But the sap was rising in Grippa's young, strong body, and Roxane was safer as a boy—safe from that travesty of natural law called Cime, safe from Randal the First Hazard, safe enough to be content to stay this way, at least until she arrived at the Festival of Man.

A boy, in Tyse, had advantages over a girl: he could stay out all night, come home with the dawn, and no one

questioned it; in all debauch and any manly escapade,
Grippa could count on his father's full support.

And Niko confided in Grippa the way he never would in
Sauni: when the Stepson, ponying a loaded pack horse,
armed and armored with shabby duty gear, dropped by to
say goodbye on his way southeast to the Festival site, it
was Grippa, not Sauni, Niko took aside.

"Take care of your sister now, Grippa," Niko advised.
"Keep a close eye on her, in case she's with child. Don't
let on you're doing it, but don't let her hurt herself—
nothing too strenuous, until it's certain one way or the
other. Get her down to the Festival unscathed, and I'll give
you this." Niko tapped the hilt of a bronze war-ax thrust
in his belt which had obviously seen a dozen battles.

As Grippa would, Roxane oohed and aahed. And then
she said, pretending naiveté: "But why are you leaving so
early, Niko? Our training's not yet done. This is the
crucial week, and you won't be here to help us."

"Don't worry, pud." Niko ruffled Grippa's hair. "You'll
do just fine. Don't overtrain, that's all."

Roxane, out by Partha's stone house, squatted down on
the thawing sod and picked up a stick: "But can't you stay
and ride down with us? What if the death squads attack us
on the way? What if we're overrun by slavers? Or rival
factions? Niko, please don't go—"

"I have to, pud." Niko hunkered down beside him.
"And you must be brave. You're a man now, not a boy
since New Year's. If you're attacked, you fight. If you
can't win, then you give your sister an easy death before
you let her be a slave or a pawn of witchcraft. Understand?"

Grippa/Roxane gulped, then nodded, eyes downcast,
saying very low, "It's a long way to the Festival."

"I know, I know." Niko sighed and brought out a little
wooden box of krrf. "Here, Grippa, try a bit of this. It'll
make you mean, but start you thinking like a man."

Roxane, curious and titillated, did as Niko showed her,
piling a pinch of brown powder in her fist's well, then

sniffing krrf. A rush of well-being overcame her manly person, so that she found herself aroused and put her hand on Niko's arm.

He misunderstood: "Don't worry, I said. I'm safe enough; I'll be with the Riddler—a rightman goes where his left-side leader goes, and Tempus wants to straighten out some things with the Rankans before the Festival. But Bashir's sending a contingent—that's the team I'm on—and you and Sauni are welcome to travel with them. Going with the warrior-priest is as good as going with the god.'' Niko's eyes were deeply sunken, his mouth tight-drawn.

Grippa, as northern boys were free to do, flung his arms around the Stepson's neck and kissed him.

Niko held him tightly for a moment, then pushed him back: "Don't tempt me. You're a man now, and that's a different matter. Krrf does strange things to men . . . we've both got your sister to consider."

His breath was warm against Grippa's neck, and Roxane first longed for her abandoned womanform, then cautioned herself that Grippa must not, under any circumstances, seem fey. And somewhere deep inside her a boyish presence struggled in its bonds. She could have erased the soul of the child whose flesh she now inhabited; she would, but not just yet: she needed to monitor his reactions, use the Grippa-personality for occasional corrections of her course.

So since Grippa couldn't bear being seen as less than manly in Niko's eyes, Roxane straightened his shoulders, blinked fiercely, and sat back. "I won't disappoint you, Stealth. I'm not afraid. And if I'm good . . . if I win my events, and prove myself worthy, would you . . . could you . . . no, it's too much to ask." Roxane/Grippa bowed his head.

"What? What is it, pud? We're friends—we have no secrets."

"If . . . you're not forever going to be the Riddler's rightman, are you? You've been a squadron leader on your own."

"That's so," Niko said uncomfortably. "It's just a temporary thing, a whim of my commander's. That's why they call him Tempus the Obscure. But what of it?"

"If. . ." Roxane peered through Grippa's eyes soulfully ". . .when you're a left-side leader again, you ever need a partner—if you'd consider an untried youth with honor and glory on his mind. . .that is, unless you go back to consorting with magicians . . ." She ended with a wicked grin as she trailed off.

This time Niko grabbed him playfully and wrestled him to the ground. "So you want to be a Stepson, do you?" Niko's elbow bore down upon his throat. "Think well before you act, young man: you're a first son, with an inheritance coming. Mercenaries tend to come from lesser fortune—second sons and third, men escaping bad love affairs and murders, or marriages they can't otherwise avoid. Your father might not like it."

"You don't think I'm good enough?" Grippa accused, his young voice as deep as she could make it with resentment, rejection, and disappointment.

Niko's quick, canny smile came and went. He released the boy he'd tutored. "I trained you, didn't I? You're more than good enough, and more than welcome, as my rightman or a single I'll gladly sponsor with the guild. When the time comes. If you're certain. It's a life from which there's little turning back. Even if you want to, once you've sacked and pillaged, hired yourself out to this army or that, given up on passing judgment, you've got too many enemies to settle down and raise a family without providing a fortress's worth of protection or looking ever to your back."

"See? You don't think I can do it." Grippa scrambled to his feet and went to the stone house wall, where he pulled a stone loose and dug inside.

"That's not what I'm saying," Niko said, frustrated and concerned, following just where Roxane led. "I'm only saying, think it over. When your father dies, you'll be a lord—''

''Partha? Die? In twenty years, or thirty. I'll be *old* by then, my life half over!''

''I understand. I'm not rejecting you. At the Festival, if you still want it, I'll arrange to have the Stepsons take you on.''

''Not you? You won't take me as your rightman?''

Niko, who'd been Grippa's age when a Syrese fighter of renown had paired with him, scratched his two-week beard: ''That's not up to me. When you're one of us, you'll understand it better. I'm Tempus's right-side partner until he frees me. Then . . .''

''Then there's Randal, isn't there?'' Roxane spat the accusation from shining eyes that said that Grippa's hero shouldn't be beholden to a wizard.

''No, there's not. Never again. Believe me. It's over. And so is this. I've got to go. The Riddler's meeting me at the Shepherd's Crook at noon.''

''Then take this, Niko. With all my love,'' Grippa said as Roxane sprung her trap and took from beneath the stone she'd pulled out from the wall a trinket—an amulet of hair and bone.

''What's this?'' Niko turned it in his fingers, one eyebrow raised. ''A talisman?''

''It will keep you safe, forever.'' Grippa's voice was proud, his demeanor noble and self-sacrificing. ''It's very old; it's been in my family for years.'' It had been—in Roxane's family. While Niko had it, no lesser witch could touch him, no warlock covet him: it marked him as Roxane's with strands of hair and shards of discarded bone.

Niko, not wanting to offend, said only, ''My thanks, Grippa. And a safe trek to you.'' With a final, manly slap on Grippa's backside he left her there, headed for his horses.

Grippa/Roxane watched him go, his fine athletic form so appealing, his gait only slightly uncertain from the krrf.

It had been risky, giving him a marking charm, but worth it: she didn't have to worry that any lesser evil might chance upon him first.

She'd been lucky all this morning: the Askelonian panoply Niko owned was wrapped in oxhide on his pack horse. If he'd been wearing any part of it, it would have warmed to warn him that magic was about.

Watching him dwindle, then crest a hillock and descend out of sight, she began to spell, calling upon what minions she still commanded from beyond the veil. She needed to steal that armor, destroy the sword and dirk he had which alone of all he owned could threaten her—or coax fate to take it from him.

She'd make sure he lost it on the way or cast it from him, or somehow down in Ranke was parted from the stigma Askelon had marked him with—not because Niko wanted to be free of it, but because the dream lord stood in Roxane's way.

* **2** *

The Shepherd's Crook was a way station on the "general's route" leading from Upper Ranke down into the heart of empire.

The Crook was at the southernmost edge of Tyse. Niko had stopped here once before, when coming home after years of roving, and found that his uncle, who'd once owned the place, was dead.

It was a favorite watering hole of Tysian "specials" —those who wore the yellow armband of Grillo's secret police and Rankan agents.

Grillo himself was in the Crook, scuffing sawdust with his boots and drinking with the Riddler when Niko arrived. Grillo was wholly owned by Tempus, though once he'd served a plentitude of interests. If not for the fact that

Grillo and his spies were crucial to the survival of Bashir's Nisibis and the Stepsons' best conduit of information from the empire, Grillo wouldn't have survived this long.

He was a handsome Rankan, treacherous, double-dealing, who'd had the corner on the drug trade when the Stepsons had arrived. He'd had brushes with the witch, too, and even Niko, who should have sympathized, was uncomfortable in his presence.

But Grillo was one of those necessary evils: his specials were the most effective force in Tyse, still; no other unit, Rankan or mercenary, knew the streets or the inhabitants as well.

It was a good thing Crit wasn't there, Niko thought, enduring a guffaw when he ordered goat's milk (the Riddler had forbidden him strong drink) at the bar and brought it to their table. Crit and Grillo hated each other as much as they dared, foiled each other's plans routinely, keeping their quarrels just below the level where Tempus would intervene.

The talk wasn't of Crit, directly; it was of holding Tyse steady while the Stepsons were out of town: "I expect," Tempus was saying patiently in response to a question Niko hadn't heard the Rankan ask, "you to do your best to keep order. I expect," Tempus leaned forward, "Randal to give a good report of your efforts when he joins us at the Festival. I expect you to take up the slack when the 3rd Commando and the task force leave. I expect Madame Bomba's caravans to continue to ply the trade routes from Caronne unmolested, if you have to draft half the Rankan garrison to give her convoys safe conduct. Is that clear?"

"And you expect," Grillo said snidely, "me to do all this without a bit of help from you? What if Ranke decides this is as good a time as any to rid itself of half a dozen troublesome factions, to liberate Wizardwall from the 'Nisibisi outlaws' and put Bashir in a lion cage and exhibit him at the Festival, as Abakithis has sworn to do? What then? Am I still to play the loyal Rankan agent and help the garrison storm Wizardwall?" Grillo looked up, his blue eyes bold, and said to Niko: "Sit down, assassin. Help me talk some sense into—"

"Grillo," Niko said quietly as he pulled back a bench and joined the pair, "would you like to have your teeth for lunch?"

"Niko." Tempus shook his head. "Have your say, Grillo—what have you heard about the projected coup?"

Grillo had come to Tyse as a Rankan spy; elements of Abakithis's opposition had tried to discredit, even kill him, but that had just made him more valuable in the emperor's eyes. And Tempus, who took advantage where he could, was using Grillo to keep abreast of what went by diplomatic pouch and secret message, as well as by the Rankan mageguild network, back and forth between Tyse and the capital.

Grillo shifted in his seat, his gaze resting on Niko's face as if on a particularly doubtful piece of intelligence. Then he said quietly: "I've heard that Brachis made this man an offer, and the offer was accepted. I've heard an oath was sworn before the gods, a token given. I've heard that though the token itself was handed back to Brachis in a slightly different form than it once had, and Brachis, too, returned to Ranke in a swine's suit, the bargain holds."

"How's that?" Niko leaned back, sipping goat's milk, wishing Grillo wasn't worth so much to Tempus.

"Brachis," Grillo said offhandedly, "was restored to human form by the capital's mageguild. He's Theron's man, remember, and a man of the god to boot. The whole opposition faction expects to be in power by the end of the third week of the Festival. And that," Grillo raised his mug to eye level, toasting Niko sardonically, "is all I've got to say about the matter, except . . ." he grinned wolfishly ". . . good luck, Stealth. You'll need it. And to you, Riddler, since your unit's slated to take the blame."

Niko was looking around for prying ears or knowing glances by them. He didn't see any, just a grimy serving wench giving mutton stew to two of Grillo's specials. It was early for dinner, late for lunch, and the Crook was nearly empty. Directly behind Niko, on the wall as decoration, was a scythe. He could have reached back, lifted it from its hooks, and cleaved Grillo on the spot.

But he didn't. He put down his mug delicately and propped both elbows on the table, conscious that Tempus was watching him through brooding eyes: "Let me tell you something, Rankan monkey. The deal I made with Brachis will result in Nisibis being recognized as a free, uncontested state with Bashir its leader—without bloodshed, without strife, with the loss of only a single life." Now he was whispering, his hands balled into fists so that, of their own accord, they didn't lash out and strangle Grillo simply to wipe the supercilious grin off his Rankan face. "And that's what we all want, isn't it? Bashir and his Successors recognized as the rightful government of the independent state of Free Nisibis. Well, Grillo, *isn't it?*"

"Easy, Niko," the Riddler warned.

Niko hadn't told Tempus about his bargain previously; if he hadn't been so angry, he wouldn't have detailed it now. But the krrf he'd sniffed this morning out at Partha's was wearing off, leaving him argumentative and ready for a fight. And there was no single man in Tyse Niko would rather have pounded into the sawdust on the Crook's floor than Grillo. The man was a liar and anybody's agent who could pay his price.

"That's right, Nikodemos—it's too late to justify it now. How much are they paying you to make hunted men out of a Sacred Band and fugitives out of—"

"That's enough!" Tempus thundered as Niko pushed back and, on his feet, suggested that Grillo accompany him outside.

Grillo, too, was standing. "My pleasure, Niko, if the Riddler will—"

"Well, I won't. Both of you sit down."

They did, and Tempus looked between them as if looking at dog vomit in a temple. "It's nice to know that
Ranke still feels it has an agent at the Festival," he said
calmly.

"You mean despite the fact that Niko's a drug addict
and a sot? They don't care about that, just about having
their murder done, and his record proves he's competent
enough at that."

"Do you want to die? I need the practice," Niko said
pleasantly, throwing stars glittering ominously between his
fingers.

"Niko," Tempus said as if to a naughty child, "wait
outside."

He couldn't disobey his commander's orders. He left
with heat prickling the back of his neck and sweat on his
upper lip and without even ordering a meal.

Outside, he curried his Askelonian with fervor, so that it
whickered and half-closed its eyes, its big ears drooping
with pleasure. He wasn't used to being a rightman. He'd
lost the knack of being quiet and standing by, of taking
orders gracefully—even from the Riddler.

Ashamed of himself and wishing he hadn't let Grillo rile
him so obviously, he fumed, so that when the grimy girl
from the Crook brought him out a tray, saying, "You're to
eat this, soldier. Your commander's orders," he snarled at
her: "Get away from me. Just leave it on the ground. That
gruel's not fit for a man to eat."

But when she'd left it and retreated into the Crook with
one eloquent, reproving backward look, the smell of lamb
and barley made him salivate.

Putting away his currycomb, an out-of-season hornet
buzzing around his head, he took the bowl and sat on a
tree stump that doubled as a mounting block, eating without tasting, his eyes on the bowl in his hand.

When feet appeared in his field of vision, feet in shiny
boots, he looked up and saw a tall man who was not
Tempus standing there.

Askelon of Meridian wore wine-dark robes; his face was virile, severe but not haughty, his mouth compassionate, his cheeks hollowed. And the eyes of the entelechy of dream, regent of the seventh sphere, who had once been an archmage of repute but now was so much more, held all the sorrows of humankind in them, and all the bravery as well.

Askelon's compassionate mouth twitched; his dream-inducing countenance, so young and yet so old, twisted as if in some awful struggle. From his lips, words tried to issue forth: there was no voice to say them, though, and Niko's lip-reading wasn't good.

It could have been "Throw it away," that the dream lord said; it might have been, "Do it my way."

It might, in fact, have been neither of those, but as Niko, spilling his food, shot to his feet and backed away, saying, "Askelon, please let me be. I can't . . . I know I promised but I can't . . ." the dream lord's apparition disappeared.

The lamb and barley stew was all over his hillman's trousers, globs of it on his boots.

Cleaning himself up as best he could with shaking hands that hardly could hold the straw with which he mopped up the mess, Niko told himself that krrf sometimes caused hallucinations, that Askelon really hadn't appeared to him, that the dream lord didn't pierce the veil in daylight.

But it was no good. When Niko had faced every other trial and surmounted every other test, he still had his failure to keep his word to Askelon to contend with: Niko had gifts from the dream lord, power gifts he was keeping in bad faith. Even though he'd built an altar to Askelon in the free zone, he himself had never worshipped there.

He just couldn't bring himself to worship a demigod who'd once been a mortal—worse, a man who'd traded his humanity for power, who'd become more of a god than some deities, who ruled the sleep of all humanity from his once-in-a-while archipelago of dreams.

When Tempus came out of the Shepherd's Crook, Niko was unlacing his pack to get out the enchanted panoply which he'd never been able to bring himself to throw away, with hopes of burying it here, in Tyse. If he could just leave it here, he could ride away and free himself of all this madness by simply never coming back.

"What are you doing, Niko?" Tempus's voice was hoarse, close by, nearly in his ear.

"What? I— Riddler, the dream lord appeared to me . . ." That sounded daft. He tried again: "I had a vision. Askelon was in it. He said words I couldn't hear." Niko shook his head miserably, aware that it sounded like the rantings of a drunkard who mixed his wine with drugs. "Never mind."

"Go on," Tempus crossed his arms.

"It said . . . something . . . 'Throw it away' or something like that. So since I've abrogated my oath to him thrice over, I thought I'd leave this accursed armor and—"

"No! Make your pack fast. Let's get out of here before anything else happens to delay us."

"But he wants it back—"

"You don't know that. You don't even know if it *was* Ash—the witch is about, remember. Perhaps she can masquerade as him, I don't know. I do know that when Ash decides to appear on earth, the signs are unmistakable. And he doesn't waste his time—if he wanted you to get a message, you'd have it, not be wondering what it was."

Niko rubbed his neck, which was beginning to ache; his hand was trembling from lack of wine. "Maybe if I had just one drink, I'd be able to tell what was happening and what was not."

"Mount up, Stepson. And don't worry about half-seen visitations or manifestations. When we've got you free of wine's yoke, you'll know what you're seeing and what you're not."

It was a direct order. Niko had to obey.

And maybe the Riddler was right. The Askelonian stal-

lion, who nuzzled him as he mounted up, would surely
have greeted the man who raised it, Askelon, lord of
shadow and of dream. And yet the horse had been silent
the whole time.

Riding out of Tyse, his pack horse ponied tight, Niko
could only hope the Riddler was right, that the whole thing
was a figment of his drink-deprived imagination, and not a
message unheeded, a warning untaken.

* 3 *

Three days south of Tyse, wizard weather combined
with storms from heaven to stop Tempus and his rightman
in their tracks.

They could see the lights of a nearby hamlet when the
wizard weather started; its chilling mist oozed up from the
ground and drifted at saddle-height through the air, icing
trees and freezing varmints in their burrows. The wind on
which it rose was so rank with salt and sea that wolves
howled their distress and foxes ran for higher ground,
yipping as they went in search of safety.

Ahead, the town's lights disappeared from view; a swirl-
ing mass of deadly cloud was all that could be seen.

"Keep going!" Tempus yelled to Niko, and they did,
though they had to whip their horses, who wanted most of
all to stop, turn head to tail, and wait out the unnatural
storm. Without shelter, movement was their only weapon
against the chilling fog that froze their eyelashes and made
their fingers numb.

They raced through it blindly, their horses on the run,
hoping that their own heat might save them from being
frozen solid in their saddles.

Somewhere ahead, the hamlet they'd seen must still
exist. Even if the mist was wound about its streets, and its
inhabitants ice-statues in their beds, ahead were barns and

hearths and doors that could be barred against the storm.
Both men had been in Sanctuary when wizard weather
roamed the streets; both knew what sort of storm this was.

Grimly, they kicked and urged their snorting horses
forward, where the little town must be.

And then, from high above the tundra-hugging mist, a
deep and throaty roar came down to shake the earth beneath so that their horses panicked and bolted wildly. The
pack animals broke their tethers and disappeared into the
fog as thunder roared and lightning flashed to earth, burning a path through the killing mist with every bolt.

It was as if heaven and hell did battle; the mist rose up,
its fingers curled, as if to rend the sky. Every lightning
bolt cast into the fog made it quiver like a living thing; the
mist drew back, hissing when it was pierced, and where
lightning struck, a stench like rotting fish began to spread.

Around the riders the lightning ranged itself like an
embattled guard, so that Tempus sawed on his maddened
Askelonian's reins, trying to bring it to a halt and signal
Niko to do the same.

But the horses wouldn't listen; they ran pall-mall right
through that corridor of ozone and blue stinking light as if
they'd scented their own stable.

And on the far side of the weather war, they halted of
their own accord, blowing hard and shivering.

Ahead of them a town sprawled, golden and enchanting,
its harbors clean, its skyline clear and crystalline, waves
lapping at its shore.

Behind them, Tempus saw as Niko turned in his saddle
and he did likewise, was a veil of mist, rent in places,
beyond which soundless lightning impotently raged.

Here the weather was more than clement—it was like a
summer's eve. The town before them was snuggled safe
and beautiful, dreaming in a twilight that made the sea
which lapped it iridescent green.

Niko urged his weary horse to sidle up to Tempus's.
They sat there silent, staring at the seaboard town where

an inland hamlet should have been until their horses began to paw the ground and champ upon their bits.

Then Niko said reluctantly, "You know what this is . . . where we are, Commander?"

Tempus had never heard Niko sound so hopeless. "Meridian, I expect. The archipelago of dreams."

"That's right," said Niko, who'd been here once before.

"Don't worry, Stealth. It's just Ash playing archmagical games."

"What do we do, Commander? Our pack animals, food, provisions, arms and armor . . ." Niko's enchanted panoply had been on his pack horse.

"Do? We ride down and find out what he wants, what else?"

They were on a little rise above the seacoast; an inland breeze brought them the sounds of hymns and chants upon the air. Beyond Meridian's quays, night was falling; in its streets, torches were being lit.

Niko took a shuddering breath, slipped off his horse, and held it by the bridle. Looking up at Tempus as if he looked at his own death, Niko said, "I can't. I can't go down there. Please . . . you don't understand. That man, if man he is, has got too much of me already—my rest-place, my valor, my self-respect. Coward I may be, but I'm not going into Meridian at nighttime, when all men's nightmares come to life."

"A wise choice, Niko. I need you here, to watch the horses. We can't have them bolting to their stable, not when we'll need them to ride out again." Tempus had to let the boy know he didn't blame him—that this was wisdom, not cowardice, in the Riddler's eyes.

Sliding off his own horse, he handed Niko its reins: "Watch them well. Don't fall asleep now," he teased.

Niko managed a shaky grin: "Sleep? Here? Not while I'm alive."

And with that Tempus left him, striding off down the hill. He looked back once and saw the boy reaching in his tunic, then fondling something in his hand—a talisman or charm, no doubt. Tempus hoped it would keep him safe, whatever it might be.

With a foul taste in his mouth, he trod the ensorceled sod of Meridian, the largest island in a chain that belonged to the entelechy of dreams and to the seventh sphere, and manifested on earth only occasionally.

Tempus tried not to wonder what the occasion was as he wandered streets paved with gold and Meridian's changeling nature became obvious: buildings shivered, shuddered, came and went; people who were doubtless sleeping in their beds some safer place dashed madly to and fro, living out their dream lives, be they horrid, wondrous, or grave, oblivious to one another's fates.

He'd just passed a woman changing into a fish-tailed girl, pursued by a handsome man with seaweed-colored hair, when Askelon appeared before him.

All the impermanence of the dreamers here and there then faded. With Askelon was a processional: drum-beaters, horn-blowers, pipe players with short horns upon their heads and ram's bottoms, rosy-cheeked children who must have died in their sleep eons past. They carried high a red-lacquered chair and in it Askelon was borne, high on the shoulders of men from every race and women of every color.

When he saw Tempus, he made a sign and his bearers all knelt down. Stepping out upon their backs and down onto his ground, Ash said, "Greetings, Tempus. I'm pleased that you could come."

The gray, sad eyes of Askelon, so like Cime's full of char and smoke and hell, impaled him.

Tempus shook the first spell off. "What do you want, Ash? That boy you've terrorized can't even bear to find out, so I've left him behind." At Tempus's hip was the sword Enlil had sanctified; with it, he was willing to try and skewer the dream lord if he had to.

On Askelon's wrist, as he raised it to finger a long-

suffering smile, was a talisman, a bracelet called the Heart
of Askelon which, should it be pierced just right, would
consign this dream and shadow lord to his fate, long
overdue.

"I want to talk to him; that's why I did this." Askelon
came close. "Come, sleepless one, let's take a walk. I'll
convince you that I mean well, show you my domain . . ."

Tempus held his ground and kept his distance. "I won't
hand him to you. I assume you can't get to him yourself.
Why is that, do you think?"

Ash only smiled and shook his head.

"For the same reason the god did battle with your mist,
I'd say," Tempus guessed.

Then the dream lord expelled a weary breath. "What is
it with that child, that you would risk my wrath to save
him, the gods battle in his stead?"

It was a rhetorical question Tempus didn't answer: if he
and Ash came to contest, the outcome—not just for them,
but for the fabric of the land of dreams—could not be
predicted.

"Won't you bring him to me? He needs counsel and
some witch has given him a token which prevents my
helping him."

"That's the best news I've heard all day," Tempus
grunted. "He doesn't want your help. You're keeping him
from his mystery, you've invaded his rest-place, he says,
driven him to drink. Aren't countless hapless souls enough
for you, benighted thing? Or have you lived so long your
wits are addled?"

"No more than yours." The dream lord rubbed the
heart upon his arm ruminatively. "Why must you spurn
my counsel? By all the powers, you surely need some.
Rattling around in the affairs of puny mortals not capable
of giving you even a contest; aren't you tired of being a
figurehead for the gods? You're as helpless as a baby,
swept by fate—and you don't have to be. I can lift your
curse and grant you mortality, if you wish it . . . Why not,

aren't you tired? Wouldn't you like a restful sleep?" The dream lord's voice was singsong, soothing.

But Tempus knew the power and the danger of Meridian's lord. "As you saved my sister from herself? She'll be young and beautiful eternally, so she tells me, yet she's as vicious and as murderous as ever."

"That's free will and human choice, no work of mine. Surely even you'll agree I've kept my bargain." But Askelon's gray eyes darkened, the light from them now cold.

"Your bargain? With my sister? You got eternal salvation—or at least salvation for a time. And now you plague my fighters. Ash, I'm warning you, stay away from Niko."

"You're warning me? As did your new god? You saw what short work I made of him—you're here, aren't you?"

Tempus's hand was on his swordbelt, but Askelon's eyes held him fast: he could not draw it out.

"Don't try me, little demigod. We have to coexist, you see. You affright them and cull their numbers with your wars; I'll take care of their dreams. Now's here's my final offer: reunite your Niko with my servant, Randal. At that time, I'll leave him be until he comes to me on his own. He'll have his mental refuge back; he can consider his word to me unspoken."

"And for this, you want what? You came to him, he says, and gave a message he couldn't understand."

The dream lord looked away, the first time Tempus had ever seen him do so: Ash was not one to shrink from a confrontation or defer a fight. "I can't get to him, I told you—he doesn't sleep, or if he does, he's too full of drink or drugs for me to help him."

"Help him to what?"

"You really don't know," Askelon said pityingly. "He's your successor, Tempus. When he takes up his burden, you can put yours down. Finally, after all these years . . . come, don't tell me it isn't tempting."

"Not one whit. And besides, you old liar, he's just a boy, nothing more."

"And what were you, one time? Or your sister? What was she?"

"So," Tempus said slowly, fighting every temptation Askelon could bring to bear. "All I have to do is hand that child to you, and I'm free of my curse? No thanks."

"You'll kill him with it, otherwise."

"Men are born to die."

"My point exactly, Riddler. Don't you long for death? Can't you see that this new god is worse than being without one? In Enlil's stead you can do no good, but only evil. I'll prove to you—"

Tempus stopped listening; far behind, amid the crowd, he saw a woman he'd once loved—Jihan, a supernal sprite, and with her, a wizard's son who could have ended the war with Mygdon if only Tempus could have brought him there.

The dream lord followed his gaze, then said: "You see, they're happy here. Their fates are sealed. They have each other; they live in pleasant dreams."

"Jihan!" Tempus bellowed. She didn't even raise her head.

"Shamshi!" he called out to the boy, the child didn't turn a hair.

"That's no use—she'd be a mere wave in an eternal sea by now, if not for me. And the boy was born to die young. They have more with me than they'd have any other way. As you may, if you just let me help you . . ."

Then Tempus heard Enlil's voice in his head: *"Strike now; strike hard; My might is with thee!"*

This time, the sword came easily from its scabbard, its metal shining redly in Meridian's fading light.

And Askelon, with a howl and a shudder, his arms up to protect his heart, gave back a pace, then two.

Tempus followed, disquiet in him: a war with Askelon would never end, but add insult to injury and complicate his fate. Yet he shouted: "Leave that boy alone, or deal with me," and leaped into the crowd of Askelon's minions as all around him the very ground began to heave.

The heavens sheeted colored light and grumbled, rumbled, split, and thundered.

Around him, the buildings and the people began to shake and break apart.

And darkness descended over everything, a dark sometimes reddish, sometimes blue, so that Tempus could find no enemy to fight, just light and cold and cloudy firmament.

As the cold began to seep into his lungs, his sword got hotter. He thrust at nothing, and something squealed like iron grating on a slate, and yielded.

Then blinding sparks showered from his sword tip, so that he had to shut his eyes.

And when he opened them, he was standing in a dell on open ground, in mud half-frozen.

Above, silhouetted in gentle moonlight, he could see four horses grazing and one man, sitting with his knees up and his head upon his arms.

When he'd climbed the tricky, wintry hill, he looked back the way he'd come: down the slope lay a hamlet, small and lit here and there with torches. No sea gleamed anywhere about; no cymbals tinkled, no drums beat.

He knew that the Meridian he'd been to was the Meridian of his own perception, that the Ash he'd met there was all things to all men. But he was glad that for the first time ever he'd tried to fight the dream lord. When Ash had swept his sister up for a year of bondage, Tempus hadn't dared to lift a hand to stop him.

He turned back and realized that Niko was dozing where he sat upon his saddle cloth.

He knelt down and touched the youth's ashy hair. Beside the boy an empty wineskin dripped out dregs, but Tempus could forgive that: he'd been beyond the veil and come back wiser, if not happier.

He was glad to be alive and in one piece and able to say to Niko, "Wake up, it's all over."

"What? Riddler! I thought I'd lost you!" Niko, for the first time, hugged him.

Tempus was so shocked it took a moment before he thought to growl and pull away. "No chance of that, Nikodemos. This time you've a partner you'll not be quit of quite so easily."

The boy, embarrassed, said, "The pack horses came back; I'll fix us something to eat."

As Niko got out pot and provisions and knelt to build a fire, Tempus pondered, then said: "Never mind that. We'll eat in town. Ash tells me you've a charm to ward him off, now. Can I see it?"

"A charm? Against Askelon? I don't . . . that is, I didn't know . . . Here."

Niko handed Tempus the bit of hair and bone.

"Where did you get this, Stealth?"

"From Grippa. It's been in his family for years," said the haunted youth. "Did the dream lord say what the message was?"

Tempus chuckled. "He wants you to throw this away—it keeps him from bedeviling you. If I were you, I'd keep it."

"You can be sure of that," Niko said, accepting it from Tempus with new reverence.

The Riddler didn't have the heart to tell Niko why the little bit of bone and hair was so potent, or who the gift was *really* from. He'd do his best to help the boy, but right then the riddles spun and spells done seemed beyond his power to avoid.

He almost advised Niko to throw the charm away and bury the panoply right here in Rankan soil, far from any they could harm. But there were too many unknowables ahead; he couldn't counsel Niko wrongly. Therefore he didn't try at all.

It was comforting, in a way, to have the youngster

beside him—another who hardly ever slept, who strove to master his own fate, who'd not ask questions that had no answers to make demands.

Off and on, those next few days, Tempus thought of the denizens of Meridian. The once-loved sprite, Jihan, had seemed happy in her unknowing way; the child-wizard beside her was better off in dreamland. But those two were special cases. Tempus couldn't bring himself, though he did try, to consider Ash's offer seriously: Meridian was not for him, or for Niko. Cime had been right when she'd called it the land of boredom; Niko knew in his heart that even his rest-place was worth the price of his freedom from that fate.

And Tempus, who craved only worthy enemies to fight and clear-cut human problems, banished all thoughts of the deal he might make with Ash for eternal peace.

He had too much to do: a war to win or at least a contest at the Festival of Man; a new god to get to know; an emperor to unseat; a youth to whom he'd pledged the Sacred Band's oath of trust and honor to help become his own man.

* **4** *

In a cavern in Meridian, the dream lord paced. Tempus was a fool, a wanton slaughterer, his sister's true soul mate.

What Niko needed was no initiation into war, not congress with foul battle gods, but an introduction to the joys of peace.

Askelon had lived on earth and waged livid wars for power in his time. He'd passed through that phase, his soul at risk, and out again to become the regent of the seventh sphere, a plane and place away from space and time.

But it was exile, if a gentle one. The dreams of mortals were wholly his; their subconscious his work place. Yet men still turned to gods and set their sacrifices on bloody altars—not just sheep and lambs, some places, but maidens and poor prisoners of war.

He didn't understand why men could not make peace within themselves—he had, and pulled himself hand over hand toward perfection, though he could only go so far.

For Askelon had traded much away for power; he'd haggled with the accountants of creation. He ruled now in Meridian as much because of the sins he'd done as the power he'd accrued.

As long as Tempus and his sister were abroad, his dream realm and his person were not safe.

Once in the misty past, Askelon had been an archmage, one of true power, not like these weakling magicians who lived now. And in extremis, if he would pay the price, he could call upon the sons and daughters of magic. He could, if he dared flout the rules of plane and sphere.

And he just might, for fate had cheated him, giving him Tempus's sister as a companion for a year. Only once each thousand years was Askelon granted a companion, a woman to warm the loneliness he'd earned from ancient bones. The rest of the millennium, he must labor, paying penance for wrongs done when he was young and foolish, bringing salving dreams to hearts his sorcery once had tortured.

He didn't mind it, most times; he'd grown accustomed to his fate.

But then Cime had come, undoing all his comfort, giving nothing, taking all, spending a year here to earn her freedom and leaving him more lonely than he'd been before she came.

She'd half-killed him once, come with her diamond wands and near destroyed him. A year with her had destroyed more than it had mended—his peace was gone, contentment no longer his.

Because of *her* he'd conceived a plan to make an avatar

on earth, a herald of the power of dream, and he could not let the plan, or Niko, who should by now have been his instrument, go.

He knew he was succumbing to a risk he shouldn't take. He knew that Cime might yet destroy him, for she'd made him lust for things beyond his realm—the love of men, the right of wisdom to triumph over ignorance. His time with Cime had made him discontent with the suffering of the race from which he'd sprung.

This was insolence he was heaping upon the gods, he knew, and he might be punished for it. But he wanted so to see an end to everything Tempus stood for—blind murder, blind allegiance to the murder gods, blind adherence to causes which existed only in the minds of some men whom others blindly followed—he told himself he didn't care.

He paced and paced and thought and thought and considered the repercussions of his fate.

At length, he stoked the fire in his cavern and began to forge a chariot fit for riding into battle: hell on wheels it was, and surely would be.

For Askelon needed something daunting, something more than the occasional mortal's weapon he'd forged before. If he were to ride out, beyond the veil in the opposite direction, take a hand in human events which affected more than dreams, he'd need this chariot, and more.

When he'd finished it, it smoked and gleamed, its sides worked with warlock's legends. Perhaps he was regressing; perhaps he was deluded, senility overcoming him, trying to regain his long-lost youth.

But a year with Cime had made him long for life as once he'd known it; all in Meridian was shadow—shadow life, shadow joy, shadows of existence.

Those he ruled over were not awake; those he longed to free from bondage and elevate forever spurned him—or simply woke up.

So when the chariot was done, Askelon began the long

and complicated process that would free him, temporarily, from the land of dreams.

He called upon Randal, his lone apprentice, called him in faraway Tyse where he lay sleeping. And in Randal's dream, Askelon appeared and made a bargain, as wizards will: Askelon would take away every one of Randal's allergies, each infirmity that plagued him, if Randal would drive this chariot down to the Festival and do certain things there when he arrived.

And the dreaming soul of Randal agreed.

* **5** *

Niko was having a hard time of it in Ranke, capital city of the empire.

Tempus was well known there but Niko was a stranger. Men coveted his position on the Riddler's right and the wondrous panoply that Tempus, after his visit with the dream lord, insisted that Niko wear.

All that Tempus would say about his reasons was that the panoply was too valuable to lose, until Niko, emboldened by krrf one night in the seraglio of a Rankan noble, pressed him.

Then Tempus, jouncing the girl on top of him, had said: "It's this way, Niko: wear the talisman and the armor both, and they cancel one another out."

The next morning Niko went to the Storm God's temple.

He bought a black lamb from a sacrificial vendor near Vashanka's temple, paying twice what it was worth even if it was certified, as the shopkeeper swore it was, by the priesthood as being perfect, free from flaw.

He led it in and up among the fluted columns, standing in a line with other penitents and afflicted souls.

When six sacrifices still remained until his turn came, the priests on duty noticed something strange—a liver the wrong color, a goat with two hearts, or something worse—for they closed down the temple for the day, sending everyone away.

Alone, with his black lamb on a tether, he wandered through the magnificence of Ranke, where he didn't know a soul but Tempus, who was having conferences with generals that a mere rightman could not attend.

The weather was heavy, full of spring's rainy musk this far south in the lowlands: a good omen, he'd heard this promissory spring called while he'd been in the temple line. He wasn't sure about that—the Festival needed the hard-packed winter ground for chariot racing; boggy muck would be a disenfranchisement from the war gods.

He'd been wandering the temple district for an hour with his bleating lamb, his cloak open to the wet warm air, when he encountered soldiers by the Mother Ea's temple.

Soldiers lounging about where women were routinely deflowered to please the gods didn't seem unusual. Niko tugged upon his lamb's leash and dragged it across the stone-paved street.

Two of half a dozen brown-cloaked regulars were talking to another whose bronze-and-leather cuirass denoted higher rank, who'd just come up the street.

Niko, gawking at the friezes on the temples, didn't hear the soldiers coming up behind him until one said, "This way, citizen, if you please."

The hands on his arms were less than polite, though, and he regretted that he'd been drinking. If not, he might have heard them, or paid more attention to what he'd seen. The Riddler was right: Niko had to give up wine and face his fate head on.

The first step on that road, he supposed, was not to struggle against the Rankan guard. If they wanted him, they must have a reason. He'd done nothing wrong, but these men might not know that.

He went along unprotesting, enduring jokes about his

lamb, until one soldier took the ax from his belt and slew it in the street.

Then Stealth's temper got the better of him and his training took command.

The soldiers, not expecting trouble from the slightly drunken, almost pretty youth who'd come so meekly despite his fancy armor and his battle-scarred face, were caught completely unawares.

One went down with a satisfying thud as Niko's elbow jabbed his sternum where the brass plates of his armor joined; another found himself tripped and sprawling on the stones.

Since there were six and no blood had yet been let, Niko, no sword drawn but throwing stars in one hand and the other on his hilt, said, "Now tell me what this is about."

"About?" said the man he'd tripped, wiping the blood from a split lip, his helmet rolling back and forth beside him. "It's about you, Stepson."

The four on their feet hesitated, awaiting orders, while Niko realized they knew who—or at least what—he was. This was no mistake, then.

"I want no trouble with you Rankans," he said, his eyes flicking from man to man, blade to ax, wondering how he was going to get out of this without killing any of them.

The other on the ground was taking gulping breaths, his head still down: "We've heard that about Stepsons. So why don't you just stop pretending to be fearsome and come along, little girl." He pushed himself to his feet.

Niko was sober enough now to be ordering his targets—those he'd take singly, those he could use to knock others off their feet.

He was saying, "Not until you tell me what this is about—who wants me and why," and looking for escape routes in a city he didn't know at all when the officer, who'd been watching from the temple steps, approached and joined his men.

"You have an appointment with a priest, Stepson—if you are one. Maybe we've made a mistake." The officer's eyes were narrowed. "Stepsons, we've heard, can't fight their way out of ladies' boudoirs. Yet you fit the description we were given." He wrinkled his nose and sniffed exaggeratedly in Niko's direction.

Niko ignored the insults. "What priest?"

The officer shook his head. "Whatever you are, you need a bit of remedial training. Soldiers, hereabouts, show respect for superior officers. Teach him, gentlemen."

Niko really didn't want to get into anything Tempus would have to get him out of, and yet the four men closing on him and the one wiping his bloody lip weren't going to back off with a superior present.

The throwing stars in his hand did for the first four: he could only think that Rankans had never seen Bandaran stars at work.

He aimed to stop, not to maim or kill, but men move and things go wrong in close quarters: one took a star in his right knee, another ducked his head and got one in the face; the third took it where Niko had sent it, to his shoulder, and the fourth got it in the neck.

Not even breathing hard, Niko drew his blade and backed away as the two remaining soldiers on their feet drew their weapons.

It was a good thing, he thought, that Rankans didn't carry crossbows—things were too "civilized" here for that.

His eyes still on the swordsmen, in case one palmed a dirk, he backed toward the building entrance behind him without daring to take a look.

Then something hit from behind and everything exploded into stars, then snow, then night.

When he awoke, he was stripped naked, bound hand

and foot, going somewhere in a wagon. He was blind-folded and expertly bound—he couldn't even sit up.

He wondered if he'd get a chance to explain, then told himself he wouldn't: he'd hurt those soldiers badly; he'd be getting only what he deserved.

After a time, the wagon slowed, then stopped. Men talked, it lurched forward once again and stopped again and chain rattled, wood creaked: the wagon's rear gate being let down.

Hands dragged him out; he struggled. He was dropped roughly and landed on hard ground.

"Oh, we're sorry, how clumsy of us," someone said; then he was kicked by booted feet and struck low in the back with a stick or stave.

He cursed and someone forced his teeth apart, pushed wadding in his mouth. "Ssh, that's it; good boy," he heard; then: "Let's get this garbage inside and get out of here."

Those who dragged him up stairs weren't careful: his knees knocked against stone and his head banged against a wall.

Then he was tossed on a floor, he thought. A man said, "Oh yes, thank you for all the spiffy gear." Then the door shut and he thought he was alone.

He tried his bonds, rolled to his side to loose the tension, and began working them.

A voice said, "You're Stealth, called Nikodemos?"

He grunted: he couldn't have answered if he wanted to with the wadding in his mouth.

But then fingers that smelled of rosewater touched his face and pulled the wadding out. The voice, a man's but high, a tenor, said again: "You *are* Stealth, called Nikodemos. Don't try to lie. The god tells us when a man is lying and we become very angry."

"He speaks the truth," a second voice, lower, said. "If you want to live, answer."

"That's right," he said. "That's who I am." His mouth felt cottony; his neck was wrenched; his head ached.

"And you're here to murder Emperor Abakithis. Don't deny it. We know all about you."

Niko didn't say anything.

The rosewater fingers touched his neck and agony laced up his spine from their pressure on a nerve. "Confess and save your soul, boy. Murder of the god's representative's a heinous crime. Only a confession can save you a maiming that will make you beg for death."

"You're wrong," he gasped in pain. And that was true—he wasn't going to kill Abakithis here; he was going to kill him at the Festival.

"We've an informer in your midst. Confess."

Again, a touch; again the pain. He gritted his teeth and waited: if they were bound to torture him, then torture him they would; there was nothing he could say or do about it. Niko had endured tortures mere Rankan priests knew little of, at the hands of the Nisibisi wizards; a witch's efforts, he presumed to think, couldn't be matched by mortal men.

But as the touching went on and on and smoke filled his nostrils with the smell of metal heating, he began to wonder.

He heard Grillo's name, he thought; he heard Theron's name, he was certain. He kept lying stolidly, hoping he could get them angry enough to simply kill him, wishing he could seek refuge in his rest-place from the pain.

But Askelon might be there, in his meadow where meditation could whisk him into glorious escape. And yet, when blazing metal touched the inside of his thigh, he had no other option.

Given a choice of betraying a trust or facing the lord of dream, Niko used the pain to escape what agony he could.

He envisioned his Bandaran master, he called his ritual to mind, he blocked the sound of his own moaning from his ears and made his breathing steady: just a little more calm, a little more pain, and he could slip his body's bonds and be away.

They gave him that, not knowing what they did, and thought that he'd passed out: his body went limp, his breathing deepened.

Somewhere in the rafters, a hornet buzzed softly.

And Niko, in another place, sat crosslegged in his meadow, sunshine beaming down on him and the smell of new grass replacing burning flesh in his nostrils.

It didn't even bother him that Askelon was there. The dream lord sat down sorrowfully beside him and shook his head, a slow tear running down his chiseled face.

"You've lost the panoply, my son; you've fled me and vacated your promise. Now look what has come to pass."

"Greetings, Ash." For the first time, Niko dared be flip with Askelon—but he was dying, and if he had to die, he wanted to reclaim the rest-place he'd worked so hard to earn. "That's right, I lost it. I wasn't what you thought I was. I've never been. I don't want to be. I just want this place of mine. I got it on my own. I don't think you have a right to take it from me."

"Don't you care about your fellows? About men's nightmares, about their dreams?"

"Not anymore. I've too many nightmares of my own and I need my soul unfettered. If I'm dying, at least that part of me should be free. Will you go, leave me, let me have what peace I've earned?"

A stab of pain so fierce it traveled even here, where Niko's body was a figment, rocked him. In his rest-place, beset by Askelon, an unwanted guest, and the pain of his person in another realm, Niko began to weep.

And his tears washed the dream lord away, falling like a rain upon his rest-place, and all Niko's maat, his comfort and his spirit, came back to make him whole there, where he had so long longed to be.

The dream lord's last words, "Call me when you want

me, Nikodemos, for one day you will,'' echoed in that
quiet place a while.

Then the wind blew them away and on that wind, come
from somewhere deep inside of him, a hawk circled overhead. The hawk was red-tailed and handsome, so beautiful
and calm, so at one with this rest-place and the world it
represented, that Niko's body's pain was replaced with a
transcendental joy.

And as he watched the hawk, on the rainy wind, it
circled, then alighted.

It cocked its head at him and then it said, ''Niko, don't
be afraid. I'm here if you want me,'' in Randal's voice
and before he could answer, beneath the hawk's feet, the
grass of Niko's rest-place turned to gravel.

And the hawk bent its beak to the gravel and traced the
spiral sign of Niko's mystery, traced it perfectly within a
circle and then took wing again to alight upon his shoulder.

It pressed its feathered head to his cheek and told him:
''It's so beautiful, don't be afraid.''

''I'm not,'' he told it softly, but then everything—the
hawk, his rest-place, the spiral pattern in the gravel, began
to fade away.

                          * 6 *

Abakithis's henchmen were holding Niko in an offering
shed out behind the state-cult's priests' retreat, on a hilltop
bathed in sunset's ruddy light.

The god had come to Tempus in his meeting with a
clutch of Rankan generals, insistent and incensed. The
voice in his head was adamant, commanding: Niko was a
favorite of Lord Storm's; on top of that, some luckless
soldier had slain a lamb the boy had bought, a lamb
destined for Vashanka's altar.

''*Servant*,'' Enlil's ringing voice decreed, ''*in the name of my brother god, Vashanka, wreak Our havoc on these infidels!''*

Then the god's wrath had come upon him, a red mask before his eyes. Enlil's strength had come into him, doubling his own. And the northern Storm God guided him unerringly to the spot where their mutual protégé was being held and tortured.

It was like the old days for Tempus. The joy of the ravening murder gods was in him, the sunset around him just a harbinger of retribution on the way and blood about to spill.

Tempus hadn't bothered to recruit a single man from that meeting of the best of Theron's faction: the god's sanction fell upon him like a mantle; the god's lightning speed was his; the Askelonian horse under him had raced Rankan streets as if it owned them, faster than light, it seemed, as true as fate.

And when blowing horse and god-sent rider galloped up the stairs of an offering shed defiled by what corrupted priests who'd stolen a sacrifice from their own god did there, the sight of Tempus, Enlil's holy light flashing around him and his horse so that it seemed the pair breathed fire and sparks flew from iron-shod hooves and cutting sword, those who saw the fearsome apparition fled for their lives, certain that the Lord of Blood and Death had come.

Those who didn't see, within the offering shed, first heard a thunderous pounding on its quaking doors.

The vaulted roof above them seemed to shake; the door burst inward and, horse and all, an avenger bore down upon them, leopard-mantled, fast as light, looking for all the world like a temple frieze come to life.

One priest brandished a poker he'd been heating in a brazier; another lifted his robes to run; a third got out his sacrificial dagger and leaped to slay the boy, now hanging, turning slowly like a pig upon a spit above banked coals.

Jumping from his horse, who took out after the fleeing

priest and cornered him against the walls, Tempus, battle-lust full upon him, slew the priest brandishing the poker in a single, vicious blow that severed head and neck and arm from shoulder.

His speed was such that the poker seemed to hit the flags and bounce in slow motion. He had ample time to catch the red-glowing poker by its tip, oblivious to the pain, flip it round and grip it by its handle, and still make it to the second priest, who thought to slay the tortured boy before Tempus could intervene.

And for an instant, seeing Niko's plight—his wounds, his blistered skin, his ruined state, Tempus almost delayed his kill until the boy was dead: even with the god in him and all the fury of the heavens animating limbs built for exactly that, he had time to think, a will of his own, and that will said that Niko ought to die—that those hurts were too severe for healing, that a hero's place in heaven was the only hope the boy had left.

But then the god spoke, saying, *"Save My faithful servant, thou who has escaped a thousand deaths and braved more awful wounds than these."* And with Enlil's words ringing in his head, Tempus leaped to intercede.

The priest was screaming curses in Vashanka's name. And that travesty, of all he saw there, steeled Tempus for what was to come.

He severed the hand that held the dagger from the arm with which a priest who didn't deserve the name sought to give unholy death.

Niko had been a better representative of Vashanka, the embattled missing god, than any of these. And since Enlil fought Vashanka's battles, and Tempus was right then the instrument of the Lords of Storm and supernal justice, he raised the poker high.

The priest, clutching his stump and screaming, stumbled backward, terror in his bulging eyes.

But there was no mercy in Tempus then; rather, the god's fury was his. He took the priest and threw him to the ground and with his sword at that blaspheming mouth and his foot upon the priest's skinny neck, he rammed the poker home, beginning a torture that lasted as long as the priest still screamed.

When that was done, he looked around, sickened by the smell of roasted entrails, and saw what his horse had done to the one remaining priest. The pile of meat under the horse's hooves was unrecognizable: this crew had met their destined fate.

Then came the hard part: he had to get Niko off the spit, and the boy by then was semi-conscious. Niko's eyelids fluttered; eyes roved under them, seeking refuge from the pain of feeling the Riddler's arms around him as Tempus cut him down and held him in his arms.

There seemed no place to put him; the entire god's house was thoroughly defiled.

Outside in the twilight, Tempus lay Niko's trembling form upon clean ground. He took his leopardskin off and covered Stealth with it, while his horse snuffled about the dying youth.

Blackened skin and blisters, serum running from open wounds and ruined loins and buttocks: there seemed no hope. It was a wonder, Tempus thought, that the boy still lived at all.

He'd recited death rites a hundred times, consigned souls to heaven that he'd loved so often that he'd thought no mortal death could hurt him.

And yet before this ravaged boy, who needed the god's blessing to send him safe to heaven, Tempus could not get the words out.

He simply knelt there. Right then he'd have gladly died, if only he could have, traded soul for soul to the hungry gods, accepted heaven or even hell in Niko's stead.

He put his hand on Niko's sweating forehead and the boy's head tossed. His mouth worked; he seemed to smile.

Niko whispered something: "Riddler? Is that you?" in a voice so faint that Tempus had to bend his head to hear it.

"Rest, Niko. I'm here."

Then: "Don't . . . worry. I didn't tell them. This time . . . I didn't tell them."

And then Tempus's eyes filled with tears and he roared to heaven: "*No!* I won't accept this, greedy god! If You have any power, any right to be, if You give your faithful anything worth having, then take away these wounds, ease this pain, give me this one soul back! I've never asked for such a thing before, and by my own word, if You deny me, I won't ever lift my arm again in Your service—"

Then he broke off, bit his lips, and tears blurred his sight—a blessing, considering what lay before him in the ravaged person of a boy he'd thought to love, and train, and save.

When, years ago, Abarsis had come to Tempus and sought death in his service, the Riddler had had to send him off to heaven, build the pyre and say the rites. And in that smoky farewell on a Sanctuary hillside, his eyes had smarted from the smoke and pain. But Abarsis had needed only death; Stealth, called Nikodemos, still loved life.

And that cut deep into the Riddler's heart so that he rejected what he saw, even when he looked up and saw the shade of dead Abarsis, wizard-haired and wise and full of grief, as elegant as a ghost can be, reaching out his arms.

"You'll *not* take him . . . not from me. This is *my* boy—the closest I've ever come to one, and I swear by all the muck in heaven, I'll do hell's service if he dies unknowing, half-awake."

Then Abarsis coalesced, his satin skin and smooth cheeks as real as life. In gleaming armor, with a silken smile, he knelt down on Niko's far side.

And the ghost said gently: "Riddler, don't give up. You who were my inspiration in life, don't threaten or defame the gods. We love you. Your place awaits in heaven and someday you will claim it." The ghost of the Slaughter Priest smiled tenderly and put a gentle, almost opaque hand on Niko's brow. "Sleep," it whispered. "Sleep, sweet fighter, your time's not come if your will is strong. Live, Stealth called Nikodemos. Live to fight again.''

And then the shade of Abarsis, who'd formed the Stepsons and brought them glory and a special place in heaven, looked again at Tempus soulfully: "Riddler, give Niko water. Give him solace. Give him time.''

In Abarsis's ethereal hand, a flask of crystal flickered into being and Tempus, reaching for it, touched the ghost's hand with both his own. And they clasped hands there, a ghost who had loved a man who saved him when he was but a boy and a man who could not die.

"Give *me* your death, Slaughter Priest," Tempus whispered. "Take me up to heaven in his stead. Death is sweet to me, and theft to him, who's just begun to live. I can't bear this soul's weight upon my heart if he's maimed, or if he dies with witches hunting him and dream lords thirsting for his spirit."

"*Listen*, Riddler . . . I'll say it once again and I must go: have faith and we can heal him, you and I, who fell out of love with life. If he loves it still, he'll mend."

Tempus felt the vial in his hand grow heavy, and as it did, the ghost who was once called Stepson began to fade.

Tempus tried to clutch that hand again, stay the ghost, but it was too late.

When Abarsis was gone, the sun was wholly set, and Tempus sat upon the ground before a youth struggling for each breath he took as the night's chill came and the darkness made it seem that perhaps the ghost was right.

So Tempus opened the vial and with his hand under Niko's head, helped him to drink.

He didn't know what else to do: Abarsis had come and not taken Niko's soul, said some words, and gone, leaving Tempus shaken, not sure of anything, distressed.

Somehow, he had to get Niko out of here, somewhere better for healing or dying, and moving that tortured body would bring great pain.

The Askelonian butted him, as if to say, "I'll gladly

bear him anywhere," but Niko's wounds were worst just where a man sat a horse.

In the end, he carried Niko in his arms, the horse following behind him, through Ranke's streets, and everywhere he went, he laid curses upon Abakithis and the Rankan empire, wishing death and destruction upon it all.

When he came to the mercenaries' hostel, where he and the boy were lodging, there was a chariot outside, a chariot worked with ancient skill, borne by horses whom Tempus's steed greeted like brothers.

And inside, sitting sorrowfully in the anteroom, grit and trail dust covering his clothes and face, was the mageling Randal, looking supremely out of place among a score of hard-bitten fighters who jumped up when they saw Tempus and his burden.

As the mercenaries crowded around him, inflamed by the sight of Niko, the little mage demanded, "Let me through! Let me pass!"

And while men ran to prepare a sickroom and others formed up a hunting party who'd look for those who'd stolen Niko's gear, the flop-eared mage, face pale and freckles like spattered blood upon his cheeks, whispered: "You've got to let me help him, Riddler."

"You think you can?" Tempus lifted up the leopardskin and Randal gasped and squeezed his eyes shut. His Adam's apple worked; he gulped. He said, "That's what I'm here for."

Tempus nodded equably. "Then that's your chariot, outside."

Miserably, the mage admitted that it was. "Don't hold it against me—where it came from, why I've got it. We're all in this together. Even your mercenary brothers know that."

And so Tempus was able to lay Niko on a bed with soft clean linen, leave him in the hands of Randal, who might do no good but could surely do no harm, and go out avenging with twenty mercenaries who knew the Rankan streets and Rankan soldiery as well as the backs of their own hands.

* **7** *

Randal, alone with Niko in a room no bigger than a cell, with one arrowloop of a window high in the facing wall, tried everything he knew to make that seared flesh whole and bring Niko's canny smile back.

Everything, that is, but call upon the lord of dreams. He brought his globe out from its bag and spun it; he spoke spells and offered deals to demons; he even offered to take Niko's wounds unto his person.

But it wasn't enough. And Randal, who'd met Niko in his rest-place in the form of a hawk, didn't think that Niko would want the dream lord's help.

"By the Writ, Niko, tell me what to do," the Hazard begged the sleeping fighter, whom he adored. Would Niko be content if he recovered, a eunuch, ruined and half a man, to live on watching his body and his nature change? Fighters couldn't take their own lives. If Randal couldn't do the job properly, Niko would hate him with good reason—not just for being what he was, but for not being good enough.

It was a wonder that Stealth lived at all. Now and then his head tossed; his eyes roved beneath pain-tightened lids.

At one point, his hand groped, and Randal took it in his, holding tightly, remembering the soaring spirit, the pure and special soul he'd met in Niko's rest-place.

"Probably you're there," Randal said out loud. "Probably you're better off there." He blinked, and turned away.

There was one interim measure he could try before calling on Askelon—Randal could summon Cime, Tempus's sister, down from Tyse.

If she didn't come, there remained only alternatives Niko wouldn't like: Askelon, or even the Nisibisi witch, could be supplicated.

So there was only Cime, Randal decided, and that was that. Niko wouldn't want to live, beholden to the dream lord or as the creature of a witch.

Summoning Cime wasn't easy: she still scared Randal. She might take offense and slay him; she despised his kind.

But he worked the words of Writ and spoke the spells as clearly as he could, trying not to think how unhappy the Riddler would be to see his sister and what kind of bargain Randal would have to make to gain Cime's aid without putting Niko in her debt.

The air thickened, glazed with blue, and spun about, a little whirlwind in the middle of the room.

And soon enough, a woman's doeskin-clad form stood there, strode forth with angry eyes. *"Yes,* foul magician? This had better be important—you've risked your life and more, calling me to—"

Then Cime saw Niko on the bed. Her winter eyes darkened; she raised her hands and pulled her diamond rods down from her hair.

Well, thought Randal, *she'll either kill me with them or heal him with them; whichever, it's too late to back out now.*

"My brother's seen this," she said, lifting the sheet over Niko and then shaking her head, "and didn't let him die? Or is this *your* idea, you sniveling little sorcerer? Come on, which is it?" She tapped her wands and they began to spark with bright blue light.

Randal held his ground. "It's my idea, but the Riddler brought him here—he didn't kill him out of kindness, or set a funeral date. It was either you—you'll excuse my being blunt—or Askelon, or Roxane."

Cime stared at him gravely, then chuckled. "You speak the truth, that's something. Well, don't just stand there, Randal—get me lots of fresh cold water, butter, horse salve from the stables. Go! Run, if you want to save your friend."

And Randal ran, thinking that all any man can do is the best he can, even when he's a mage.

* **8** *

It took all night to find the soldiers who'd brought Niko
to Abakithis's priests.

But the god was whispering in Tempus's ear the whole
time, and though the culprits had hidden pieces of the
enchanted panoply in bunks and barracks and stableyards,
the Riddler *knew* just which soldiers he was seeking.

By dawn, the mercenaries had all six and their commanding officer tied in a coffle, the man who'd slain the
god's lamb at its head.

They took them out beyond the city limits and on the
shores of a river began the ritual of Neverending Deaths,
which Rankans mete out to their captives.

Though Tempus hadn't seen it done for more than twenty
years, he ordered the rites and closed his ears to the
doomed men's screams: the god wanted His sacrifice,
seven-fold, as gods are wont when they've been slighted.

By sunup the river ran pink with blood and the mercenaries rode in age-old fashion between the pieces of their
enemies.

And when they did, a hawk flew over, right to left,
sanctifying all in the Storm God's name—or names, if
Enlil was taking over Vashanka's duties, the way He'd
said, until the missing god came back.

Then it was time for Tempus, after thanking the men, to
visit Theron, the leader of the faction that wanted Abakithis
dead.

He'd stayed out of Rankan politics as best he could till
then, but this was a different matter: when priests betray
their gods and emperors go too far, it's always up to the
armies to set things right.

At Theron's home, the staff was serving breakfast.

The appearance of a huge man in blood-stained leopardskin with a boar's tooth helm and the god's own high-browed face sent menials scurrying.

But Theron, short and dark and windscored from years of honest battle, greeted Tempus with equanimity: general to general, as once they'd fought together in the field.

"Some food, Tempus? A bowl? A posset?"

Tempus took a bowl of winter wine thick with barley and goat's cheese and sat on Theron's terrace with a man, now aged and wizened, nearly sixty, who'd helped make Abakithis's empire the greatest in the world.

"What brings you here, old friend?" asked Theron, his thick lips working, his upslanted eyes sharp and wary. On his forehead was a dark gray callus from years of bowing his head to the god of war.

"You sent a priest," Tempus said without preamble, "up to Tyse to recruit a Stepson of mine for an assassination, bypassing me. Is that because you don't want my help?"

Theron snorted like an old warhorse. "By Vashanka's blazing eye, it's not that. We're short on funds and the priests yet fear you. They didn't tell me until afterward what they'd done. I won't apologize . . . this whole political business makes me queasy. If Abakithis were a man, I could call him out to single combat. But since he's not, I'm at the mercy of the manipulators and my backers . . . you know how coups are, and empires . . ."

"The boy can't fulfill his promise. He's badly hurt and may not live out the day."

Theron frowned. "From the way you say that, it happened here . . . not my men, I hope?"

"Your enemy's, *I* hope—Abakithis's priests in league with certain soldiers of the emperor's guard."

Theron's dark face grew darker. He put down his milk-and-goat's-blood drink and stood up. "Come on, then, let's go avenge it. It's about time things came out in the open. We're not quite ready, but then, if I leave it to the priests, we'll never be. For old times' sake, and with you at my side, let's split some faggot heads—"

"Sit down, Theron," Tempus grinned bleakly. "They're all deceased, gone down to some dark hell. I don't like to let vengeance wait—anticipation rots the soul."

"I should have known." Theron picked his teeth, then grimaced. "Do you need help? Support troops? What kind of trouble are you in?"

"None I can't handle. It was a mercenary matter, handled according to mercenary law."

"Then this is just a social visit?" the would-be emperor scoffed.

"You need a new assassin. I'll find you one . . . if the deal remains the same."

"The same?" said Theron, innocence like a jest upon his wise old face, where battlescars crosshatched squint lines and dissolution showed like pain.

"A recognized state of Free Nisibis, with Bashir as its independent ruler—an ally, if he wishes it; if not, not."

"Done."

"Good."

They shook hands in the fashion of the armies, a three-turn grip.

"And I can count on your support, Riddler? If so, the coup's assured."

Then Tempus's hoarse laughter echoed: "It's not that easy, the way the gods are now. You'll have my advice, but not my direct participation beyond enlisting an assassin for your cause."

Theron fingered his lips. "We'll do the best we can with that. I'm a servant of fate in this matter; if I were younger and wiser, I'd not let the priests use me either. But I'm old, my joints creak, I get angry at the way the empire's being driven full-tilt to ruin."

"So you'll give me free rein in the matter of Abakithis?"

"Of course. And I wish you well with it. And you, in your turn, won't blame me for doing what I have to do to save the empire?"

Tempus rose up and Theron walked him to the door.

"Not if you're the same man I remember. Life to you, old friend, and everlasting glory."

"And to you, Riddler," said the one-time mercenary who would be king.

* 9 *

Roxane, in her Grippa-form, lay tossing sleepless in her bed. Something was very wrong, she could feel it. Somewhere far away, the talisman of her protection was in the wrong hands.

She couldn't sleep; she couldn't leave this form. She wasn't strong enough. She had no globe to spin and few undeads; she couldn't keep snakes here, in Partha's holy, god-sworn home.

The god-taint everywhere was all she could contend with; she was busy keeping her disguise intact.

She longed to subdue the souls around her, take them as her instruments, bring evil back to its rightful place, but she needed time . . . time to grow strong again, time to make her plans.

Soon enough, she'd be able to hold her own.

Right now, all she could do was wonder, and weigh the consequences of leaving this just-claimed body, though an ancient part of her longed to change to eagle form, take wing, fly on down to Ranke where somewhere Niko, her beloved erstwhile minion, hovered close to death.

If she were there, perhaps she could claim his dying soul, lure him into service . . . even offer him an everlasting simulacrum of life.

But it was too risky; it was too soon. And there were others close around him, powerful forces she couldn't fight right now.

So she had to wait.

And if she had to wait, then Niko must not die.

So she told herself, rationalizing the stirrings of compassion and a purer love than Death's Queen ought to feel.

And in her bed, though it was risky to do good when evil owns your soul, she sat up straight and spoke some ancient words, sending what strength she could to Nikodemos, in the way of her kind, telling herself it was for evil that she'd save him.

She was only saving him for herself.

* 10 *

Niko was dreaming about wasps. They were buzzing around his head in his rest-place, bringing him caterpillars and fresh flowers to eat. The Hornet King had a white head, and when it hovered near his face it looked a lot like Randal.

But Niko was happy in the springtime of his rest-place, and if Randal wanted to be there as a hornet, he was welcome.

Here nothing hurt and everything was beautiful and new. His life, he remembered vaguely, was full of strife but he'd deal with it some other time.

Now he was content to recall all the good things, remember lessons learned on the islands of Bandara, walk the tiny islet of Ennina with his mentors, claiming his maat and trying not to be too proud that he had done so.

Those times were the best he'd ever had, on Bandara, away from war. He knew that *maat* would shield him, when he left again and walked in the world outside, from the desperate loss and loneliness of a war-orphan's youth. And he was willing to be an instrument of the discipline he'd mastered, embody the principles of truth and equilibrium in a dishonest and unsettled world. Maat was only peaceful where peace was: where disorder reigned, it struggled to bring things into balance.

That was fine with Niko; balance and a quiet heart were all he craved. He wanted to be the best that he could make himself, strive ever upward, seek perfection without ever demanding to attain it.

He wanted only to be free to try.

And in his rest-place, maat's finest gift, he was all of these—content to be discontent, peacefully struggling to attain impossible perfection, exulting in life by withdrawing from it.

Then his first left-side leader came walking across his star-shaped meadow, a man whom he respected with all his heart, a Syrese fighter a decade older who'd taught him much of what he knew of war, a man who'd died in Sanctuary and left Niko on his own.

"Time to go back, Stealth," said the suntanned ghost, scratching in his short gray hair as he'd always done when announcing a new mission.

"Now?" Niko hesitated. He was so comfortable, so happy here. But then, that was the way it always was. He couldn't disappoint his partner; he'd sworn an oath and never faltered. He'd do as he was bid, this one more time.

And when he thought that thought, and got to his feet in his rest-place with one regretful look around at the sweet green meadow of his mind's creation, it dissolved around him, dropping him into dark and pain, a struggle to survive his maat had let him forget a while, to rest and gain his strength.

When he opened his eyes next, he saw Randal's swimming face, and other faces: Tempus, he was almost certain, and the Riddler's sister, standing by.

And though he couldn't seem to remember how to speak, the faces floating in his vision obviously were pleased enough to see him.

At his bedside, some sort of celebration began.

Book Four:

————

FESTIVAL OF MAN

Three days before the Festival officially began, Tempus sent Randal out to the Festival village, which once had been pasture for the cattle of the gods, to greet Bashir's contingent and the mixed cadre of Stepsons and 3rd Commando rangers Crit led when they arrived.

The Riddler's timing was exquisite—Randal had promised the dream lord he'd drive that hell-forged chariot across the newly sanctified grounds and speak certain words at compass points to create a portal through which Askelon might enter into the Festival village when and where he willed.

But Randal had been too busy nursing Niko. He'd told himself he didn't care if he had his allergies forever—he'd lived with them this long. It was Niko's health which mattered to the Hazard, mattered more than self-interest or promises made to dream lords.

Niko was healing slowly, his wounds so grave that no spell could just erase them—even Cime warned that Niko might never be the man he'd been before.

So Randal had put off this matter of a promise made to the entelechy of dreams indefinitely—truth be known, Randal blamed the dream lord for not taking better care of Niko.

Though Stealth was now the Riddler's partner, it was to

Nikodemos Randal had sworn an oath and given his heart. Seeing Niko toss and turn in search of a comfortable way to lie abed, greased like a ceremonial pig and his clear eyes shrouded with pain whenever he was awake, Randal had second thoughts about his chosen way of life. If a First Hazard couldn't conjure health for a beloved friend, perhaps there was no such thing as white magic, no power which could circumvent the cruel and angry gods.

But when Tempus sent him out to the Festival grounds, adamant like fate, he'd come. Once here, he'd driven the Askelonian team in the requisite arabesques, said the words and chanted where he should, then come up above the village on a hill from which the capital, fifteen miles behind, and the general's route due north could both be seen.

He half expected to see Askelon materialize, striding down the road, but it was Bashir's contingent who raised the dust in sunrise, with Crit's mixed cadre alongside.

And for some reason Randal didn't understand, as Bashir's party neared the hill crest, Randal's kris began to rattle in its scabbard, as it did when an enemy was near.

"Hush," he told it, hand firmly on its hilt to keep the sword from jumping from its scabbard. "Bashir doesn't hate me that much, he's just the god's man, and the Stepsons are my friends."

But the kris kept jittering and nudging his hand as the wagon with the Partha children in it and Bashir beside it stopped before him.

Bashir took one look at the sable stallions from the dream lord's stable and the chariot with its graven sides, low war flute, its bracers gilded with raised demons of the brood, and made godsign before his face.

It was all Randal could do not to counter with a ritual of his own. But he said, instead, "Niko's badly hurt, Bashir. The Riddler requests your presence as soon as possible. I'm here to take you—"

A commotion came from inside the wagon; then a scuffle ended and Sauni scrambled out, her brother close behind her.

"Niko's hurt?" Her face was pale; she hugged herself.

Grippa had her by the shoulder as if to pull her back inside. "If he is, it's not for *you* to see, sister *dear*; you've a god's child to think of, not yourself. Now get back inside before I—"

Randal was holding his kris still with all his might.

Bashir turned in his saddle. "Grippa, I won't tell you again: your sister is a holy vessel, not to be chastised by such as you. *Get* your hands off her, and respect her person, or in the name of Enlil I, myself, will teach you reverence—and you won't soon forget it if I do."

Grippa, flustered, his cheeks as red as the sunrise, let go his sister with a little push that almost sent her sprawling.

But Bashir had already looked away, saying to Randal, "These children feel they have a vested interest—Sauni for obvious reasons, Grippa because Stealth was going to sponsor him with the Stepsons. If it's possible, I'd like to bring them both along."

"That's . . . up to you, Bashir. But it's nothing for young eyes to see."

Bashir urged his horse up beside the chariot. Leaning down, the priest said, "Then perhaps it's time those eyes grew up."

From that, Randal deduced that the children had been troublesome on the trek and that Bashir, despite his priestly calm, was worried about Niko, though no man of the god would ever ask a mage for information and admit that there were some things the god hadn't told His servant in advance.

"I'll just get Crit and we'll be off, then," Randal said smoothly, trying to pretend he didn't see Bashir's shocked expression as the warrior-priest of Free Nisibis looked over the hilltop, down at the Festival village for the first time.

Bashir had never been farther south than Tyse, never seen the might of the overlords he flouted. The miniature

city Abakithis had built on the Storm God's pastureland
was supposed to cow, to convince the treaty signatories
and rival states who came to win the game that they
couldn't win a war against Imperial Ranke, that the empire
was not so disarrayed or so penurious as they'd been told.
And one look at Bashir told Randal that the gilt-domed,
lacquered Festival village had done just that.

Randal was glad to leave the priest alone there and head
on down the line to check in with Critias.

Crit asked all the questions Bashir was too proud to
voice: "How? When? Has he been avenged? How badly is
Niko hurt?"

When Randal said, "Badly. We're doing our best—he'll
live, if that's a comfort. The Riddler won't leave him,
though—you know Sacred Band oaths. You're to come
with me, and bring Sync with you."

"Sync? Why Sync?"

Then Randal realized that Crit was actually upset, that
Stepsons did love one another, that the whole Sacred Band
mystique was really true. "Because," Randal said as gently
as he could, "the Riddler ordered it, task force leader.
You're to leave Straton in command, get Sync, Kama, a
pair or two who care more for Niko than winning some
silly game, and come along."

* **2** *

Niko's sickroom smelled of camphor, sweat, and rancid
butter and, now that Bashir was present, incense and
offerings to the gods.

Tempus was glad enough to see the priest and the
endless stream of visitors he had in tow.

Until then, he'd been virtually alone with Niko, who
slept a lot, and with Cime, the temptress of his soul.

So even the pair of Partha children, when they arrived,

were a timely distraction. He told Cime of his suspicions and bade her watch young Grippa well.

The boy stood, pale-faced, while at Niko's bedside Sauni knelt and wept, her cheek pressed against Stealth's hand while the healing fighter tried to focus on her, half-raised his head and let it fall, then whispered, frowning with the effort: "Sauni . . . don't cry. It's the will of gods and . . ."

Then she sobbed so that Tempus didn't hear the rest, telling Niko she bore his baby, not the god's, and he must get well to see it born, so that Bashir put down his censer and intervened, lifting her bodily away and ejecting her.

Then Tempus caught Grippa smiling, and when the boy's turn came to kneel beside the sickbed, Grippa reminded Niko that Stealth had promised to sponsor him as a Stepson.

Cime stepped in quickly, saying, "Selfish brat. Don't tire him with this—"

But Tempus had a better idea: "Lie back, Stealth, it's as good as done."

Niko did. He was waxen and as ashen as his hair; the regrowth of so much flesh took time. Tempus would have given Niko his own regenerative nature if he could. He'd half-hoped that if Grippa was the witch, the sight of Niko in this state would flush her.

But if Roxane was Grippa, she was too canny for that. So Tempus added, when no one asked him to explain, "Grippa will be Randal's new partner; Randal's good enough to lead a team."

Niko groaned softly in his bed, but didn't argue.

If Grippa had been a normal boy, he would have: the rightman of a wizard wasn't what a young man joined the Stepsons to become.

"Riddler!" Randal was horror-struck, an hour later, when in a private conference room in the basement of the ancient Rankan mercenaries' hostel, the Riddler told him of his plan.

"I think it's a great idea," Crit glowered at Randal. "A masterstroke of a plan. If Grippa's Roxane, she won't be able to hide it long from you."

"That's no plan at all," Randal objected. "It's a sacrifice—of *me*!"

"Don't argue, Randal," Crit warned. "Just do what you're assigned to do, or you'll be mucking stables out at Hidden Valley all next season, Niko or no Niko."

"Well! You can't tell me—" Then Randal got control of himself, saying, "Yes, task force leader, sir!" and adding only one more objection: "I wish someone would tell me how I can abrogate my former oath, make an ersatz one to a possible witch, and still keep my integrity intact."

Tempus said nothing, just watched the mage whom he was putting in mortal jeopardy.

When the formal meeting was over, Tempus took the slight First Hazard aside. "Randal, I have something for you, to help with this assignment. If you can make it fit, it might just save you, or give you an edge, at least."

"Fit? Whatever it is, I'll manage. Anything that helps, I'll try." Randal's eyes were round with worry; First Hazard or not, keeping tabs on Grippa might be a killing task.

Taking Randal by the arm, Tempus led the mageling to his quarters, got a hide-wrapped bundle from beneath his bed, and uncovered Niko's charmed panoply—cuirass, dagger, and sword.

"There you go, Randal. Armor fit for a prince of magic, a fighting mage."

"But that's Niko's." Randal was aghast, blinking back sudden tears. "Let's not give up hope. He might recover, be able to—"

"Right now, this gear's no use to him. He wants you to have it—we discussed it."

"You mean you told him what to do and he nodded his head."

"Randal, that's the way of the armies. Your oath to

Niko, you insist, is yet binding. Therefore, subsequent oaths you take are just like any of Crit's covert games. Now,'' Tempus sat back on his haunches, ''let's see if we can make this cuirass fit you. You're going to need all the help you can get, and Askelon's given you other . . . things . . .'' Tempus alluded to the hell-chariot Randal now drove. ''He won't begrudge you these.''

* 3 *

Kama knew Ranke in a way Crit was never settled long enough to learn anyplace. She could change from her uniform into a bronze-beaded gown in a twinkling and take him among the movers and shakers of Rankan society he'd never have had access to otherwise.

She was risking a lot, letting Crit see her as she was—politically connected, sophisticated, well known to the priests of Theron's faction and to the old war horse himself as only a trusted agent could be.

She knew Crit would make the obvious deductions. Whether he would forgive her lies of omission was another matter.

So when he broached the subject, at the festivities on the night before the games' official start in a chandeliered hall filled with Rankan nobility, she braced herself: tonight she might lose Crit's respect, if not his love, forever.

He said quietly, dancing close while a quartet played just loud enough for folk to talk freely, ''You could have told me you were a Rankan agent. Or did you just assume a simple country boy wouldn't understand?''

Now that the moment had come, her silver tongue failed her; she didn't know what to say. She said nothing at all, just brushed his close-bearded cheek with her lips.

''Some of it must have been real, between us,'' Crit said then. ''Surely you wouldn't get pregnant and lose a child for the good of empire?'' He stopped dancing and his grip on her was firm. ''Say something, damn it, before I have to conclude that I've been had by an expert and there's nothing more to it than that—that Strat's been right all along and you'll disappear when you're done using us for—''

"I can help you with things here, Crit," she said numbly. "I've been helping you all along."

"The lady and the barbarian? I don't need etiquette lessons, I need to know what the big secret is that all of you are keeping, how Brachis fits in now that Niko's out of commission, a list of the dramatis personae, at least . . ."

They were conspicuous, standing motionless on the dance floor.

She said, "You can have all of that, and more." And, though it was opportune, she would have told him anything, that night, even if it wasn't. "Let's go somewhere quiet and talk. Then I want to introduce you to some people."

Kama took Critias through crowded streets full of strangers gathered for the games: natives of Uraete, Sivis, Altoch and Mygdonia (here under a flag of truce), sporting the intricate turbans that made the Rankan army call them Rag-heads, rubbed shoulders with athletes from Caronne and Azehur; dusky Ilsigs from as far south as Sanctuary reeled drunkenly down bunting-hung streets arm-in-arm with Machadi nationals; here and there the sibilances of Nisi mixed with the rolling r's of Crit's own mother-tongue, Syrese. There were even a few Bandaran initiates, here for the weaponry competition, their hands in their sleeves and their eyes downcast, their mystery surrounding them like guardians so that men gave them room unconsciously.

Some gamers had their pets with them: hawks on padded shoulders, leopards on jeweled leashes, hunting dogs as big as ponies who bayed at the leopards who hissed at the hawks who screamed wild challenges into the crisp night air of winter's end.

At the house Kama's mother had bequeathed her, she stopped, took a deep breath, and told the Syrese fighter whom she loved: "This where I live; it's been shut-up but it's safe inside—and empty. Come on."

She slit a ward she'd bought from a friendly witch, untied her knot, keyed her lock, and opened the wrought iron gate doors wide. Her home was going to seem too rich to him; his impression of her as a woman of the armies might be canceled out by its opulence, its silk rugs, it silver mirrors.

She lit oil panniers borne by agate lions, and in their light, she watched Crit reassess her: there was nothing else to do. Critias's patrician nose drew down with his frown: mercenaries disdained inherited wealth—most of them had turned their back on it, or been cheated out of it.

He said, "Am I now supposed to call you 'my lady'? Or be impressed? Forgive near a year of lies?"

She'd bought a charm this morning, a spell to pacify him if he'd drink a cup of wine with her. The flagon and the goblets were waiting, but she found she couldn't do it. She wanted Critias, but not that way.

She said, "My mother earned all this. She was a leading courtesan, a confidant of politicians, a whore-mistress. I'm not proud of it, but I won't reject her legacy. Anyway, it's not what I have, but what I am, that ought to matter."

"That's right," he said, the slap of his oxhide boots as loud as her heartbeat as he made a circuit of her front room, touching scrolls and tapestries, then came back to her again: "And you're a Rankan spy. I ought to denounce you to your father . . ."

"Crit," said Kama, "give me a chance to explain . . ."

"What's to explain? You've wormed your way into my confidence. I went against the Riddler's counsel, against orders, and took up with you. Now I know why he disapproved so. I'm feeling a little bit foolish. I should have known."

She was afraid he was going to leave. She said: "There's

no way I can prove to you that you're jumping to conclusions if you won't give me a chance." She unlatched her woolen cloak and let it fall, longing to touch him. But she had a job to do, interests to serve that were more important than her own.

And he said, as she'd hoped he would: "Right. Then you explain. I'll listen."

She told him she hadn't gone in Tyse in bad faith. "Theron's faction seeks to restore the empire, not destroy it. The Riddler's worked for him before. He knew what I was from the beginning," she half-lied, for god and country. "And now the coup's nearly a reality. Except . . ."

"Except?" Arms crossed, he waited, chin tucked in, stern and unyielding.

"Except that Niko's not . . . competent. I helped to choose him. I have to help find another."

"Don't look at me—that's a suicide mission. We know all about it; we've known since Tyse."

She hid her surprise. What, then, did he expect that she could tell him? She took a chance: "My father's said he'd find another, someone willing. But with the war god missing, and Abakithis's faction sworn to revenge their dead priests upon the Riddler, it might go awry. We need someone else, ready in the wings, prepared to step in if . . ."

"So that's the point, then? Help you find an assassin? And that's the secret—that Abakithis plots against us? Any child could have guessed all this. Surely, you can do better than that."

But she couldn't. She shrugged miserably, raised her eyes to him and said softly: "I'm a 3rd Commando first; I'm everything I said. I've never lied to you, just held back things. Crit . . . I love you. You have your duty and I've never questioned it—to my father, to Straton, to your Sacred Band. I've found room for my love in the cracks of your life and never pushed for more. Can't you do the same for me?"

"Woman, if I heard you right, you're asking the Stepsons to involve themselves in treason. I can't allow that. Not my unit, especially when the coup's not sure . . ."

"I trusted you with this." She stood up and they were eye to eye. "I wanted you to know, now—not find yourself tricked into something later."

And that made Crit look away. "I know, Kama . . . but this thing can't go on, between us. I don't want to light your pyre or have to give your eulogy."

He backed a pace. She followed. "I'll resign," she whispered. "From the 3rd, from everything . . . for you."

She hadn't meant to say it. She didn't believe her own ears.

But it must have been exactly the right thing to say and she thought the god must have prompted her, for he put his arms around her and held her close, unspeaking.

Since it might be the last time, she was content with that. Recruiting Crit, whose honor was worth more to him than life itself, had been an assignment she'd half-known she couldn't carry out. A part of her was proud of him; a part wanted to be like him.

But she had to do what she'd been ordered: alert him to the threat Abakithis posed; put the Stepsons on their guard; make sure that her enemy was theirs.

When he touched her throat, she put her hand on his swordbelt. When he whispered harshly, "We shouldn't do this. We ought to make a clean break," she hushed him.

Perhaps it was because their love was doomed, but no man's touch had ever been so sweet to her.

Afterward, when she shed tears, he didn't understand why. He consoled her, told her she wouldn't have to be dishonored; they'd find a way for her to resign from the 3rd and he'd induct her into his own task force.

From that moment, Kama commanded Critias, Tempus's task force leader—and the coup, finally, was as sure as Kama's victory in the bard's contest at the Festival of Man.

* 4 *

Grippa formally became a Stepson on the second day of the games, the same day that Sauni's footrace was being held.

Roxane had been horrified when she'd learned she was to be Randal's partner, but there was nothing to do but see the matter through to its conclusion.

Out behind the red-lacquered Festival barracks, where Bashir's Successor team had pitched black tents rather than spend their nights inside, the pairing ritual took place with Bashir, not Tempus, presiding.

This too was trouble: the warrior-priest of Free Nisibis looked at Grippa as if he were looking through the manly guise to Roxane underneath.

Tempus was there, leopard-mantled as if going into battle, and Niko lay inside a black tent on a stretcher, where he could see the bonfire of the ceremony and all the Stepsons who attended, and the Riddler's sister Cime, in scale-armor and doeskin, knelt by Niko's side.

Enjoying the hospitality of her enemies, with the mightiest of them watching her through narrowed eyes, shook the valor of even Nisibis's finest witch.

Grippa's big hands were trembling as he took the cup of blood wine and he stumbled over the words that bound him to Randal as a Sacred Bander and a member of the Stepsons.

Swearing to die, shoulder to shoulder, to never shirk or quail or run, to defend his partner's honor as his own and protect the hated First Hazard with Grippa's last breath was difficult in the extreme for Roxane.

The oath of allegiance to Tempus was so foreign to her nature she could barely get the words out.

But under Bashir's watchful eye she promised all in the name of a god she hated and a goddess she despised.

When the blood wine was passed a second time, she could hardly bear to let it touch her lips. And as it did a rain began to fall from heaven that was black and greasy, full of pumice.

It rained upon the bonfire and the flames there sputtered out. It rained upon the soldiers and they began to mutter restlessly among themselves.

But the ritual was nearly over, the celebration to follow in the black tents about to start.

Randal came forward for her to embrace him, and as he did the mageling cast aside his fur-lined cloak.

And there, upon Randal's person, was the armor forged by Askelon, entelechy of dreams. Its raised snakes and enameled demons seemed to writhe and hiss at her.

She almost broke and ran: she was expected to embrace this Hazard, who wore armor that heated up in the presence of hostile magic.

Grippa began to sweat as Randal advanced, one foot before the other at a ritual's slow pace with his arms outstretched, a strained but welcoming smile upon his freckled face as the grimy rain streaked down it.

Should she refuse to embrace the wizard, all her effort would be lost. And there were too many forces here—Tempus, Cime, Bashir, the Storm God's priest—to chance being unmasked there and then.

She knew it was going to hurt her; she could see the armor heating up.

Bracing Grippa's flesh for the searing contact, she went to hug the wizard, all her skill marshaled to make sure Grippa wouldn't faint, or blister, or even burn. The rain, heavier now, was oily, greasy, unnatural as the meeting of two hostile magics before the eyes of men.

Then Randal's arms enfolded Grippa and there was a hiss as Grippa's skin began to sear.

Fighting the pain and spelling furiously, Roxane protected the flesh which was her flesh, the bone which was her home, from the conjured panoply of the entelechy of dreams.

Anguish rippled through her in waves as she took the damage to her inner person to avoid the boy whose shape she shared being marked as a witch before so many onlookers.

And Randal, who surely knew what was happening, said not one word about it, but just hugged her tight, mouthing ritual welcoming phrases, until she couldn't stand the pain, and stumbled backward.

Weaving momentarily on her feet, she caught herself, then straightened; in an instant, the raw, blistered skin no one could be sure they'd seen was gone, replaced by smooth and youthful flesh as Grippa ought to have.

The crowd broke into a half-hearted cheer, some squinting at the sky, and hurried into the celebration tent.

Sauni came running up, threw her arms around Grippa's neck, and wailed, "Oh, it's awful—what a heinous omen, what a shame."

And Randal was standing right there, just watching Grippa, when Roxane made the boy say: "What do you mean?"

"My event—it might be canceled. A pox on whatever's brought this rain."

"It won't be, Sauni, never fear," said Randal. "And my rightman will be there to cheer you on." Then the mage turned to Grippa, an evil twinkle in his eye as he picked dry film like sunbaked snakeskin from his armor: "Coming, Stepson? It's your party you're missing."

Roxane had no alternative but to follow Randal, Sauni hanging on him, chattering as she went, not realizing the pain she caused flesh which looked unmarred, but really was burned deep.

Inside the tent, the revel lasted well past the trumpet calling contestants to their first events. Men came up and congratulated Grippa with hearty slaps upon the back and foul jokes.

Cime and the Riddler, together, wished Grippa well and drifted back into the crowd. Bashir was the only one who kept his distance, and Roxane was relieved at this one small favor from the lords of hell.

When Sauni's event was called, Grippa hurried to his sister. "Let's go. You can't be late. You didn't eat or drink too much, did you, sister dear?"

And the brainless receptacle of the god's child said, "Oh, no. I wouldn't do that. I'll just kiss Niko . . ."

And off she went, fluttering like a butterfly from Niko to the Riddler, to the Stepson Gayle who'd become her bodyguard, and back.

Outside the tent, the rain had stopped, leaving the ground treacherous and slick.

But this was the moment Roxane had been waiting for: Randal was otherwise engaged; his stolen globe of power, a rightful Nisibisi heirloom, was snug in his barracks.

When Sauni, with a final peck on Grippa's cheek, trotted to the starting line, Grippa edged backward against the press of the crowd.

And then, free of it, she turned to trot back to the barracks.

"Forgotten something?" came a tenor voice beside her as she reached its door.

It was Randal's voice. The scrawny mage, spiteful and smug, stood on the threshold, an oilskin cloak held out.

"I was just . . . looking for that, Ran—left-side leader," Grippa said.

"That, rightman, is what a partner's for," said Randal, and tossed the cloak to Grippa. "Hurry now, rightman, or we'll miss your sister's contest."

She almost hissed; she nearly cast a spell to char the wizard where he gloated: he knew who and what she was, she had no doubt.

But two could play this game. The globe was there, she

could feel it, waiting for her to reclaim it. And tomorrow
was another day.

Tonight she'd meditate on a fate fit for a First Hazard,
and contemplate how well she'd feel when Randal's soul
was on her plate.

* 5 *

Bashir had chanced upon a Bandaran master on the
Rankan Street of Temples. Bashir had come into town to
lay a sacrifice before Vashanka, the Rankan equivalent of
Enlil.

What the Bandaran, a secular adept, was doing here, he
couldn't say. Bandara wasn't threatened by renegade wizards looking to reclaim their mountain home, or the godless Mygdonians fomenting revolution and training troops
for spring assaults. Nor was Ranke an enemy of Bandara:
the island chain was independent, uncontested, a place of
elder gods and spiritual wealth.

The two fell in together naturally, once Bashir had said,
"What brings a teacher to the Street of Students?"

The Bandaran, a man easily fifty, looked calmly up at
him. "A priest's question from a fighting man? Perhaps
it's you I seek then," his sea-change gaze serene and
introspective.

"Perhaps," Bashir agreed. "I've long wondered about
the relationship of the elder gods to the islands of human
mystery. I have a friend who trained there . . ."

"You do." The Bandaran, barefoot, paced Bashir as
they passed Vashanka's state-cult temple. It wasn't a question, but an affirmation. "Then you are just the man I'd
hoped to meet. Could your friend be a full initiate of maat,
a worthy soul called Nikodemos?"

"Shrivel me, that's Stealth, all right!" Bashir clapped

the Bandaran on the back and felt muscle like a bull beneath. "You know him, then?"

"We've met. I hoped he'd be here himself. We . . . want to tender him an invitation."

"You do?" Bashir's natural caution was aroused. "Well, I'll take a message to him. I'd heard that he was cast out of Bandara in disgrace. He's a favorite of Enlil, you know—you do respect the elder gods, you men who vie with the lesser ones."

"Tell him that his master died, when a boat with rainbow sails came back. And tell him that on his deathbed the sun shone and the teacher wished to see his student."

Bashir knew that something serious was being entrusted to him, a message more important than it appeared. He could feel the god, restless inside him, as Enlil listened through his ears. "Anything more—a name? Yours? The dead adept's?"

"My name is unimportant," said the sea-eyed Bandaran. "But Nikodemos's is not. Is the student well?"

Bashir considered lying: Niko was the god's now, not the property of any mind-reading plane-climbers who fooled with powers men shouldn't covet. But he didn't; he could feel the spirit animating this Bandaran master, and it was strong.

Bashir said honestly, "He's beset by demons, witches, even the entelechy of dreams. He's been ill; he's healing slowly."

The Bandaran nodded again as if this, too, were no surprise. "A purge. We sensed it. When one of us suffers, all know it. He should know that his teacher asked for him—by name."

They were on the corner of a main thoroughfare; there was a Rankan alehouse near. "Let's get a drink, friend Bandaran. Then you can tell me what all this means. I'm Bashir, priest of Enlil, warlord of the Successors, keeper of Wizardwall and Father of Free Nisibis. Any message for my blood brother, Nikodemos, is safe with me."

But the Bandaran declined to drink, saying: "If there's a response, you can find me with my delegation. If it pleases you, we'll meditate upon Niko's swift recovery . . ."

It was definitely a petition for permission. Bashir said, a bit uncomfortably, "Whatever Niko's fate, it's in the god's hands. But meditate all you will."

"We'll do that," said the Bandaran, his beatific smile beaming in the torchlight. "Farewell, priest. And luck to you in your event."

Watching the Bandaran disappear into the crowd, Bashir reflected that he hadn't told the adept he was competing. But then, it was a natural assumption, given Bashir's fighting stature and his god's love for arms, he told himself.

It wasn't until much later that he returned to the Festival grounds; he'd drunk off his disquiet at all this Rankan might and met Straton, who was entered in the boxing tomorrow, calming his nerves in a drug parlor.

Together they lurched into the Festival village an hour before the dawn.

"Take this, Strat, lest someone see you snookered." Bashir held out a little box of pulcis, shared it with Straton, and then, as the drug knifed through to clear his brain, remembered the Bandaran he'd chanced to meet.

"Bless you, Bashir," Strat called out, stumbling on the stairs to the Stepsons' barracks, "and your god in my god's name." Strat paused, retched on the lacquered balcony, and with exaggerated poise, shouldered his way inside.

Bashir heard a crash, then some curses as he walked away.

Niko was billeted with the Riddler and his sister, in the team leaders' houses away from the raucous contestants.

With a squint at the lightening sky, Bashir decided that it might not be too late to look in on Niko, and knocked on the Riddler's door.

Tempus, who never slept, invited him in, openly curious: "You need your rest, too, priest. What is it?"

"I met a Bandaran in town who gave me a message for Niko. Who knows what it means, but it might mean something to Stealth . . ."

Then Bashir realized he'd interrupted something. Tempus was disarrayed, half-clothed, and somewhat sheepish. Such an expression on the Riddler's face could mean only one thing: Cime, who collected men and had long been after Tempus as a trophy, was close to winning.

"Do *you* need the god's help to avoid temptation, Riddler?" Bashir said bluntly. "Anyone can ask; the god is generous."

"The god?" Tempus nearly spat. "Enlil? It's the god who wants what's forbidden me, as gods do. Stay out of this, Bashir, it's not your business. Go say goodnight to your little lamb, Nikodemos, and leave me to wrestle with my fate in peace."

"Ah . . . as you wish, my friend. But my door is always open, my house your house, my arm your strength."

"I'll keep it in mind, Bashir," Tempus said impatiently, holding Niko's door open.

Inside, alone with the smell of healing and in the light of a single taper, Bashir regretted having come. Embarrassing the Riddler was something he'd never meant to do. And Niko, Bashir thought, was sleeping.

But when he sat down beside Stealth's bed on an elephant-foot stool, Stealth turned his head and opened his eyes.

"Bashir," said Niko in a voice barely audible, "good."

"How are you, Stealth?"

"Dreaming . . ." His eyes blinked, steadied. "Witches in my dreams. And gods." He tried to smile and put out a hand as if to sit up. He couldn't manage it, but at least he tried. "Sauni won her race . . ."

"I know. Niko, in town I met a Bandaran."

Niko closed his eyes.

"Niko? Stealth?"

"I'm listening," Stealth said, and Bashir saw a drop of sweat or a tear run from the corner of his eye.

"The Bandaran said to tell you that your master died when a rainbow-sailed ship came in, and that as the sun shone the master asked for you—by name. I don't know what it means, but he seemed to think *you* would."

Niko turned his head and looked up at Bashir, smiling for the first time in far too long. "It means," Stealth said, "that I can . . . go home . . . if I want. That I'm forgiven."

*   **∗ 6 ∗**

Tempus was just about to rape his sister when Crit came pounding on the door.

Cime had been his only love for years; he'd stayed away from her for many reasons—her curse, his, their kinship, etc.

But if she was a whore now, with her curse lifted, it was by choice and no fault of his. And if she teased him any longer, with her parted lips and bull-whip tongue, he was going to vent his wrath on some innocent, which she assuredly was not.

Nor was she his sister, he told himself—no relationship of blood, but only marriage, had ever been proved, since their mothers weren't the same.

And Enlil wanted Cime badly; Tempus was deep in godbond, hardly capable of holding back the urge to rape another day.

So when Crit's knock came, he released Cime's hair, took his hand out from between her thighs, and told her: "Get up, while you still can, Cime. Get out of here and go back whence you came. This is no place to tempt the gods."

Breathing hard, her eyes wide with something—treachery, triumph, fear, or lust, he couldn't tell—she scampered like a maiden from his front room, leaving nothing on the table where he'd thought to have her but a slick of sweat.

So much for that, he thought—for now—and let Crit in, not really surprised by the consternated look on his first officer's face: since Tempus had cursed Ranke, carrying Niko's savaged body through the capital's streets, he'd been expecting trouble. The black rain that had fallen when Grippa had been inducted into the Stepsons and the fact that, well into the second week of the games, Ranke had yet to win one event, told him that he hadn't cursed the empire in vain.

"Commander, sorry to disturb you, but there's trouble over at the Nisibisi tents." Crit's eyes were bleak and icy; behind him, on the doorstep, Sync, the 3rd's colonel, stood with ready crossbow, policing the night.

"Rag-heads slew the sentries," Critias continued. "They've taken the Nisibisi athletes hostage . . . Bashir and Sauni, too. They want an end to Free Nisibis and they want the Mygdonian boy we had last season delivered there by morning or they'll kill every prisoner they've got."

"Mygdonians? Are you certain?" Tempus gathered up his panoply, his sharkskin-hilted sword. The Mygdonian boy in question, Shamshi, was the wizard-child Tempus had seen languishing in Meridian under the dream lord's spell. And the Mygdonians knew as well as Tempus that no mortal power could produce the child.

Crit shrugged cynically. "Hardly. Anybody could be under those turbans. Their message said 'blood for blood; priest for priest.' The Mygdonians are godless still, so far as we know."

"What do the Mygdonians say?" Tempus demanded, buckling on his cuirass.

"I sent Strat over to interrogate the leader of the Mygdonian delegation." Crit squinted at Tempus ruefully: "Nobody lies to Straton; the Mygdonians say it's not their doing and they've offered to help. That's why I'm here

. . . I know you're . . . ah . . . busy; I wouldn't have disturbed you if it wasn't ticklish. Orders?''

"Could it be the witch-caste, the rebel Nisibisi? Was Grippa taken hostage?"

"Grippa? No, he was with Randal the whole time. Commander, we think—Kama and I, that is . . . Vashanka's balls, Riddler, it seems like Abakithis's faction, avenging the priests you slew and sending us a message to stay clear of Theron, not resurrect the coup. Kama says we can ask for help from Theron's—"

"Surround the Nisibisi tents. We'll burn them out. If we lose Bashir and the girl, it's a kinder death than they'll get otherwise. Make sure Randal's there, and Grippa. Go on, I'll meet you there. And send Sync in here."

"Commander?"

"Crit?"

'Is there some reason you haven't mentioned finding a replacement for Niko . . . will you accept a volunteer?''

"Not you, Stepson, nor any one of yours. If I didn't know you wouldn't disobey my orders, I'd think you'd been letting my daughter whisper in your ear. Now go on, let's see if we can't roast those bastards, whoever they are. And don't worry about Bashir—a martyr's death will suit him."

Crit grinned without humor and saluted, opened the door and called Sync in, then left, closing it.

"You wanted to see me, Commander?" said the rangy commando colonel warily, crested helmet in his hands.

"Sync, I have a task for you, if you'll accept it. One that should be done by a Rankan, a man who remembers what Ranke used to be, and wants to be proud of the empire once again."

The Rankan ranger watched the quasi-immortal he'd deserted Abakithis to serve without emotion. Then he said: "Something the Stepsons can't handle, Commander?"

"A special mission that Niko was to have performed."

Sync's eyes glinted. "I was hoping you'd ask."

When they'd discussed the details and the commando had gone, Tempus threw open the door to his back rooms and found his sister right behind it, still half-naked.

She came to him and said, pressed against him, her hand on his loinguard: "So? You've sent your boys out to do men's work. Now you come to me to save you once again. . . . What is it this time, brother, that you can't accomplish without my help?" A finger traced his lips; her breath was warm against his throat. "Shall I call upon Askelon and secure the Mygdonian boy for you?"

He knew he shouldn't bargain with his sister, yet he had little choice. He meant to ask her for help, to make a deal with this creature half siren, half witch. But the god came into him, full force.

He put a hand on her; she closed her eyes.

The god wanted rape; he wanted peace between them.

Too long they'd fought and spat at one another. She leaned against his hand and spoke his name, her voice soft and nothing like the harpy she'd become.

"You're free of everything but me, is that it, sister? Am I the curse that even the dream lord couldn't lift?" It was no good, he knew: the time was right, and after three centuries of longing, he couldn't deny his feelings—calling her "sister" wasn't even helping.

"I could make him free you, too."

"Of everything but you?" The god deepened his voice and in his head, silently, he fought a battle with Enlil. He'd do anything but rape her, if the god would settle for less than that.

But the god was adamant and Tempus had fought this battle so many times—it was a matter of personal import, of self-respect. If she'd come to him before the god had, and begged him then, as she did now, to make her truly free by consummating what had lain undone between them for three hundred years, he could have done it. Done it even though the girl he'd loved—a girl so beautiful in mind and body that he'd stepped between her and a wizard, knowing full well he'd suffer eternally for what he did—no longer existed in this twisted creature who sought to mount him as if she were a man and he her conquest.

Had she not been so bent on his seduction, she might have had him, damned him in his own terms, brought him at last as low as she. But she was too forward, too much the courtesan for him. And she always would be. This final time, when he could have taken her with a god to blame, he turned away from Cime, just disgusted.

And all the love he'd nursed forever, which had kept him from loving women and constrained him from making an accommodation with his fate, bled out of him.

* **7** *

Roxane, in her Grippa-form, slipped away from Randal in the confusion before the Nisibisi tents.

The dark lords had smiled upon her; Bashir, her hated enemy, was in the hands of the Rankan priesthood. Even as she sneaked away, she heard tortured screams and moans from inside the tent where the hostages were being held.

And it was hard to leave: inside, a man was dying, being bled over a barrel sacred to Vashanka, the missing god. And since there was no god to take his soul, Roxane could have had it.

Nor was that the extent of the feast at hand: the girl Sauni, Enlil's pregnant priestess, was learning that all men were not as gentle or as loving as Nikodemos, that more could happen in a man's arms than ecstasy. And Bashir was suffering most, watching his flock suffer under Rankan torture and his young priestess defiled by Rankan hands.

The psychic anguish emanating from that tent was so extreme she was giddy from it, so that she didn't notice that Randal saw her slip away, and went to Crit, or that Crit sent Straton after her.

Grippa's young, strong form seemed to glide among the shadows and the tents. Full of bloodlust and nearly sated from the suffering on the air, she hurried him through the crowd, avoiding Stepsons, 3rd Commando rangers, and onlookers held back by Rankan soldiers.

From the scuffles among the crowd and the mutters of the factions, a war might break out this night.

But it wasn't Grippa's war—she had no trouble moving away from the black tents of Nisibis, where brush and oil were being set to make a flaming pyre out of hostages and hostage-takers.

At the Stepsons' billet, all was deserted; in Randal's quarters, she didn't have to slit a single ward.

She spent long minutes searching for the globe before she realized it wasn't there. Then she looked at the mess she'd made, cursed herself, and began to put the little room to rights.

She thought she heard a footstep, stopped still, heard nothing more, and began again.

Where was the globe? Where would the accursed Hazard have secreted it? As she put mageguild robes and finery away, she could think of nothing but the power globe, made from Nisibisi clay with precious inset stones and a stand of gold with glyphs her race alone knew how to read.

And then she thought of another place that it might be.

She dashed out of Randal's room and collided with Straton, the Stepsons' chief interrogator.

"Grippa!" Strat's huge hands caught Grippa by the arms. "Randal's out at the Nisibisi tent. Come on, boy, your partner's waiting."

She almost struck him dead. She had the strength in her, from all the pain abroad tonight, to do it. But Strat was stupid—she thought to get around him.

"But Straton, someone's got to be with Niko—look in on him at least. He doesn't know about my sister—my . . ." She made Grippa's lip quiver, his eyes fill with tears

". . . poor, benighted sister. I've got to go to Stealth!"
She jerked Grippa's arms free and turned and ran—a thing
the grief-stricken brother of a captive girl might easily
have done.

Cursing folly, Strat pounded after Grippa. She didn't try
to lose him in the crowd, just ran full-tilt among the
lacquered buildings until she came to the one where Niko
lay abed.

Inside, she barred the door behind her and halted, panting.

The outer room seemed deserted; there was no one here.

With a spell on her tongue, she searched for the magic
globe of power; she thought she felt it near.

If it was here, it was in the rear room, where Niko slept.

She cautioned herself—Niko made her do things and
dare things and feel things no witch should try.

She pushed open one door, then another. In the second
room, Niko lay.

Inside, she closed the door behind her and leaned upon
it, just looking at the sleeping fighter who'd bound her to
him as surely as once she'd bound him to her with a string
of magic.

He must have sensed her; his head tossed on his pillow;
he ran a hand through tousled, ashen hair and raised his
head.

In the light of one candle burning low, his eyes seemed
sunken; yet she could sense the vitality in him, the vigor
coming back again.

And for the first time since she'd changed her shape,
she regretted taking man-form.

"Who's there?" he called out.

"Grippa," she had to say, the name foul upon her
tongue.

"What's wrong out there, Grippa? I heard commotion—no one's here . . ."

He pushed himself up on his elbows and she realized
how well Niko was healing: the pain that came to her was
faint, the will behind the movement sure, determined.

She found herself kneeling at his bedside, wanting most
of all to take a form he'd recognize, a woman's form, and
bestow herself upon him.

She took his hand and kissed it; he caressed her cheek.
"Grippa, you didn't answer me. What's wrong?"

"It's . . . Sauni." Grippa's voice *should* tremble, she
told herself; she hadn't given anything away.

"Sauni?" Niko took his hand away and sat up. What it
cost him made Roxane shiver with delight.

As the covers fell away and he swung his legs over the
side of the low cot, she saw the deep scars and half healed
wounds on his thighs and groin.

She closed her eyes, realizing that Niko might never
love another girl. Once, she would have gloried in such a
revelation. Now, she almost wept. And compassion was
too dangerous for a witch.

Niko's hands were on her, shaking Grippa's shoulders.
"What happened? Tell me."

"Sauni . . . Bashir . . . they're hostages of the Mygdonians. Oh, Niko . . ." She threw her arms around him,
the globe forgotten.

"Ssh, pud, we'll think of something. Just help me up.
We'll see what we can do."

And though she hadn't meant to, she did something so
perverted, so painful to her person, so twisted for a witch,
that she staggered with its gravity: all the strength she'd
gathered, all the soul-meat she'd eaten, everything she had
beyond the strength to live, she wound into a net of power
and cast it over Nikodemos.

He'd think he'd dreamed that Grippa came, she told him
softly; she touched his face and traced a sign upon his
brow.

He was so weak, it took very little of her power to
control him. Shaking his head as if bemused, Niko sat
back on his cot, eyes half-closed.

Then Roxane, her net of spell and privacy cast about the
room, took an even greater risk: she conjured health, she

conjured strength, she took the maleness from Grippa's youthful body and gave to Niko what the Rankan priests had stolen.

And her Grippa-self cried out in loss and pain. The boy she inhabited shivered and sobbed while Niko, unseeing, uncomprehending, ensorceled, sat quietly.

Roxane fought the Grippa-form, forced it over into a corner. And there she left it, whining like a beaten pup.

She knew she might bring down the wrath of hell upon herself; she should have sought out the globe of Nisibisi power for purely evil purpose.

But, wraithlike, discorporate in the middle of Niko's room, she took on a woman's form—like her own, but not that crippled body she'd left dying in a Tysian alley. This was a Roxane fully hale, a conjured Roxane.

And in it, breathing heavily, she could see the globe, a plane away, secreted between realities where Randal had hidden it.

If Niko could have seen, he would have seen a translucent Nisibisi witch pull a globe of power from midair, as if opening an invisible box.

But Niko saw nothing, heard nothing: she didn't want him to know a witch had helped him. She was asking nothing for her aid. She was trading something, though: the Grippa-form was dying, emasculated, evanescently evincing every wound that Niko had taken, every wound that lesser magicians and weakling gods had tried to heal but could only lessen.

And Roxane heard a rumble deep from underground, a rumble her inner ear knew to be a discontented accountant in the bank of souls.

With her not-quite-corporeal hands on the Nisibisi globe of power, she set it spinning so that colored light spun webs about the room.

And in their midst a stinking, scale-footed demon lord came to be, so powerful a one that Roxane bowed her head.

"Creature," its voice boomed, "thou art close to dissolution. Saving souls is stealing from the lord of hell."

"I have this Grippa-soul to offer, meager penance. I
promise others by the score. Let me have this one boy to
. . ." She'd almost said, 'to love.' She couldn't say that,
couldn't dare even to think it. She made promises, instead,
which would keep her busy for a score of years. And at the
end of that time, Roxane would face her judgment. All
this, for Nikodemos.

It didn't seem like quite so much until the demon lord
was gone and she sat alone with the mewling Grippa-form,
the power globe in her lap, her Roxane-body fully realized.

She looked back once at Niko, who still saw nothing but
what she wished him to see: he looked inward, onto his
pacific rest-place, a half-smile upon his face.

The Grippa-form, as it was, was useless. There was
only one thing to do: consume it, make a simulacrum of it,
and be Roxane once again.

If she'd had longer, she would have lain with Niko. She
wanted to, but she heard voices right outside.

She had time enough only to spin her globe, speak to it
in words it loved to hear, words it hadn't heard for far too
long, then spirit it to a safe place where no puny Hazard
would ever find it, kiss Niko once upon the brow, and bid
him: "Sleep, sleep, beloved."

He lay back, his face peaceful. On his body, scars were
fading as she watched. One tear of hers fell on him, a tear
for herself, who'd become tainted with self-sacrifice and
weakened by this unwanted love for a mortal which had
taken Death's Queen and reduced her to a mere slave of
hell with only twenty years to live.

Then she went and knelt before the Grippa-form, made
passes over it and, hunched there, began to eat.

* 8 *

When Tempus gave the order, Crit himself set the Nisibisi tent aflame.

Crit didn't like it. He told Strat so as they prepared to rush inside as soon as the 3rd Commando cut the tenting and Tempus gave the word.

"It's a big tent, don't worry," Strat told him.

"That's not the point, Strat. What if we can't save Bashir?" Strat had reported back to Crit when Grippa had gone into Niko's quarters. Crit needed Strat—Niko would have to take his chances with the witch, if Grippa still was one, as everybody thought.

"Then Bashir will be a martyr, with a special place in Nisi heaven, and we'll have some fried priests to show for it," Strat said sensibly, wetting himself down with soda water. "Here, partner." Strat gave him a wet turban-cloth to wrap around his face. "Compliments of our Mygdonian friends. Funny, what kind of allies we've got these days."

Strat's first boxing match was tomorrow; luckily, his opponent was a Mygdonian, who'd also have been up all night. "At least they're human," Crit groused.

Close by, Tempus's sister and Randal had their heads together.

Strat said, "What's with you, Crit? The Riddler's right—this is the only way. I've never seen you like this . . ." Then Strat peered into the smoke and saw Kama striding their way. "Unless it's *her*—I know she's done her best to turn you against everyone, but against the Riddler? Is that it? If it is, I'm going to crack her skull right here and now—"

"No, it's not—it's . . . I'm confused, that's all. Bashir's our ally; we could have tried to negotiate. Nobody wants a

Free Nisibis more than Tempus. And there's the Rankan factions. . . .''

"Just follow your orders, leftman, and leave those other stones unturned."

Then Crit had his hands full, assuring Strat that he'd do just that, keeping his partner from saying or doing anything to Kama, and forming up the task force for the imminent assault.

They had "help" from the 3rd Commando and a contingent of Rankan guards. The 3rd's job was to keep the guards from turning on them in the dark and smoke, or from killing any hostages instead of saving them, or from letting any of the Mygdonians-who-might-be-Rankans escape.

Cime and Randal were to part the fire—Randal swore that his kris was capable of that.

Tempus, with a battle cry and a torch held high, leaped forward suddenly and the tent went up like tinder.

Then there was a general rush in which Crit's job was to keep track of all his people, call formation orders, and sortie forth, hopeful of getting to Bashir before the kidnappers inside could kill him.

Some magician—Cime or Randal—was as good as the god's word: the flaming tent lifted into the heavens, dragging tentpoles, stakes and all, as the mixed militia rushed it.

The fire parted before Crit; then he and Strat, coughing and their eyes streaming tears, tried to sight their targets in the melee: targets to rescue, not to kill.

The first discernible thing Crit saw was Tempus, running past him with Sauni in his arms.

Then Strat punched him, yelling through the din of combat and howling, burning men: "There's Bashir—tied to that pole!"

They fought their way together toward the warrior-priest of Free Nisibis, half-conscious, a pig ready to roast upon its spit.

Strat thrice saved Crit—once with an ax-blow that sev-

ered a swordhand from the arm that swung it, once with a
timely: "Behind you," as a man whose head was wrapped
in a burning turban jumped for his back and Crit had time
to see the Rankan armor beneath the Mygdonian costume
as he slit his attacker's throat. The third time, Strat pushed
Crit from his feet in time to dodge an arrow that would
have got him in the head.

They reached Bashir about the same time that Sync, the
3rd's colonel, did.

The warrior-priest was overcome with smoke, showing
signs of Rankan and not Mygdonian-style torture, but he'd
live. As they cut him down, Crit had time to yell: "Sync,
what are you doing here? You're supposed to be outside.
Can't you follow simple orders?"

"Sorry, Stepdaughter," Sync yelled back. "In all the
excitement, I forgot."

Then there were enemies to slay and captives to take—
Tempus wanted at least two of the hostage-takers alive.

Crit and Strat let Sync finish rescuing Bashir and col-
lared two fleeing enemies, reasoning that those who ran
the fastest were those with the most to lose.

But from somewhere, arrows whizzed, and both their
captives died on the spot.

When they'd sorted out the mess and put out the fire,
and coughed the soot out of their lungs, it developed that
not one of the hostage-takers had survived.

Whether this was due, as Tempus generously proclaimed,
to Rankan interference and no fault of Crit's task force, or
from "overzealousness," as Sync suggested, it was done
and nothing could undo it.

A bunch of corpses in Rankan-made undergarments and
an occasional piece of Rankan armor proved nothing.

They had to be content with having saved Bashir, who'd
been tortured the least of all, since his captors were saving
him for last, and Sauni, who Cime said needed "rest,
away from men," and nearly fifteen of Bashir's contingent.

Later, when the Stepsons went in a body to cool their

throats and talk about the evening's work, Randal pulled Crit and Strat aside:

"My globe's gone. I can feel it," the Hazard said, looking at them both with worried eyes.

"What are we supposed to do about that, witchy-ears?" Straton growled.

"Strat, Randal did a good job tonight. No more 'witchy-ears,' where I can hear it. Randal, will that sword of yours do that for any man—control fire?"

"What does it matter? Strat, did you let Grippa alone with Niko long?"

Crit intervened: "Randal, we can't fight your battles for you—it's not that we wouldn't like to, it's that we can't . . . we're not able. If you want us to go with you now, to find Grippa . . ."

The scrawny mage looked relieved. "I'd like that, task force leader. I don't want to *hurt* Grippa, you see . . ."

"Right," Crit said, while Strat guffawed.

But when they got to Niko's quarters, Grippa wasn't there.

Niko was alone, sleeping deeper, looking better than he had in weeks.

"It's gone, by the Writ; it's gone without a trace," Randal moaned, feeling around in a hole in the middle of the air.

"What's gone? Your hands?"

Randal's hands reappeared from nowhere and he slammed nothing down as if it were the lid of a box that had failed in its purpose.

"The globe. She's got it now. Oh drat and—"

"Randal," Straton said companionably, putting a huge arm over the mage's shoulders, "Crit says you're really one of us now, and because he's right, I'm going to teach you to curse—properly, like the Stepson you are. Now repeat after me . . ."

Crit, watching Niko sleep, noticed something: an open

window over the Stepson's bed. He went to close it and
heard a noise outside.

"I'll be right back," he told Strat and Randal. "And do
that in the other room, will you? Niko needs his rest."

Behind the lacquer cabin, hunkered down against the
building wall, sat Grippa, sobbing his heart out.

Crit couldn't get a coherent word out of the boy or witch
or whatever it was, but since he was supposed to treat
Grippa like a Stepson, he invited the boy to have a drink
with them, assuring him that his sister would be all right.

And when the youth had wiped his nose and palmed his
eyes and gained his feet, Crit noticed something different
about young Grippa, but for the life of him he couldn't
have said exactly what.

* 9 *

The crowd was especially large and especially polarized
for Straton's match with the Mygdonian champion, a boxer
half-again his weight.

Men that big were often clumsy. Watching Crit watch
Straton, Tempus wished his first officer had more faith.
Crit was clearly nervous, though the six Sacred Band pairs
around him in Strat's corner, oiled and silked and sporting
their finest panoplies, were clearly anticipating a victory
celebration.

The Band had taken last night's successful rescue of
Bashir and Enlil's priestess as a sign from heaven, a
reconsecration of their bond to the warlords of the afterlife. Had they not triumphed over the Rankan priesthood?

The Stepsons loitered near the ring in twos and threes,
full of all their former surety, arrogance, and grace. Since
Tempus and the cadre had saved Bashir, the omen for the
coming season was clear: Bashir would reign on Wizardwall, the Rankan-based 3rd Commando would be revealed

as unworthy of the Riddler's favor, and Mygdonia as a
paper tiger. This, the pairs declared and the singles nodded
sagely, was the only proper reading of last night's events.

Tempus wished he felt as comfortable with sidetaking
by the gods. Bashir, next to him watching the match,
assuredly did not. Bashir had questions clouding eyes once
clear with god-given wisdom, questions Tempus didn't
want to answer.

Beyond, in the sand ring, Straton grabbed the Mygdonian
contestant by the hair with one hand and thumped savagely
on his opponent's skull with his other fist.

As the man staggered and his head went down, Straton's
knee came up and connected with the Mygdonian's chin,
lifting the unfortunate a full foot into the air: they were
fighting combat-style, with only field rules enforced.

When a roar came up from the crowd, Bashir leaned
over and wondered, "Has my god forsaken me? That is
the question."

"The Lord Thunderbolt steers all things—scatters and
gathers, comes together and goes away, approaches and
departs."

"So you are saying that I've fallen from grace?"

"I'm saying, Bashir, that sometimes it is necessary to
depart from the mountain to see its heights. Wisdom
is separate from other things; separate yourself from
judgment, pride, and questions."

The god had sacrificed Bashir's complacency for a purpose, no doubt. What that purpose was, Tempus wasn't
sure. Nor did he wish to dwell upon the intricacies of
theomachy or the riddle of the hidden god. Whether Enlil
thought to absorb the hidden god, take his place, or only
his followers, was not the business of Tempus, or Bashir,
who for the first time had been led by a god into folly.

Tempus, who knew that folly was the only possible
result of religion, of philosophy, and of magic, was concerned only that Bashir come to terms with treachery from

on high, not seek a flaw within himself or imagine that punishment had been meted out.

The warrior-priest was badly shaken, so much so that he'd withdrawn from his own events and insisted his followers do likewise: all the freemen of Nisibis were in mourning for their dead.

This serendipity suited Tempus: none of Bashir's Successors would be at the winners' feast, where an emperor would die, and thus none could take the blame for it.

Straton, on the other hand, might well be among the victors that night: lifting up the Mygdonian once more with a blow so that the man landed flat upon his back, spread-eagled, Strat put a sandaled foot upon his chest.

The crowd cheered hoarsely in delight as Strat was declared the winner.

Tempus, edging away from Bashir, who kept trying to make sense out of the senseless fury of the gods, found himself face-to-face with Theron and Brachis, the revolutionary priest.

"Ho, Riddler! Congratulations," Theron bawled. "You still find the finest and hone their mettle. There won't be much joy for Ranke in next week's winners' night if your men keep winning everything they enter." The Rankan general was as gleeful as if Straton had been a man of his.

And Brachis, in a priestly, covert whisper, demanded: "Have we a consecrated tool or not, Riddler? The time is right, the purpose—"

"I can't be seen with you, god-mouth," Tempus rumbled as quietly as he might; the very sight of the priest made his blood boil. "Trust in the Storm God . . . practice what you preach."

He pushed by them roughly, toward the Sacred Banders crowded around Straton, each vying to attend the winner.

"Life, Straton—the glory's yours already," said Tempus to his Stepson.

Strat's big chest, covered with bruises, dirt, and sweat, puffed out. Before the Riddler's approbation, Strat turned shy, and mumbled. Crit, a wet towel in hand, grinned fondly down upon his partner and caught Tempus's eye: "Let's wait and see if we can beat Sync—that's Strat's match for the finals. Then we'll talk about glory."

Tempus hadn't known it would be Sync—no one had until this morning, he found out when he pulled Critias aside.

"Crit," Tempus said slowly, "Strat must lose to Sync.

"What's this? Is Enlil whispering in your ear, now that Vashanka's gone?"

"You might say that."

Crit's face fell. "What's the use, then, of him taking so much punishment if losing's his fate?"

"Not fate," Tempus explained, hating to compromise his Stepsons, but knowing that Crit, if any man, would understand. "Politics—I need Sync in the winners' tent. I'd also like it if neither one of you two were there."

"What? Why? Oh." Crit's quick mind stilled his tongue. "Rankan justice for Rankans, if I hear you right?"

Tempus said nothing, thinking to let it go at that.

But Crit couldn't. "Is that it, Commander? If so, some-one ought to tell Kama, who's—"

"Tell Kama nothing. Volunteer for nothing. Your or-ders, Stepson, come only from me—and you've just heard them."

Tempus turned away.

Crit fell in beside him: "Make Strat throw the match? That's what you're asking—there's no chance Sync can beat him otherwise. And I can't tell him that . . . he's put his heart into this. And there's cadre honor. It had better come from you, if such an order—"

"Crit, I don't care how you do it. Drug him. Get him drunk. Push him down a well. Let's not leave it to the gods, this time . . . someone might get hurt."

"I . . ." Crit had long been Tempus's covert task force leader. He was a man who understood things more com-plex than simple honor, honest glory. Crit's mouth twisted;

he looked at his booted feet in the Rankan mud. "I'll take care of it, Commander."

"Life to you, Crit," Tempus said, and veered away through the Festival crowd without giving the matter more thought than he had to: Crit was always as good as his word.

And the Band was right: the omens *were* auspicious—the sort of omens in which the man called the Riddler believed: he'd finally shaken the hold Cime had had on him for centuries; he'd put even a god in His place to do it. He went now to the field altars by the food tents, to find a likely girl, some temple hopeful, to rape and consecrate as required by ritual—a consolation prize he was glad enough to award Enlil.

Whatever happened from now on at the Festival, Tempus had already won the most coveted prize of all: freedom to a degree he'd thought he might never claim.

There were problems still—there always were. There was the matter of his rightman, his sworn partner, Nikodemos, whose freedom must likewise be assured. Sacred Band pairs were bound to strive for parity, and one thing Tempus was unwilling to accept was Askelon's prognostication that Niko would take the Riddler's place as a slave to forces beyond Stealth's comprehension so that Tempus could be free.

* **10** *

Each night, Niko was getting stronger. He could feel it in the mornings, as he sorted through the strangeness of his dreams.

For five nights running, in his sleep, he'd proved his manhood, made love to a long-lost wench named Cybele, a girl he'd loved and lost who some said had been a witch.

She came to him in his sleep and he was always ready;

none of the impotence he'd feared, then glumly told himself he'd have to live with, marred those dreams.

Tonight, he was determined to stay awake—to see if there was any substance to the dreams or if they were just his body's trick to hasten its return to health.

Helping him, unknowing of his plan, was Randal, whom Niko had asked a Sacred Bander to summon when a pair came by with news of bouts won and events to come.

Randal was uneasy, his ears tinged with red, his glance flitting everywhere but incapable of meeting Niko's.

Finally, Randal said, "Your armor, Stealth. Tempus gave it to me for safekeeping. Now you're well enough, you ought to take it back."

"Lord Storm forfend!" Niko shrank back in exaggerated fear, then sat up again on his cot, where the Hazard and he were sharing the small ration of wine Nikodemos was allowed. "You keep it, Randal. It suits you. And you've earned it. Call it a parting gift, to a right-side partner I'll never forget."

"It's . . . permanent, then—" Randal's voice was suddenly thick, his face turned away "—your pairing with Riddler?"

"Nothing's permanent for mortals. It's all lend-lease—you magicians, and even Tempus, keep forgetting that. In Bandara we learn that you can't own anything, so why delude yourself?"

"There's trust . . . affection . . . love—honest feelings. Those belong to each of us," Randal said very low. "That sable horse of yours wouldn't eat and kept snapping horselines until they tethered him outside this place last night."

"There's that."

"You should let Sauni come to see you, Stealth. She's had a terrible time here and all she wants is for you to—"

"That's why I can't see her. She had a claim on me before, by virtue of the way she got with child. But now the god has claimed her as truly his—vessel of the Lord of Rape."

"You fighters." Randal swung around and glared at Niko. "Everything's so pat, so easy—a woman's raped, and she's consecrated to the gods. A man's heart is torn apart, and it's fine . . . just what's needed. Oaths are sworn and broken and none of you—"

"Randal, we've had some good times. Don't do this," Niko warned. "Don't judge me. You, a mageguild Hazard, who ought never to have taken up with fighters in the first place, shouldn't talk to anyone about oaths broken or fit behavior. How many spells have you cast that were benign? How many lives have you ruined with the taint of magic? Didn't you break every law of man and god and devil to ride with us and claim that Nisibisi globe of—"

"It's gone," Randal blurted. "She's got it. She came and took it back."

"*She?*" Niko was suddenly cold. "She's here?"

"We . . . didn't want to tell you. What good would it have done?" Randal was peevish, angry, striking back. "But since once you were my partner, I'll warn you— she's about, is Roxane, and she'll lurk and work her evil wherever *you* are, probably until you're dead. So you see, former leftman, you might need me sometime . . ."

Randal shot to his feet and, face averted once more, swept toward the door in a flurry of lacy mageguild robes.

"And where will I find you, if that's the case?" Niko said as gently as he could. "In the Tysian mageguild?"

Back still turned, Randal stopped, his hand on the doorlatch. "*I* keep my word. I've sent my request for an extended sabbatical up to Tyse—it's that or resignation. The Riddler, unlike you, thinks he needs me. I'm going on a special mission."

"Where? When?" Niko almost went to the little mage and put his arms around him. But that, Randal might have misconstrued. Helplessly, Niko peered through the gloom at the mage who couldn't even face him, who'd kept from him the news that Roxane was on the Festival grounds, and who knew what else?

Randal's response was brusque. "I can't tell you that. If the Riddler wants you to know, he'll tell you. As for when—soon. This may well be goodbye, Stealth." Then Randal glanced over his shoulder and Niko thought he saw a reddened nose, trembling lips, the glint of tears: "No matter what happens, Stealth—Niko—I'll never, ever, forget you. You've changed my life."

Then in a rush the mage was gone, slamming the door behind him.

Niko lay back, staring at the now-familiar ceiling. Randal on a secret mission? Roxane here? He didn't know which news bothered him more.

But then he realized that what bothered him the most was that his new partner, Tempus, hadn't told him. Tempus had kept secrets from Niko in the past, but then they hadn't been paired. Pairing brought with it *mutual* responsibility. The Riddler might treat a Stepson thus, but a right-side partner could expect better from his leftman.

In the morning, Niko thought, he'd confront his left-side leader and find out what had been going on while he'd been bedridden. He was well enough now.

Tomorrow he'd get dressed, go outside, watch the games, and reenter the fellowship so long denied him—he wanted to be among his Sacred Band when Kama told her tale, and celebrate with the winners. It was his right, even if Cime kept insisting that no man so soon returned from death's door had any rights whatever.

Perhaps, if he went among the crowd, he'd meet a Bandaran and confirm what Bashir had told him—that Niko's name was no longer forgotten among the islands where he'd trained.

He closed his eyes, not to sleep, just to envision the Bandaran islands in their veil of mist, marvelous Ennina jutting out from the sea, her pines whispering and her gravel raked and smooth, the sparkling waves lapping her coastline . . .

Something touched him, soft as a bird's wing; warm breath tickled his neck.

He opened his eyes and there was his dream girl, solemn-eyed and glowing softly in the candlelight—Cybele. But since he must have fallen asleep dreaming about Ennina, he didn't worry about it.

Her hand on him was cool and nothing that felt so good could possibly be bad, even if Randal was right and Roxane lurked close by. Cybele was a witch and Roxane was a witch and though they might be the same witch, it was only a dream, a dream in which no witch would do him harm.

* 11 *

Crit and Kama, the same night, went into Ranke. She thought it was to tryst in her ancestral home and to twist Critias to her will in the matter of the coming assassination.

Crit knew it, but he had other things on his mind. He took her to an uptown bar and proceeded to get as drunk as he could manage.

When he'd borrowed what courage he could from wine, he mustered enough bravado to say: "I need your help, Commando—help without question."

Kama could drink most men under their horses. She peered into her wineglass, then stared around the barroom, where gamers and foreigners from all over empire drank and watched a pair of dancers wax erotic with long-haired monkeys: Rankan entertainment hadn't changed while she'd been upcountry.

A house-slave served them warily: any Rankan slave, eunuch or girl, lived in peril. And here, where the drunks were rich and their tastes eclectic, any night of work might be their last.

When the girl was gone, Kama said, "Out with it, Crit.

Or shall I guess—your commander's forbidden you to even look on me and I'm to poke out both your eyes? You've quit the Stepsons, dissolved your pairbond, and want an honest post in the 3rd as my—"

"Kama, this is serious."

"You think I'm not?"

"Strat can't win his match tomorrow."

"Ah, you want to place a surreptitious bet? No problem," she waved a hand magnanimously. "I can arrange it without any of the Stepsons knowing you've come to your senses and realized Syncy's going to make Straton eat enough dirt to fill his—"

Syncy? Kama was drunk. "Kama, look at me."

She did, blinking owlishly.

"How drunk are you? Do you remember that conversation we had—about the fate of empire?"

She scowled: "Of course." She brushed an errant curl out of her eyes. "I'm not that drunk, only trying to get you drunk enough to take you home and tumble—"

"Strat can't win his match tomorrow," he said again, slowly, precisely.

She stirred her wine with a finger. "Yes. Of course. I see. You don't want to leave it to the gods." Solemnly, she waggled the finger at him. "Sync will probably win anyway, but this smells of my father's intervention." She hitched herself up, put her chin in her fists. "Let's see, isn't that some sort of mortal sin—a left-side leader conspiring to— *Ouch!*"

Crit, having kicked her under the table, said levelly, "We've got to find a way to assure it. I'll worry about my immortal soul, you worry about your friends Brachis and—"

It was her turn to hush him. "I under*stand*, Crit, what you're saying. Now let's see . . . You wouldn't settle for Strat having an accident . . . a broken wrist, even a finger would do the— No, I see you wouldn't." Kama was intrigued, her expression mischievous, her nostrils flaring as she suggested vicious but not fatal ways to keep Straton from entering the ring.

Watching her, for the first time Crit wondered how he ever could have imagined her feminine and soft. But then, they'd never shared a covert enterprise together. She was so much her father's daughter in that moment that she seemed inhuman. He found himself wishing he'd taken the Riddler's advice.

When she'd agreed to help him lure Straton out and administer a drug to make him slow and weak on the morrow, she laughed girlishly and said: "Don't get any ideas about doing this to me—I've got the bard's contest, you'll remember. And I expect you to be there to give me moral—well, that isn't quite the right word, is it?—let's say, spiritual support."

They rode out to the Festival village once Kama had stopped by a chemist attached to the Rankan army; while there, she'd pulled rank as shamelessly as any man he'd ever seen bully a subordinate.

And when, arm in arm with Straton, they sashayed through the makeshift village streets to "toast your prowess, and your luck," as Kama said, Crit left the talking to this woman who seemed suddenly like a soulless manipulator and not the girl he'd loved.

She poured the packet in Strat's drink so neatly that no one not informed before the fact would have noticed.

Strat drank the mug down, on her challenge, in one deep draught.

Crit squeezed his eyes shut, thinking it was all for the good of empire . . . or at least it was for Tempus, which had to be the same thing. Stepsons follow orders.

Once the deed was done, Kama excused herself: "Well, loves, I'm off to find Sync. It's only fair to wish my unit leader all the luck I've wished his opponent."

When she left them, Strat was already beginning to sway and shake his head.

Half-carrying his rightman back to their billet, Crit told

himself that he was lucky he'd seen this side of Kama so early—while he still had time enough to break away.

Strat, who deserved better, was going to need him badly in the morning and thereafter.

Levering the huge, snoring Stepson onto his cot, Crit promised himself that if any permanent ill befell Straton because of the drug Kama had administered, he'd collect from the Riddler's daughter in kind.

* 12 *

Randal drove the hell-wheeled chariot out to the highest hill above the Festival grounds at dawn.

The sable horses pulled on their bits until his arms ached in their sockets and he wrapped the reins around his wrists to hold them.

The sunrise was purple, red, and gold; it slit the night like rents, spilling through the clouds in rays.

And from the east, out of the sun, a dark shape came walking toward him, rainbow-hued around its edges, man-like but seemingly twice the size of any man.

Seeing it, the horses slowed to a walk and snorted as they approached their master, Askelon, the lord of dreams.

"Is she here, apprentice?" Askelon said while still a dark shape with light glittering through the foxfur of his robe.

"They're *both* here—the witch Roxane and the Riddler's sister." Chilled and nervous, Randal fumbled with the bracers, set the chariot's brakes, and stepped down, handing the reins to Askelon.

"Thank you, Randal. Well done. I trust the globe of Nisibisi power serves you well?"

"I . . . ah . . . I lost it. Or, that is, she took it. It's hers, after all—I don't really want it. Or *need* it—I've got power enough, without it, to be an adept who travels with

the armies." Askelon hadn't known—he wasn't omni-
scient, then, wasn't perfect. Somehow, this made Randal
feel better.

Askelon, without a word, stepped up into the chariot
and released its brakes. The horses snorted; the lead horse
pawed the ground. A team they were, like a Sacred Band
team, trained to pull together, each with his job to do, not
contesting, but coexisting and cooperating for the good of
both.

As the horses surged forward, Randal raised a hand in
farewell, relieved. He hadn't expected to ride down onto
the Festival grounds with Askelon—hadn't wanted to, truth
be known.

But the dream lord swung the team around and drove
the chariot back, encircling Randal once, twice, then saying:
"Do you wish to be relieved of your apprenticeship, young
master mage? Have you learned enough to suit you?"

"It's not that, you see, Regent . . . it's—well, yes, I
do. It's causing me no end of trouble, being yours. The
dream realm isn't . . . *here,* you see—I have to be."

Askelon raised his palm toward the sunrise, cupped light
in his hand, and spilled it down on Randal's head. "You're
free, but not rejected, adept. Anytime you need me,
dream of me."

And he was gone to wreak his havoc upon the Riddler's
sister, or work his will upon the unsuspecting throng, or
whatever lords of dream and shadow did when they walked
in the world of men.

A sharp pang of guilt shot through Randal, for making it
possible for Askelon to manifest in the world without even
the warning of wizard weather, the disturbance of the
planes that preceded him, most times.

Randal knew the Riddler wanted him to undertake a
special mission; what kind, the Riddler hadn't said. And
he was to prepare for it by the means a wizard uses to
purify himself. Even if reneging on his apprenticeship to

Askelon meant that his allergies might return, he felt cleansed already.

But considering that he had a witch for a rightside partner, Randal still had quite a bit to do before he could tell the Riddler he was ready.

* **13** *

Niko was up early and out at the sand ring in the morning with Grippa and Sauni—early enough to see Sync win the boxing match and see Crit and Kama have some sort of lover's quarrel.

The match was over almost as soon as it began: Strat wasn't himself, some Stepsons growled afterward; Sync landed a decisive blow straightaway, the 3rd Commando Rangers insisted.

If Niko hadn't known better, he'd have thought some witch or god was at the root of Straton's loss. But Crit helped his partner from the ring and the Sacred Band pairs crowded around the loser, as loving in defeat as they'd have been in victory.

Niko, leaning on Grippa for support, told the boy: "That's what it's all about. Not performance, but endurance; not pride, but loyalty," and went to join the defeat celebration, taking Grippa, but not Sauni, with him. "Sauni, that much blood and sweat aren't fitting for a woman to see. Go find Bashir, or Kama. I'll meet you at Kama's event at sunset."

Sauni was quieter since the hostage-taking; she'd learned that life was not always so beautiful or so kind as it had been when Partha's estate comprised her world. "If you say so, Stealth," she answered in a melancholy way.

"That's right," Grippa preened. "He says so. And don't try to make us feel guilty, either. This is *men's* business—no place for a *girl*."

Some remnant of the fiery Sauni Niko once had known remained; she drew herself up tall: "Don't you talk to me that way, you nasty boy. I'm a priestess of Enlil and I can bring His wrath down upon you—like that." She snapped her fingers under Grippa's nose. "Remember what happened to those who dared violate my person—they're all suffering for it eternally in hell—and draw your own conclusions, brother!"

"Stop it, both of you. Sauni, that's close to sacrilege. Grippa, she's right—you should have more respect for a vessel of the gods." Niko, between brother and sister, wished he didn't feel in some way responsible for them both.

But Sauni flounced off, then, and as he and Grippa joined the Stepsons, while Niko was trying to explain that women cleaved to gods when men displeased them, Grippa held out something in his hand.

"What's this?" Niko took his arm from the boy's shoulders and stood unsupported.

"It's yours, isn't it?" Grippa seemed almost coy as he offered the amulet in his palm—a bit of hair, a shard of bone. "I found it in the city, on the Street of Temples, yesterday."

And indeed, it looked like the very amulet that Grippa had given Niko out at Partha's stone house that day in Tyse.

"You keep it, pud—a family heirloom works for the family to whom it belongs. If you'd had it, perhaps Sauni wouldn't be so much the priestess as she is now."

Grippa was crestfallen, but Stealth insisted. "Come on, let's find your partner and help Straton drink away his loss."

"*Randal!*" Grippa's face fell, then he pouted. "I don't want to drink with him—he hates me. I'm a burden. He never wanted to be my—"

"Hush. He's your left-side leader. He deserves honor from you, respect."

"But it's true, he—''

Niko would hear no more of that and, with Grippa, joined the fellowship of his peers, who needed help in cheering up Crit, though Strat was taking his loss with wry good humor.

Hours later, well plied with drink, Strat was still wondering how it was that he never even saw Sync's first punch coming, when Randal came to remind Niko that Kama's event was about to start.

Grippa and Randal eyed each other with such obvious distaste that Niko pulled the mage aside as they were heading toward the little stage where the bards, in torchlight, would contest.

"That's no way to treat your rightman, Randal. You know better than to let personal matters between us intrude upon your oath. Grippa's well-meaning, harmless—just a boy.''

"You're wrong, Stealth,'' Randal said harshly. Dressed in Nisibisi freeman's mottled garb, the mage looked more like a guerrilla than a sorcerer; in fact, Randal's tone of voice and stance were so fierce that Niko looked at him askance.

"Wrong? What do you mean?''

"Wrong. And if you can't imagine what I mean, then it's not time for you to know,'' Randal retorted portentously, then added: "Don't worry, Stealth. We'll take care of things—the Riddler and I. You just regain your health.''

Grippa was waiting at a polite distance, watching them.

"Well, when it is time for me to know, I expect you to tell me what's going on here. Right now, let's not make the boy feel any worse than he does already.''

"I . . . can't . . . go with you, Niko. And I really can't explain. You'll see . . . things will work out.'' And the little mage put a commiserating hand on Niko's shoulder as if comforting a troubled child.

Rather than start an argument, Niko walked away. His temper, when aroused, was hard to hold; he didn't want to fight with Randal. If the Hazard was deceptive, it was just the nature of his kind. And it was the Riddler, more than Randal, who'd been keeping things from Niko—Tempus, who demanded unqualified, uninformed loyalty without giving back in kind.

On the slow walk through the crowd of Festival onlookers and contestants to the bard's stage, Niko brooded. In his stomach was a hollowness that came from knowing that by omission he'd been betrayed. Niko still loved Tempus the way a Stepson should love his commander, and a rightman his left-side leader, and yet his faith in Tempus was shaken. Perhaps his valor was, too. Right now, he was feeling fragile, afraid of something nameless, a spectre that might not even exist except in Randal's mind.

And whenever he encountered the witch in his dreams, she didn't seem evil to him. In daylight, this frightened him as much as Randal's innuendo.

So when Grippa and he chanced across a shaven-headed Bandaran as they entered the wooden stands set aside for the bard's contest, Niko introduced himself: "I'm Stealth, called Nikodemos, friend Bandaran. May I speak to you?"

The Bandaran stared at Niko, then at Grippa, and his sea-changed eyes grew hard. But he nodded and said, with ritual precision, "Nikodemos. I know the name. Greetings from us all."

By this, Niko knew that the prohibition which had banned his name, his memory, and his person from Bandara had been lifted—a parting gift from Niko's master. "May we talk?"

"Privately, whenever you wish. But we have not softened our attitude toward magicians," the Bandaran replied, looking straight at Grippa.

Niko was about to introduce Grippa to the Bandaran when the youth pulled on his arm. "There she is, Stealth. Oh, she looks glorious! I'll get us a seat up front!" and the boy dashed up the aisle between the wooden benches.

Then the Bandaran seemed to relax. "Shed these ties, initiate, and you're welcome anytime. Or come before your tests are done—but come alone. We won't have another incident like the last, when you brought sorcery among us."

"Ties?" Niko was going to ask the Bandaran his name, but the man's comments made him forget. "I'm no longer paired with Randal, the adept—"

"We know that, student. You should shed this one, too." The Bandaran looked after Grippa, and his words floated back to Niko: "We return home on Winners' Day. If you like, you are welcome to come with us." Then he faced Niko, and his expression was compassionate: "Don't worry about your future, student. You're prepared for what's to come."

And with a touch which told Niko that this must be his dead master's successor, so calming and pleasant was it upon Niko's arm, the Bandaran glided away.

Watching him go, Niko felt a renewed sense of purpose: not an external purpose of accomplishment, but an internal purpose—one of centering the perfectible being that he was without so much concern as to how others saw him or what others thought of his behavior, or even what his fate might be in human terms. Maat made him recall that he was building a different Niko, a spiritual abode in another place, and that, in extremis, he'd been able to protect that place from even the intrusion of Askelon, lord of dreams.

Feeling much calmer, much clearer, he took his seat beside Grippa, who looked at him with an odd, troubled expression on his face, and waited for the bard's contest to begin.

Six bards stood on the stage together, and Grippa was right: none looked so fine as Kama, in her 3rd Commando dress blacks with every buckle shining.

She was the fourth to spin her tale, and so she left the stage with the others when they'd been introduced and sat quietly beside it, the only woman there, until her turn came.

"Even if she wins," Grippa whispered as the man before her finished his tale and bowed his head to the stomping of feet and thunderous applause, "it won't be because she's better—it'll be because she's a girl."

Someone from behind hissed at them to be quiet.

On the stage, the drum beaters on either side began to pound a muffled rhythm and Kama stepped up to the front of the stage.

"Come muse," she began, "sing to me of mighty men and witches' ken and the wind of stones on Wizardwall."

Then Niko realized that Kama's tale was going to be about him, and about his struggles with Roxane, the Nisibisi witch, and he slid down in his seat, his neck hot and his palms suddenly sweaty, embarrassed and proud of all he'd suffered and all he'd done.

And when Kama was finished relating the tale of the war for Wizardwall and Niko's battles during it, men got to their feet and cheered themselves hoarse.

Not for one moment, from the beginning of her story, was the outcome in doubt: Kama would be among the celebrants in the winners' tent at the Festival of Man.

* **14** *

The celebration that had begun, for some Stepsons, with Straton's defeat that morning, lasted well into the night. Kama's win brought everyone their second wind and even brought the 3rd Commando and the Stepsons together on better terms than the two units had ever enjoyed.

In the largest Nisibisi tent, men milled and caroused, some with girls they'd met at the games, some with boys; everyone smoked krrf and drank whatever could be found.

Outside, where Tempus had gone to escape his sister, men and women reeled and laughed toward their beds.

It was on nights like these that Tempus regretted most

that sleep was never his. The moon had risen and under it folk snored with lovers well known or lovers just met.

Only he was solitary, he presumed to think, having left the sweet camaraderie of his fighters because Cime was intent on bestowing her favors on Sync: "to set a good example for your men—this rivalry between the 3rd and your Stepsons serves no purpose," she'd told him venomously, smiling with all her vicious beauty. "And you, who could have stopped it, just make things worse by allowing the Stepsons to think you love them best."

Alone now in the companionable night, he chanced across Randal. "A fine night for celebrating, Hazard. Why aren't you with the other Stepsons?"

"I . . ." In the moonlight, Randal's freckles looked like mud spattered across his cheeks. "It's— Well, Riddler . . . you see—"

"Out with it, mage. Whatever it is, it can't be that bad."

"Bad?" Randal almost whined. "It's worse. I didn't know how to tell you, but . . . Askelon's here."

Tempus almost lifted the mageling off the ground. He controlled himself, cracking his knuckles with a sound like breaking bones in the night. "Here," he said calmly. "I see. And just how long has he been here?"

"Ah . . . a day or two." Randal's shoulders straightened. "And since he's here, I thought I'd just look in on Niko—see if he's sleeping all right. He drank more wine than was prudent this evening but—you never know."

"I'll go with you, Randal," Tempus said, and with as gentle a hand as possible, pointed Randal in the direction of Niko's quarters.

For a while they walked in silence, then Tempus said, "Is there anything else you haven't told me? Anything I should know?"

"Not really, Commander."

"How goes your pairing with Grippa? Have you determined yet if he's a boy or just a simulacrum made by the witch?''

''No, not for certain. I mean, yes, I have,'' the words came out of Randal in a rush, ''to my own satisfaction, but there's no proof and you told me proof was what you—''

''Yes, yes. *Quiet.*'' Tempus hadn't meant to snap, but he had heard squealing in the night, squealing more like a horse's than a girl's.

''Do you hear that, Randal?''

''Hear—? Yes. It's coming from Niko's— His horse is tethered there . . .''

But Tempus was already running at full speed, far too fast for Randal to keep up.

When he reached the lacquered building in which Niko was billeted, he skidded to a halt outside, not believing what he saw.

There, in the fading moonlight, was Niko's sable, rearing up and plunging down, repeatedly, trampling something, a dark shape in a heap under Niko's window.

And, a short distance away, another shape—this one tall, manlike, but exuding a palpable aura brighter than any man's—was watching the horse but making no move to intervene.

Tempus did, lunging at the crazed stallion, grabbing for its halter, from which a snapped tether swung.

The horse was so furious at whatever it was killing that it dragged Tempus up into the air as it reared again and he hung there for a second, suspended.

Then he grabbed it by the ear and brought it down, his other hand on its muzzle. The maddened horse fought him briefly, but eventually it calmed.

''Back, back,'' he told it, conscious of the robed figure watching him from the shadows.

When he'd secured it to the horse line it had snapped, it pawed the ground and whinnied, an ear-splitting trumpet of triumph.

By then, there was a light in Niko's window.

Tempus moved quickly toward the wetly gleaming pile below.

It quivered, but residually: it was dead.

Once it had been a boy; now it was a pile of human wreckage.

Knowing what he would see, certain of its identity now, Tempus bent down: enough of the skull remained intact to identify Grippa, Partha's son. And even if the skull had been shattered beyond recognition, the corpse held something in a clenched fist which, when Tempus pried it open, turned out to be a little talisman of hair and bone.

"Not even a civil greeting, sleepless one?" came a rich, bass voice from above.

Tempus, crouched by the corpse, looked up. "Hello, Ash. I was hoping you'd disappear now that your filthy work is done."

"Disappear?" The lord of dreams put his hands on his hips. "Do you know what it cost me to get there? On a mission of mercy? *Someone* had to act to free Nikodemos from the witch. You didn't."

"Mercy, you call this? And are you so sure it was a witch—it's nothing now, that's certain. Hardly enough to be worth a funerary pyre."

The stallion stamped its forefoot and whickered, its neck arched. The horse had been bred by Askelon. Tempus had no doubt that the dream lord had sicced it upon Grippa—or the simulacrum of Grippa.

"I call it a necessary evil. Surely, you've heard the term. Admit it, Tempus, I've done you a favor."

An awful feeling of foreboding came over Tempus as he rose to his full height and faced Askelon, an archmage the like of which existed nowhere else anymore.

"Admitted," he sighed, not liking this one bit. The magicians all played the same game: put you in their debt, then exacted triple payment. "What is it you want, Ash? There must be some reason for this humanitarian act on your part."

"So suspicious, old friend? Or is it that humanitarianism is something you've forgotten?"

"Don't press me tonight, Ash. I'm not in the mood for it. As a matter of fact, I'm not in the mood for *you*. If you want to do me a favor I'll respect, absent yourself from this place, from my life and the lives of my fighters, and let us all forget that a travesty like you exists at all."

"Tsk. The same old Tempus. Walk with me, before I speak your true name where you'd not like it spoken."

Tempus had to do so: they knew too much about each other, Tempus and this shadow lord who'd risen by evil to become regent of the seventh sphere. True names lent true power. Should Askelon speak Tempus's, a war between these two who were not men any longer would begin, one that might make the heavens crash to earth.

Almost, Tempus longed for it: the chance of death, a worthy foe, havoc of immense proportions to be wreaked. Just a few more words, and they'd begin it. Tempus had been good for a very long time.

But there were innocents to consider—his Sacred Band, his Stepsons, even the 3rd Commando in their way. And all the hapless, helpless Festival-goers, sleeping in one another's arms.

"Name your price, Ash, for this favor given but not requested," Tempus said carefully.

"Once again, I seek your sister."

"You've had her! By all the gods, haven't you learned your lesson? Isn't a year with her enough?" Tempus was genuinely astonished that Askelon could covet Cime after so long being in her company.

The dream lord smiled a smile that was unmistakably fond. "The circumstances under which she stayed with me weren't the best. I come now as an honest suitor. I'm asking you, her brother, her only living relative, for permission to court the lovely Cime . . ."

Tempus's gusting laughter interrupted Askelon. Tempus

couldn't help it: he laughed aloud until his sides ached, until his eyes filled with tears, until he gasped for breath.

When he got control of himself, he looked back and saw Niko's door open, two shapes—Niko's and Randal's, from their relative sizes—under the window, collecting Grippa's remains.

"Now, Riddler, what say you? I've given you a wedding gift already—that witch who bedevils Nikodemos won't trouble him here again. I can't guarantee his soul forever, but for the nonce he's safe."

Tempus started to say that being safe from one witch but in Ash's debt wasn't safe.

The dream lord intervened, hands up: "Don't thank me. It's quite all right. I've freed the boy from all commitment to me. He may seek me later in life, but as of now, he owes me nothing. This I do to prove good faith."

"And what am *I* supposed to do? Hand you Cime, trussed and basted?" He couldn't consign even his sister's wizened soul to Askelon's insubstantial hell, he realized with a sinking heart. Oh, he'd like to, but he just couldn't.

"The favor I did you, in ridding you of the witch, is conditional."

"Ah," Tempus said, thinking: here comes the trick.

"It's conditional," said Ash with a reproving glance, "only because she may take other forms—her spirit lives although the Grippa-simulacrum is gone. Therefore, all I can ask in return is a conditional permission: *if* I can woo your sister—convince her, by whatever means, to come away with me—just allow it. Don't stand in my way."

"I won't mix in," he agreed, thinking that this would never work, that Ash was not the vehicle of his freedom—Cime would never go off to live in dreams when she could torture him in the flesh.

It seemed as if Askelon could read his mind: "Don't worry about me convincing her—there are ways. Just don't 'protect' her from me."

That was a difficult thing to agree to: she was still his

sibling, he told himself. If she came to him begging
protection from the heinous dream lord, what was he to
do? But he said, "Then keep her from asking for protection. It shouldn't be that hard. She's continually telling me
she's protecting me."

Askelon clapped Tempus on the back like an old war-
friend. "Thank you, sleepless one. And since you've agreed
to this, no matter the outcome, I offer a boon—no strings,
no tricks, no matter what you think of me."

This time, Tempus's hackles rose. "And may I ask
what this gift of gratitude is?"

"Your curse—I'll lift it. You can love your nasty little
murderers without bringing death to any one of them. You
can take any girl in passion, without needing the stimulus
of rape."

"Wait—"

But Askelon's hand was already risen, making signs that
hung in blue trails in the dark long after his fingers had
finished moving.

"Wait!" Tempus said again.

But Askelon was gone; the dream lord had winked out
of existence like a doused candle.

Tempus put his hand through the space which Ash had
so recently inhabited to make sure. There was nothing
there.

Then, whistling tonelessly, he ambled down the hill to
comfort Niko in the matter of the dead boy, Grippa; make
sure that Randal pretended appropriate bereavement; and
that the horse didn't take the blame.

The sable stallion, after all, was only following his
nature: the horse hated witches. And besides, with Ash
about, things were never what they seemed.

As he approached Stealth and Randal, he wondered if it
could be true: if his curse could be lifted so simply, and
unequivocally; if good could be done by the archmage of
evil; if, given that it were true, he shouldn't feel somehow
different, or at least released.

But he didn't feel any different, except that he was a little bit tired. Deep within his mind, he heard a godly chuckle.

Yawning, he took Randal under one arm and Niko under the other and shepherded them into Niko's quarters, saying: "Let me tell you two Stepsons a story about men and mages, about nights like these, which you may find it in your hearts to believe . . ."

Book Five:

———————

WINNERS' DAY

If Tempus was without his curse, he surely was not without his new god, Enlil. The curse had constrained him from loving the living: those he chose rejected him, those who chose him suffered unto death. The god loved only gods' games and the gift of death.

Had he known Askelon would come and lift the curse, Tempus would never have made a pact with Father Enlil. As it was now, he struggled to determine just what, if anything, he'd gained when Askelon had done him this "favor": god and curse, together, balanced one another. With the curse gone, the godbond became an affliction he'd as soon have been without.

Sometimes now when he got angry, as he did over the politics-in-religion's-robes which were at the root of the Festival of Man, the sky grew dark and thunder rolled as if Enlil seconded His servant's displeasure.

It was disconcerting, to say the least, for a man whose anger had sustained him for centuries.

Riding back toward the Festival site from the hilltop where he'd gone to soothe his ire, Tempus had to admit that he felt no better than he had when he'd languished under his old, familiar curse.

The last week of the Festival was upon them, Winners' Day soon to dawn. He'd kept as busy as he could, per-

forming funerary rites for Grippa as if the slain boy had
been a Stepson and not a witch. He'd done this at Niko's
urging and because Partha's daughter was deep in mourning and Bashir needed Partha's good will. But even the
most elaborate funeral, with its own games and testimonial
rites, can only take so long.

When it was done, Abakithis's politicking priests still
roamed the Festival site, harassing Stepsons and 3rd Commando where they could; Theron's faction was still no
better than those they sought to replace, with the possible
exception of Theron himself, who drank these nights with
Tempus, recalling simpler times and simpler wars like the
old man he'd become.

And Cime, Tempus's nemesis, still inhabited his fanta-
sies and the tents of the Nisibisi, as well as the beds of
whatever 3rd Commando rangers or Stepsons she could
find.

He'd just about decided that Askelon had tricked him
after all, that the curse wasn't lifted, but only made to
seem so by some dream lord's spell. He'd done some tests:
he'd slit his palm down to the bone and watched the cut
heal in an afternoon; he'd lain awake one whole night in
his billet waiting for sleep to come; he'd found a whore he
fancied but he scared her half to death; he'd even tried to
talk to Niko about his feelings, with no success.

But then, he'd lived so long and fought so long that it
was hard to tell what was habit, what was nature, what
was god and what was man. He had no memories of adult
life before the curse, nothing to compare its absence to.
For all he knew, he was his own curse, one that neither
god nor archmage could ever lift.

Halting his steel-gray Trôs horse before the designated
bush, he waited, not for a god or wizard, but for Brachis,
priest of Vashanka the Hidden, the missing god.

With a roar the bush burst into flame and Tempus's
horse danced backward, snorting, while within his head,
Enlil growled in godly displeasure.

Then, as the horse plunged and shivered, out from behind the bush strode Brachis, Theron's premier priest of revolution, his pink cheeks plump and his feminine bottom swishing.

"Priest," Tempus snarled, "if the gods don't punish you for a pretender to godhead, I will, if you ever scare my horse again. If you called that fire from heaven, put it out."

Brachis smirked and stepped away from the burning bush. "It will burn out, by and by." Approaching, he rubbed his hands together, then took Tempus's horse by its reins. "Let us not spar with each other, Riddler. If the gods exist, they work through men. As one man of the god to another, I say to you that the time has come for you to reveal the chosen assassin's name to me."

"Why? So you can prepare a bier? Ready your men to arrest and torture a scapegoat? I'm facilitating a coup, not a purge. My man's willing to put Theron on the Lion Throne, but not to take the blame for it alone. If any of mine are singled out for so-called Rankan justice, there'll be at least one fat, impotent priest roasting alongside—"

"Now, Riddler, would we do that to you?"

"Not and live through it," said Tempus, sliding from his saddle. As he did, the Trôs whose reins the priest held, feeling Tempus's anger or the god's, snapped at Brachis, catching the priest's fleshy forearm between its teeth, then shaking his head.

"*Aiiee!*" roared the priest in pain as the horse, ears flattened, shook his head savagely and Brachis's arm with it. Brachis batted at the jowly stallion as if at a dog caught in a temple.

"Hold still, fat fool," Tempus ordered, but neither Brachis nor the horse did that, so that it took longer than it should have for Tempus to grab the horse by one ear and stick his thumb in its mouth, behind the teeth, to pry those jaws apart.

Bloody teethmarks were deep in Brachis's arm as he

staggered backward, rubbing it, his pale eyes full of fury. "You'll pay for this, sleepless one. Mark me!"

"Done," Tempus muttered, but the priest was gone behind the bush. When Tempus went around to see where he might have disappeared to, he saw a hidey-hole disguised with sod and leaves that led down into a tunnel.

Thinking that at least things were out in the open now, and that the horse wasn't to blame, Tempus mounted and rode toward the Festival village with the god's chuckle ringing in his ears.

And that made him angry, that the god should be so petty, and willing to subject Tempus's fighters to the retribution of a man like Brachis, who had power, though it came not from heaven but from his faction.

"Show Yourself, craven Lord of Strife!" he demanded aloud. "Give me one good reason why I shouldn't pull my troops out now and lead them north, leave this empire to perish as then it must!"

And what happened then reminded Tempus of the old days, when the hidden god wasn't hiding: clouds boiled up from a clean blue sky, lightning ripped down from heaven and snaked along the ground, corraling the Trôs horse, which closed its eyes and stood still, shivering.

"You wish to see Me, foundling son? Look upon Mine Glory!"

And Tempus, who'd never closed his eyes before any god or turned his head, who'd stared hell in the face and farted under demons' noses, found his arm up to protect his face, so fierce was Enlil shining.

The god was tall, a lightning shape of manlike splendor, all crackling and golden as it trod the Rankan hillside toward him. In one hand it held a thunderbolt, and in the other, a globe that spun upon its palm.

And the man who'd never once been cowed or cowered before a deity felt his throat close up.

"Well, mortal? Your wish is granted, yet you hide your

*face. Does My Majesty offend thine eyes? Look upon Me,
who asked to see Me."*

So Tempus tried again, but the sight of Father Enlil
made his eyes tear. Still, he saw the globe as the war god
threw it toward him, saying, *"Catch, foster child, and be
you warned: as long as the Nisibisi globe of evil is abroad
in the world, godhead itself is threatened. The reason you
asked for is simply this: the globe must be shattered, its
stones separated, its clay made into tableware, before any
of your beloved little men can truly claim salvation."*

Then Tempus found his voice. "Now you say this.
Before, you made no such demands. And why me—why
my men? I don't accept the challenge." And with his
sword, drawn without thought and as fast as even a god
could move, he batted the hurtling globe away so that it hit
the ground, and bounced, and rolled, and everywhere it
went the earth was scoured and scored in its wake.

*"Your Stepsons, as you call them, insolent mortal, loosed
that globe upon the world, destroying its owner but not its
own self, which is a potent evil. Remove it, destroy it, and
your forces and your person may live in peace. Until then,
seek no rest, for you will not find it. And all the blood shed
for evil's sake will be upon your hands until you've ground
it into My good clay!"*

And then, before Tempus could retort that he wasn't
interested in any quest nor convinced that the god had the
right to force him, Father Enlil disappeared, and the rolling globe of lightning with him.

This pleased Tempus's horse, who stopped shivering
and pawed the ground, ready to trot home to his stable.

But neither he nor the horse could pretend that nothing
had happened here: the horse's flanks were black with
sweat and the ground where the god had walked was
pocked with giant, blackened footprints and crisscrossed
with lines like chariot tracks where the lightning ball had
rolled.

* 2 *

Few souls attend their own funerals. Roxane had been at
Grippa's, which was much the same thing, discorporate
and ghostlike.

She'd seen Sauni wail and blacken her face with ashes,
tear at her breast and try to throw herself upon Grippa's
bier.

She'd seen Niko break a javelin across his knee and
throw it onto Grippa's pyre, a javelin he'd won during the
special funerary games in honor of Grippa . . . or of
Roxane, so far as she was concerned.

Bashir had said his/her eulogy, praising the loyalty,
youth, and honor of the departed Grippa, calling him his
father's son. Bashir had shed tears for a youth he called a
friend, and recommended Grippa's soul to heaven.

Even Randal, her enemy, the mage, seemed sad now
that she was "dead." And Randal knew exactly who and
what Grippa was, had known from the very beginning.

All this praise and love, this outpouring of affection
from these mortals, had its effect on Roxane. It made her
melancholy and it made her long for human form once
again.

At first she'd thought she might be content without a
body, the better to harass her enemies. But during the rites
she grew morose and lonely, and during the eulogies she
became unsure of just who her enemies were.

So she flitted from mortal to mortal, peering into eyes
that couldn't see her, looking for hidden hatred, despite, or
worse.

But not even in Randal could she find it, and Randal
was the mage who'd had a hand in killing her Grippa-
form, who'd brought Askelon through a portal to this time
and space.

Confused, she was distressed; distressed, she spent her nights in Niko's quarters, a noncorporeal ghost, until one night Sauni, the priestess of Enlil, crept in there, and all of Roxane's feelings began to change.

The sight of Sauni seducing Niko hardened her heart but it also decided Roxane upon a plan of action: she couldn't just hover about, a ghost, a wisp of wind, and caress her beloved Nikodemos ectoplasmically. He'd find other girls—girls with bodies, flesh and blood. And why shouldn't he? Roxane, or the Cybele-form in which he'd loved her, was long gone as far as Niko knew.

So she went out summoning on Winners' Day eve, which meant she went out hunting on the Festival grounds first: Roxane had to eat a soul or two to gather strength enough to take human form again.

She chose a minor priest of Ranke from the priestly enclave at the Festival, since Rankans were her enemies—a Rankan of Abakithis's faction, since these were enemies of Niko's.

And she sucked out his soul before his missing god's untenanted field altar, to make it sweeter. When the priest had clutched his chest and foamed at the mouth and died, a shape began to coalesce around him, a shape with sorcerous eyes.

First it was misty, then it was milky, then it became a girl. And this girl had the innocence of a waif, Cybele—the silken hair, the comely limbs, the flawless skin—but the soul of Roxane, and the face was a cross between Roxane's own and a face Niko had come to love.

Rising up, naked, from the cold dead priest, she looked about her.

Defiling the god's altar further became her evening's work. Upon it, nude, she crouched, and there she began to chant, summoning what she could lay claim to from the underworld.

A portal spun against the twilight, brightened. Foul odors told her that in its depths, a presence stirred. She called it forth, saying: "Come, demon, fiend, or devil. We've a prank to play, souls to suck, a globe of power to spin."

When she'd said that last word, a head poked out of the hole in heaven, two hands upon emptiness's edge like a marsupial peeking from its mother's pouch.

"I swear," intoned Roxane, hands raised in invocation, her legs widespread upon the altar of a hated god, "to feed you well with innocent souls, to use you well, to wreak revenge upon all of Ranke's filthy, god-loving priests."

The silhouetted form in the rent cocked its head; pointed ears twitched and pricked. Teeth gnashed—a sound not soon forgotten by any who'd ever heard a fiend devour anyone.

"Come, come, my pretty, my instrument, my pet," she crooned. She didn't call it "slave"—she wasn't strong enough to summon a horde of fiends, a raft of demons, or a clutch of devils: this one minion must be all she'd need.

"Urp!" came a hoarse voice from the paunch of hell. "Urp? Whozzat?"

"It's Roxane, your mistress. Aren't you hungry, servant mine? It's time to flay our supper." The hole was beginning to flicker, to quiver: it was hard to hold eternities apart.

She was sweating with the effort. She wasn't used to working so hard for what she wanted—she hoped soon things would be easier, then banished all depressing thoughts and in her best commanding voice, said, "Speak thy name, fiend, and come forth, or I'll close that hole upon your head and lop it from your body! Come! Come forth!"

And forth it came, a trifle awkwardly: a long-limbed, gray-skinned fiend of the warty sort, whose eyes looked every way at once and who might pass for human wherever birth defects were the rule, with a prognathic jaw and an orange shock of hair.

She thanked devils it didn't have a tail as it climbed down from the hole in heaven, then hung by one long arm, swinging there. "I can't climb down," it grated. "I'll fall!"

Now she had it—or him, from what hung between its bony legs. "Speak thy name, creature, and I'll help thee. My creature, dependent upon me for life and breath, tell me truly who you are!"

It gnashed its teeth again, then surrendered to her. "Argh; umph. My name's Snapper Jo, and now you've got me. So help me—don't leave me hanging here like fruit upon a tree."

"Snapper Jo," she repeated, "swear to me that you're my obedient servant!"

"Aw—do I have to?" It turned its head and rolled its eyes at her. It sighed again and its mouth worked. "I swear. Now get me down."

Roxane lowered her arms and the hole from hell floated groundward, until the fiend's feet touched the sod.

Immediately, it let go of the hole and dropped to all fours as above, the rent in nature telescoped in upon itself and ceased to be.

Then it gained its feet and rubbed its crotch. "So this is it?" It looked around, absently cracking its jaws. Then it rubbed its arms. "I'm cold. It's much colder here than—"

"Where you're from. I know. Come right this way, Snapper Jo. We'll find some innocents, murder them, take their clothing, and I'll start teaching you about the world of men."

"Murder? Right now?" The fiend's sharp eyes narrowed; it pulled on its lip. "But I just got here. I'd like to—"

She pointed a finger at it and it cowered. "Right away," it said. "We'll murder lots of . . . what are they? Rankans, that's right. Murder Rankans, yes. Hungry."

She looked at the fiend, who would protect the globe of Nisibisi power and her person, now that she had one, all the way down to Sanctuary, where Roxane was planning to go to hide and gain back her strength. In Sanctuary, anguish flowed freely and magic was tolerated. Witches were safe, respected, feared.

"Now, Snapper," she said, locking arms with the fiend as she led him toward a part of the village she knew was filled with priestlets, "we've a feast in store the next few days—there'll be murder aplenty, done by men. So ours must look as if men did it: no wholesale slaughtering, no throats bitten out, no bones split for marrow."

The fiend frowned earnestly, trying to understand. Fiends were stupid, from the lowest echelon of hell. But this one, who scratched himself and grinned inhumanly as she talked of breaking bones, would be just the right sort to get her through Winners' Day and safe away, on the road to Sanctuary, where she could reclaim some old undeads and marked souls she'd cached there for just this sort of emergency.

And since she was going there in part because of Randal, Tempus's Hazard, and in part because it was the safest place for a witch with a Nisibisi globe, she knew the lords of hell would assist her every step of the way.

* 3 *

The night before Winners' Day, Tempus revealed to Randal the nature of the secret mission the Hazard was to undertake for his commander.

"I want you to go into town, to the Rankan mageguild, Randal, and warn the Hazards to stay clear of the winners' tent tomorrow—to keep out of the coup coming, to take no side and lend no aid to either faction."

Randal's jaw dropped open. "Me? In the Rankan—"

"You're First Hazard of Tyse. Pull rank. I'm warning these mages of their own good." Tempus bared his teeth in that smile which all Stepsons knew presaged blood about to spill and carnage in the offing.

"Let's hope *they* realize that—adepts don't take well to threats from mere mortals . . . that is, my lord commander, from secular types." Randal shifted on his cot, toying with his kris nervously. "I'll have to be polite, not deliver a verbatim message . . ."

"Then be polite. And be careful. Hell's own fury is going to break loose when Abakithis dies. I'll need you back by then, in case I have to spirit all our fighters—the 3rd, as well as Stepsons—away from here by magic. You're up to that, if the need arises, aren't you?"

"I'll . . . have to be." Randal tried to smile, be brave, nonchalant, but intruding in another mageguild's matters was not a thing to take lightly. And there was something Tempus didn't understand. "Do you know? That is . . . you surely know that Askelon, the lord of dreams, is quartered in with the Rankan mages."

"Don't worry about the shadow lord—he and I have an understanding of a sort. And if you see my sister there, don't let it trouble you. Just deliver my warning and then come back again." With that, Tempus got up, stretched widely, and left Randal alone in his Festival billet.

Absently, Randal caressed his kris, thinking that he'd go say goodbye to Niko, just in case something went wrong and he didn't come back from the Rankan mageguild in time for the winners' fete—or didn't come back at all. No such message from an adept who had defected to the side of fighters would be well-received.

And then he heard a buzzing, as if an insect had waked from winter's sleep.

Ignoring it, he decided he'd wear the enchanted panoply, just in case. It would be hot and uncomfortable in a citadel of magic, but no hostile force could touch him, except perhaps the dream lord himself.

Again he heard the buzzing, this time louder, as he buckled on his cuirass. This time, the sound seemed closer and as the Hazard, his kris discarded on the bed, buckled on the sword which once was Niko's, a white-headed hornet landed on his nose.

The Hornet King's antennae twitched; its stinger was poised against Randal's skin. "Well, where's my honey? My caterpillars?"

"What are you doing here, Lord Hornet? I didn't call you." Randal thought quickly: he had some honey, a bit left from sweetening his tea. "Is it Niko?"

"Honey first, you welshing wizard. And be quick about it."

Carefully, his head held high so as not to offend the big wasp standing on his nose, Randal eased over to his table. "Careful with that stinger, King. I might be allergic." Eyes on the hornet, he groped around for the honeypot, fumbled with its clay top, then said, "Here's your honey. Now, what brings you here, Hornet King?"

The hornet took wing and Randal, with a heartfelt sigh of relief, backed away from the table, his hand on his dream-forged sword, thinking he could probably swat the hornet before it knew what he had in mind.

But its next words stopped him cold. "The witch, the one that haunts Nikodemos, is abroad on the Festival grounds tonight, in human form, with a summoned fiend beside her, killing priests of the Storm God in great numbers." On the honeypot's rim, it rubbed its wings together, then dipped into the pot.

"So?" Randal said nastily. "What's that to me, if she kills priests? They're no friends of mine."

"But Nikodemos, the one I've been watching all this time, is at this moment headed toward the compound where the witch and fiend are at their killing. And so is a contingent of Festival guards and—"

Randal was already running for the door, swearing softly in the name of a tutelary demon, so that he didn't hear the Hornet King's plaintive, "I thought you'd be pleased to know, and grateful," as he careened down the steps and into the Festival village lanes.

At a dead run, headed for the priests' quarters, he told himself that Niko wasn't his partner any longer, that it wasn't his business, that he had a secret mission to perform for the Riddler.

But if Niko was caught by the witch, it would then be the business of the entire Sacred Band. And the Hornet King's arrival was a sign: no matter how Niko felt, or what the Riddler declared, or even what Randal wanted, in some mystical way the kris—and even the Hornet King—understood that Randal and Niko were still a pair.

As he skidded onto the grounds of the priests' compound and smelled the sulphur and saw the sick, greenish light, he almost quailed, nearly ran: Roxane the indomitable, Roxane, Death's Queen, Roxane the Unkillable, was surely there. Despair overswept him: Niko was cursed with this witch forever.

But Randal had been a Stepson long enough that he couldn't accept defeat, not even in his mind. The witch was Randal's rightful foe, not the opponent of fragile human fighters.

Drawing the Askelonian sword of power, which glowed as it heated in his hand, sensing fielded sorcery, he ran up the way, yelling war cries but not knowing that he did, chanting counterspells as he went that woke the priests who'd been sleeping ensorceled in their billets and brought lights to every window that he passed.

As he neared the source of the sick green light, he saw Roxane, big as life, and a gray-skinned fiend crouched over three corpses in the street, with a fourth victim struggling in the fiend's grasp.

And beyond he saw Nikodemos, with Sauni the priestess of Enlil, not running away as would have been prudent, but approaching the hell-wreakers.

Yelling at the top of his lungs to divert the witch's attention, Randal leaped to intervene.

And Roxane rose up, hands spread like claws upon the air, calling him by name.

He had only enough time to wish he'd found another name, a pseudonym, a protective alias, before the spell struck him like an avalanche, a mudfall or a freezing rain, and everything slowed down.

It was hard to move: he struggled. Her words sounded too slow and deep for him to understand. Each step he took as he forced his legs to move took years to complete, each word he uttered sounded like the groaning of the earth beneath his feet.

She came toward him, did Roxane, pinwheel-eyes agleam, beckoning him with open arms.

And he couldn't check his progress: Randal felt himself being drawn into Roxane's arms as inexorably as a living man draws breath.

His armor was white-hot against his flesh: surely that would stop her. He brandished his sword but it only wavered in his hand.

Then the fiend, the warty-gray monster, approached with clacking jaws and wall-eyed stare, intent on stripping him naked where he stood.

Struggle! he told himself. But his limbs were too heavy and the witch was promising him an eternity of servitude in which all evil would be his. It sounded better and better as the fiend began to unbuckle Randal's cuirass.

And just as he was about to utter the words that Roxane demanded he speak, he remembered he ought not to do this, that he wasn't the same kind of mage as she, and that there was something very wrong about this.

Someone else thought so, too: from behind Roxane, a concerned face loomed, a mouth opened wide and shouted.

The witch turned her gaze away from Randal, and the mesmerizing spell which had made him tractable, slow, and weak was broken as Roxane faced Nikodemos, who stood in front of Enlil's priestess, Sauni, who was calling upon the god for help.

What had been slow turned lightning-fast, and confus-

ing: Niko's face contorted; he shouted, "Randal, get away!
Get out of here! Now!"

Stealth's words echoed in Randal's ears. And from down
the row, the pounding of men's feet could be heard.

Randal risked a look behind him and saw priests and
soldiers with lit torches rushing toward them.

He looked back in time to see Sauni, her hands out and
crawling with a godlike nimbus, her face masked with
sparks, casting thunderbolts like a veritable god.

She cast one at the fiend's feet and it howled: "Argh!
Get back, wicked thing!" and jumped away from Randal
to protect its bloody prey.

But it was Niko and the witch, both motionless, staring
at each other, neither drawing weapons or saying a single
word, which kept Randal there an instant longer than he
should have stayed: he saw Niko reach back without taking
his eyes from Roxane and imprison Sauni's hands in his.

He saw Roxane smile and blow Stealth a kiss, then
gather fiend and milk-white tortured souls issuing from her
victims before she waved her hands and disappeared.

By then the priests and soldiers were close upon them,
brandishing torches and weapons, bawling confused orders
and milling around the space where the witch had been and
now only corpses remained—corpses and a single fighter
who'd sunk down on the ground and sat, with the priestess
bent over him, his head down, wordless.

Randal knew that Niko was barely well, still recuperating. And he knew that what he'd seen, no wizard should
have witnessed.

He pushed his way through the priests and guards, and
when he got to Niko, he said, "Stealth, what did she say
to you? What did she make you promise? Why did you
stop Sauni?"

Niko raised his head, an exhausted, disgusted look upon
his face. "We just said farewell, if it's any business of
yours. You're alive, aren't you? Safe to magic what you
will? Go on, Hazard. Get away from me. And don't thank

me, either—I didn't do it for you. I did it for myself: we're even now, life for life."

And Sauni met Randal's gaze over Niko's head as the guards began demanding proof that witches' work had killed the priests, not men's, and shook her head sadly: what was done, was done.

Randal spent what seemed like months letting guardsmen touch his cuirass, still hot from proximity to hostile magic, and assuring the priests that he'd seen the whole thing and that the fighter, Stealth, was innocent of blame—in fact, had routed Roxane.

Then he hitched up his swordbelt and headed through the night to penetrate the Rankan mageguild and make sure no adept raised a hand to help Abakithis avoid the coup or Theron straddle the Lion Throne of Ranke.

* **4** *

Kama had contrived to spend the night before Winners' Day with Sync. She'd promised Brachis that if Tempus had treachery up his sleeve, she'd make good the coup, and she was trying to get Sync to tell her what he knew—who, and where, and when.

But she'd no more than gotten the Rankan colonel's clothes off when no less than Bashir came pounding at the door.

"Crap," Sync breathed, struggling into his breech, looking from Kama to the door and back. "Go hide somewhere, woman. I'll get back to you as soon as I can."

He'd wanted her a long time; it hadn't been that difficult to get him drunk and compromise him. She even liked him, after a fashion, though no one would ever replace Critias in her heart.

Part of her was glad they'd been interrupted—that someone would find out she was with Sync and Crit would hear of it: she still hoped against hope that the Stepsons' task force leader had feelings for her. Hers for him would take a long time, and many men, to put to rest.

So she didn't hide, just covered her breasts and lay there, watching, her limbs arranged in a fetching but passionate pose.

Bashir, in the doorway, studiously avoided her. "Niko's at the guard station: something about dead Rankan priests, and him on the scene. Sauni was with him, and she says he had nothing to do with it, that it was witchcraft, and that Randal was there and told the guards that. But they say Niko's motive is so clear they're going to hold him overnight unless one of the commanders comes and takes him into his personal custody."

Sync scratched his spine. "He's a Stepson. It's not my problem. Get Crit or Tempus." He started to close the door.

By then Kama was up, nakedness forgotten, finding her clothes and donning them hurriedly.

Bashir, in his most ringing, priestly voice, said, "Niko can't withstand a Rankan interrogation, even a mild one, not in his condition. And you, Rankan, ought to know that."

Kama, tightening her belt, looked up. Bashir, at times, seemed like just another guerrilla leader, a hillman with pretensions. But at other times, like this moment, she had no doubt that the god whispered in his ear.

"Look here, Bashir," Sync said, unmoved, "Niko killed 3rd Commando fighters back in Tyse. Maybe this is the retribution of the gods. It's not my business, I told you. Get Tempus . . . Niko's his favorite Stepdaughter—"

"Sync," Kama came up beside him, "please."

"Sync," Bashir said at the same time, "neither Critias nor Tempus can be found. Overcome this old hatred—for all our sakes. It belittles you and all of us. Do it not to please the god, but because it's right."

"Yeah, well," Sync put a proprietary hand on Kama, "maybe you're right—Niko wasn't a Stepson that time in Tyse. And it's time the rivalry between us ended. Give me a moment to change, Bashir, and I'll go with you. Come in."

So instead of spending the night before the coup gathering intelligence and making love to the 3rd's colonel, Kama was going to spend it witnessing affidavits releasing Niko into Sync's custody.

By the time they saw him, Niko was wearing a Rankan signature or two: bruises on his temples, rope burns on his wrists.

Sync had some harsh words with the guards' duty officer over jumping to insupportable conclusions, and the man replied, "They ought to count their blessings they could turn up a decent Rankan officer to take this Bandaran slime off our hands—there's plenty others, priestly types, who'd have slipped me a month's wage under the table to have a go at him."

Then Sync replied in soldierly fashion that Niko would be available at Sync's billet for any further questions: "Of the polite sort, that is. The Stepsons are a unit beyond reproach. Take my word for it. They're godfearing and the best fighters, outside of the 3rd, I've ever served with. If this soldier slew a priest, he'd have good reason, admit it on the spot, and fight you to the death before he'd let himself be taken. So he didn't do it. You have my word and that of the 3rd Commando. Take it to the priesthood and let them know that the army doesn't take kindly to any erosion of the separation between church and state."

The duty officer chuckled, "Wouldn't I love to tell them that! Take care of your prisoner, Colonel. I'm sure we'll get this settled in the morning."

Sync turned away and Kama saw a mischievous grin on his stubbled face. "Let's go, Terror," he said to Niko, a hand on the Stepson's arm, "before you scare anybody else. As it is,'' he confided as they left the guardpost, ''you've got the entire priesthood piddling in their pants.''

''What did happen?'' Kama asked, when Bashir's whisper prompted her.

Until then, Niko had said not one word of thanks or anything at all.

He shrugged, looked at Sync's hand on his arm, and replied, ''The witch had what she'd come for. She left.''

Bashir mumbled a prayer and then said aloud, ''The god calls me to my duty. Stealth, take care. Tomorrow night we ride for the high peaks. You've a mare with foal at Hidden Valley who needs her master.''

Then Niko stopped, on the torchlit way, and embraced Bashir, saying, ''I'm all right, Bashir, don't worry. A witch for a friend is better than one for an enemy. Tell Sauni that. And tell her I *will* ride north with you tomorrow, if the Riddler will . . .''

The two men stood that way, arms about each other, long enough that Sync turned to Kama with a disgusted shake of head: the 3rd didn't feel expressions of manly love were seemly, as the Stepsons and the northern fighters did.

When the long farewell was done, Niko went with Kama and Sync, and Bashir went his own way, off to do what priests did.

When it was clear that, with Niko at Sync's for the night's duration, no advantage could be gained or passion consummated, Kama left them, saying lightly, ''I'll see you in the winners' tent, Sync,'' as if she had no idea what was afoot.

* 5 *

Tempus was in town with Theron, trying to wrest a
promise from the wily old fighter of safe passage for all
his men once the deed was done.

"But how can I, Riddler?" Theron was pacing back and
forth, his brow furrowed up into his balding pate. "I'm
not in a position to write such a paper now. If I do, it'll be
clear that I'm involved with the plan for Abakithis's assassination. And afterwards, you shouldn't need any promise
of safe conduct, if all goes well."

"I've got close to two hundred men, counting Bashir's
Successors, to look out for. Don't force me to resort to
means I'd rather not employ, or violence after the fact. If
we have to fight our way out, you may not have an army
when we're done. And fight we will if even one man of
mine is implicated."

Theron came back to the table on his portico, where the
two men were watching the sunrise and eating cheese and
winter grapes. "Don't you think I'd like to live in a world
where a man's word, even if he's about to become emperor through nefarious means, could be his bond? Don't
you understand that I don't have control of the priesthood—
that they've got me? I'm just doing what the gods say,
what the omens have requested. I hate to admit it, Riddler,
but this thing's out of my control."

"Not out of mine. If my man doesn't perform this . . .
sacrifice, as your priests euphemistically call it, then I
have no problem."

"But I do? Not so. If they've got it in their minds to
blame you, as you seem to think, then what's the truth got
to do with that? They'll falsify the omens—it's not un-
heard of—and hang it around your necks anyway."

Theron's liver spots showed bright in the morning light;

his crepy neck quivered as he spoke. "I'm sorry I got you into this, old friend. Because of your . . . durability, it didn't seem to be the trap you fear."

"Brachis is too anxious to know just who among my men is going to do the deed. There's only one reason that could be so important to him."

"Riddler, I—" Theron stopped, his eyes bugged out, he bent and hacked up phlegm into a handkerchief. "Excuse me, my health's not what it once was. You have my permission to do whatever you think will help—kill a priest or two, if it makes you feel better. You'll be doing me a favor if you do. I'll even let you off the hook afterward. And when I'm emperor, once the priests have performed the rites and my word is law, I'll take care of you and yours. It's just those first few hours . . ." Theron's watery eyes were pleading. He said very quietly, "You know that I don't want this for myself. I want it for the empire, whatever that is—for the vision of the empire that I grew up with, which sustained me all these years, made me proud to serve her. This Mygdonian war's taken all the stuffing out of us—we can't win it and we can't declare ourselves defeated. And after the hostage-taking incident at the games, this season's warring looks like it will be worse, not better: they lost men, we lost men . . . it's been all we could do to keep order at the games . . ."

Almost, Tempus told Theron that it didn't matter: that Ranke was doomed to fail until the missing god was found, that without Vashanka, no hand at the helm of empire could be steady enough to put her back on course. But he didn't: valor in a man's heart was something he'd long ago learned to respect, regardless of its futility. Events weren't honorable or dishonorable; men were.

So he gently told Theron that no man of his could take the risk, but that Theron would still be emperor.

"What?" Theron's weathered face folded as he considered that. "Not a riddle, though you're famous for them—

not now when every step's so dear and everyone about me's having second thoughts but the damnable priests. . . ."

"Nevertheless, make sure they get this message: no man of mine, but the deed will still be done."

Again Theron sighed, and it was a deeper, more rattling sigh than even Tempus had ever sighed. "Whatever you want, old friend. My fate, as it's turned out, is in your hands."

And as Tempus held out one empty hand to clasp Theron's in a gesture meant to be encouraging, a runner came gasping to the portico. "Sirs! A message, if it pleases you!"

"It doesn't look like it will, but go ahead, man, deliver it," Theron said, sitting back in his chair and squinting as if against a too-bright sun.

"Five priests were killed last night, some say by witch-craft, some say by the Stepson Nikodemos, who has reason to kill Abakithis's priests. This Nikodemos is under house arrest, released in the custody of the 3rd Commando's colonel, Sync. An inquiry is under way and—"

"Why wasn't I informed?" Tempus blustered, on his feet.

"You were in conference, and couldn't be disturbed," Theron soothed as best he could, also getting to his feet. "Come on, Riddler. Just like former times—let's go get one of our boys out of jail."

* 6 *

In the Rankan mageguild was such splendor and wealth as Randal had never seen.

These were mages who'd had a place in court for de-cades, whose astrologers and seers and sybils whispered in the ear of Abakithis, the Rankan emperor.

The spells they'd cast and the wars they'd helped fight

with alchemical devices against the empire's enemies had
been exorbitantly priced, or else the empire had been
excessively grateful when things were going well.

In its halls Randal gawked like an apprentice at man-
high statues of elementals cast from gold, at tapestries
depicting past mageguild masters and changelings of whom
they were inordinately fond. Its halls were carpeted with
silken rugs depicting gargoyles at the hunt and archmages
in gilded canopies riding on elephants with Rankan kings.

But here and there, signs of a failing empire could be
seen: peeling paint and warped woods on doorsills, chalked
warding signs on brassbound doors.

The apprentice leading Randal ever deeper into the laby-
rinthine mageguild never spoke to him beyond an initial:
"To see the First Hazard? Right this way, then, honorable
mage."

It was flattering to be called "honorable mage" in
Ranke, where the most honored mages dwelt. But it would
have been more so if these sorcerers hadn't proved inade-
quate to deal with Nisibisi wizardry of the like Death's
Queen could field.

They crossed an inner court and the morning sun shone
down. Randal squinted up at it, trying to determine the
lateness of the hour: it had taken time to ride into town,
find the mageguild, be admitted, and soon the Winners'
Day fete would begin out at the Festival site.

He wanted to be there in case something else went
wrong. And he wanted to be with Niko, although he knew
he wasn't welcome.

Across the court, as they entered the central citadel of
magic, protected from the outside world by walls and
shimmering wards Randal could glimpse even in bright
daylight, which made his panoply begin to warm, he
chastised himself: after Niko's behavior on the street last
night, no renewal of their pairbond was possible, despite
what the Riddler had said. He was going to have to get
used to it.

So immersed in his own thoughts was Randal that he
didn't notice until he'd trod several corridors that the inner
citadel was filled with dogs: cinnabar dogs on lapis plinths,
rosewood dogs carved on pillars, and real dogs. Thick-
furred dogs which looked like giant cats; long-furred dogs
with pointed hunting noses; giant dogs as big as ponies;
hairless tiny dogs with mouselike ears; dogs with wrinkled
skin that seemed a size too large.

And the place smelled of dog, smelled rank and fetid.
Dogs were anathema in temples and so, Randal supposed,
dogs were the mascots of the Rankan mageguild, here
where the battle between religion and sorcery had been
ongoing for centuries.

Rankan mages vied with priests for the hearts and minds
of the populace; their war was barely under wraps. Only
the empire's war with Mygdonia had cooled the struggle
between the mages and the priests, for the Rankan people
and the Rankan nobility's allegiance.

Things weren't like that in Tyse, where Ranke's rule
was tenuous at best.

The dog dander in the air was a difficulty Randal hadn't
expected: his nose stuffed up, his eyes began to water, his
lungs labored for breath. When he'd lost Askelon's patron-
age, he'd lost his immunity to fur and feathers.

Glumly, he was thinking that he'd probably lose his
First Hazardship if he went back to Tyse and the wizards
there found out he couldn't control his allergies anymore,
when he realized that the apprentice leading him through
the corridors had stopped before a particular door.

"Here we are, noble Hazard. Shall I introduce you, or
is your Presence enough introduction on its own?"

Randal looked sharply at the apprentice, but the boy
wasn't being snide. "Announce me," Randal decided.
"I'll wait here."

So in went the apprentice and Randal had time to blow
his nose on his sleeve and swallow what he could of his
pride's denouement and wish he'd never come.

Then the boy came back and, with a sweeping bow, stood aside and told him, "Please go in."

Within the Rankan First Hazard's chamber, three people, not one, awaited him.

All three were backlit by a wall that glowed amber as if behind it a fire were contained.

He couldn't see their faces; they were black shapes against the glow.

Wishing the Riddler wouldn't get him into these things, he strode up to the raised dais on which they sat and said, though he hadn't meant to: "I'm Tyse's First Hazard and I've come here, as is my right, to claim your assistance in a matter of some gravity."

"We know of you, Hazard," one voice boomed out, basso profundo and distinctly amused. "What aid do you request?"

Somewhere nearby, a dog whined.

Randal was supposed to tell these Hazards not to mix in, not to interfere on one side or another in the coming coup. But the appearance of the Nisibisi witch and the vulnerability of the Stepsons to witchcraft made Randal want to do more. The Riddler, who couldn't die, didn't understand what death meant to men—or mages. The idea of fighting his way out of Ranke with all of Tempus's mixed militia to protect, or of ensorceling that many men so far all by himself, was more than distasteful—it was frightening.

So he said: "There's a coup coming, in case you didn't know. There'll be a new emperor on the throne tomorrow, and if we don't help—*achoo!*— things along, we'll be the enemies of the new regime."

One figure sat up; the other two didn't move.

Randal wiped his nose and continued, wishing the dog in here would leave as his nose closed up completely and his t's turned into d's. "And if you'll dake my word for id, dere's someding we can do dad mighd make da difference."

"Go on," said a feminine voice, and Randal was startled: it wasn't usual for a female to be a ranking Hazard, but these were obviously Ranke's top three.

"Well, we can keep da prieds from inderfering, dad's whad—Abakidis's prieds. Make id clear which side we're on."

"Obviously, you have a plan," said the bass-voice Hazard, "some machination in mind by way of which we can prove ourselves an essential adjunct to this new administration?"

"Of course," Randal lied, though he didn't have a plan, not a clue, just wanted some help transporting all those fighters if push came to shove and the onus fell upon him. "Bud you've god do ged rid of dese dogs, if you wand my help."

The female tittered, waved a hand, and something gave a forlorn, receding howl as if it were falling through a long tunnel.

"Done," said the basso profundo voice. "And now, your plan, honorable Hazard." This adept, too, raised a hand and, as it waved, from the four corners of the room light sprang into being: a dozen torches lit.

And there, upon the First Hazard's elegant dogheaded throne, sat Askelon, lord of dreams, with Tempus's sister Cime beside him, and a wizened Rankan adept beside her.

"Come, come, Hazard," Askelon said, and by the dream lord's face Randal knew he was to pretend they weren't acquainted. "Let's hear this plan of yours, by which the mageguild's value to empire can be demonstrated, and the priesthood brought to its knees."

The dream lord fingered his own nose and Randal could breathe again.

"I'm not talking about bringing anyone to his knees, Hazards," Randal said, "just helping things along a little." With intense foreboding and extreme disquiet, he looked from Askelon to Cime and realized that he'd made a mistake—that with Askelon and Cime involved, things were already out of hand.

It was too late to back out now.

* 7 *

"Kama, I want to talk to you and Sync after I'm finished with Niko, so please stay," said Tempus when the two brought Niko before an ad hoc tribunal consisting of one priest from Abakithis's faction, one from Theron's, and three generals, of which Tempus was one at Theron's request.

Kama and Sync, in their dress blacks, settled down uneasily next to Sauni and Bashir. They were late to the Winners' Day celebration because of this matter of Niko's alleged crime.

The priests got out their divining bowls, their holy water, and their sacrificial birds, and proceeded to "determine the guilt of the accused" by swishing tea leaves in the bowls, sprinkling Niko with water that was supposed to burn him if he was guilty or if he was consorting with a witch, and pinning the birds to boards with copper nails to see where their wingtips pointed when they died.

Intermittently, as the priests mumbled their prayers, Sync coughed in the incense-heavy air of the guardhouse and Kama looked out the window wistfully.

When the priests had reached their verdicts, they spoke them:

"He's unequivocally guilty," said the priest of Abakithis's faction, an albino in a lightning-spangled velvet robe, whose "holy water" had burned the back of Niko's hand when sprinkled on it.

"He's indubitably innocent," said the red-haired priest of Theron's faction who wore a plain robe suitable for a priest of the armies, and whose "holy water" had taken away the angry red spots on Niko's hand when sprinkled on the burns.

"Well," said Tempus, "that's encouraging—the priests are leaving it up to us, gentlemen."

The other two generals, one from each faction, shifted restlessly in their seats.

Abakithis's general said, "The testimony is inconclusive without the appearance of this Randal, who saw the whole thing."

Theron's general said, "What good is a magician's testimony in a matter of magic? The priestess, there, is above reproach—" he pointed at Sauni, white-faced at the back of the room "—and so are all of Nikodemos's character witnesses. I vote for acquittal."

Both generals looked at Tempus, who said nothing, but approached the two priests. "Sprinkle your holy water on the table, priest," he said to the albino who served Abakithis.

"The water of the gods is too precious to waste," the priest objected.

"I'll gladly sprinkle mine there," said the priest of Theron's faction.

"Do it or I'll do it myself," Tempus said with a little smile.

When Abakithis's priest sprinkled his "water" on the table, the finish began to bubble where the drops hit it.

"If Nikodemos is guilty of murdering priests, then so is this table," Tempus said loudly, stepping away so that the others could see the bubbles. "Nikodemos is innocent, but this priest is not."

"The condition of the priesthood isn't what we're here to determine," the albino spat.

Tempus would have argued that, but the other two generals, seeing mayhem in the offing, interposed themselves.

When the inquiry was officially ended, Tempus thought he saw a gray face with a shock of orange hair peering in the window as everyone but Abakithis's lackeys congratulated Niko.

"Niko," Tempus said carefully, "I want you to go with Bashir and *stay* with Bashir. Prepare your gear and your horses and be ready to ride. You're not to go to the winners' tent and you're not to be alone at any time."

"Yes, Commander," Niko said, eyes downcast, abashed at having caused so much trouble.

"Bashir, Sauni, you heard me. Keep a close watch on my partner, who can't seem to stay out of trouble on his own." It was harsh, but for Niko's own good. Tempus had more to worry about this day than just his right-side partner.

As Bashir and Sauni were ushering Niko out, Tempus thought he saw a grayish form flit by the door, but he wasn't certain.

And he had other things on his mind. "Kama, Sync, come here."

"We're late," Sync said without preamble, eyeing Kama significantly. "She's got a prize to collect."

"So does he," said Kama. His daughter's face was full of suppressed excitement.

"Sync," Tempus said slowly. "There's too much risk in this for you—and for the 3rd. I've changed my mind and you're relieved of your assignment. Go enjoy the fete—you've earned it—but ready your men for a quick exit when I give the signal."

"This is all your fault, your doing." Sync crossed his arms and glared at Kama.

"Me?" Tempus's daughter rejoined. "I don't know what you're talking about, Sync. But I know I don't like your tone!" She turned to Tempus, big-eyed and guileless. "Perhaps my father will explain just what it is I'm being accused of?"

"Are you two soldiers or an old married couple, bickering over who will prepare the dinner? You'll follow orders exactly as I give them, both of you. And those orders are to collect your prizes, your gear and horses, and protect yourselves. That's all."

Dismissed, the two stalked off toward the winners' tent, arguing with one another.

Tempus went another way, out behind the guardhouse shed where he'd seen the gray face with its orange shock of hair.

In his hand he had a talisman, a bit of hair and bone, and since there was nothing behind the guardhouse station but some brush and dirt, he hunkered down there and began to build a little fire.

Just as he put the talisman on the pile of sticks and leaves and was getting out his flints to strike a spark, a cold wind chilled his neck.

A voice said, "Yessss . . . you called, my ancient enemy?"

Calmly, Tempus turned to face Roxane, Death's Queen, who had an orange-haired fiend attending her.

"You want this back, don't you, witchy?" He picked up the talisman and held it tightly in his fist.

To give Roxane credit, she didn't pale or quail, just sat down on the ground beside him. "Could be, Riddler. What will you take for it? A nap? An eternity of sleep?"

"I'd like your help with something," he said. "And I think that, because of Nikodemos, you'll see that our interests have converged."

Roxane's fiend hadn't sat down; it stood at a sort of attention, its gangly arms swinging between its knees. It clacked its jaws now. "Murder? Is it murder? We like murder, we do." Its eyes were rolling every which way as it tried to watch for intruders.

"Shush, Snapper." The witch was beautiful, lovelier than Tempus remembered, and when she didn't try to ensorcel him straightaway, but said, "Make your proposition, Riddler, if you dare," Tempus knew his plan was going to work.

* 8 *

It didn't take Niko long to get around Bashir. "What can it hurt, Bashir, just to go and watch? Sauni must collect her prize, or snub the empire. And we should be there to see it."

They were drinking in Bashir's quarters—the warrior-priest's first mistake. And both Bashir and Sauni, who almost never drank, had drunk too much, considering it a consolation prize for missing the fete because of Niko.

Soon enough they were strolling through the crowd together, arm in arm, Sauni's head resting on Niko's shoulder as she admitted how glad she was she'd get to go.

Niko had drunk nearly nothing, just pretended to be tractable and drunk. Drink had served him ill; he'd stay away from it henceforth. He'd had time to think about his life while awaiting judgment for a crime he hadn't done. He'd thought about Randal and Roxane, the pair of mages who loved him, and decided that neither one had any claim on him.

He was a child of maat, son of the armies, and it made sense that the legions of evil would be drawn to him, try to turn him to their cause. It was hard to think of Randal as evil, and lately he could say the same of the Nisibisi witch. But he'd learned, this winter season, not to fear sorcery as all-powerful or unnatural. And this meant that it couldn't compromise him as once it had: Bandaran lore taught that once a problem was defined, its nature understood, it was halfway to being solved.

And turning away from the seductive lure of Askelon, from Randal's help, from the witch's caress, had brought his maat and his secular center together: he was feeling as if his life had just begun.

But there remained the matter of a promise he'd made to

Brachis, priest of empire, in order to secure Free Nisibis for Bashir, whom Niko loved despite the amount of god which had crept into the soul of his oldest, dearest friend.

He had to be there, close enough and ready to lend a hand, take command, do what he'd said he'd do, even if it killed him. An entire state, a country where freedom reigned and men didn't prey upon their brothers was worth his life, and more.

He considered himself lucky to have the opportunity to give it for such a worthy cause. Life would be taken from him eventually, probably for some mean or meaningless transgression, or for no reason at all but time. Loving life as Niko did, within the harmony of his mystery, made it a gift he'd be honored to give to Free Nisibis, if things turned out that way.

Niko didn't want to die, nor to assassinate an emperor, but it was his bargain, his responsibility, and his opportunity now at hand. If the gods willed otherwise, it would be shown to him and he'd ride up to Wizardwall and then on to Bandara for a well-deserved rest.

Inside the winners' tent, Sauni gasped at the magnificence of the decorations that Abakithis's staff had collected to honor the winners of the games. The tent itself was thrice as high as any Niko had ever seen. A stout young tree was its center pole and its tenting was black and red, emblazoned here and there with the gilt lion-tearing-the-world of Ranke. Inside were chairs, not bleachers—chairs like miniature thrones with lion-headed arms and claw-feet, each one gilded with red-velvet seats. On a sideboard five yards long were pigs and lambs and ducks roasted with caterpillars, all seasonable fruits from the empire's southernmost reaches, samovars of tea and great urns of wine, as well as casks of beer.

Nearly fifty winners filled their plates, opposite the presentation stand. On this, below pleats of bunting, was Abakithis's own Lion Throne of Empire, plus three lesser thrones for courtiers. And beside the stand was a silver bathtub on claw-and-ball feet, the prize to give the overall champion of the games.

Abakithis and his courtiers were not yet in attendance, but two squadrons of pretorians were, and nearly twenty Rankan slaves, their collars burnished, from all over empire circulated among the celebrants.

And the slaves made Niko's throat tighten. He'd been a slave for a time when Ranke conquered Tyse; he'd been a child, and terrified. Once a man feels a collar, he knows no man should ever wear one. And every time he saw one, it reminded him of Abarsis, the departed Slaughter Priest, who'd been gelded by the Rankans and made a slave, though he was a king's son, when his father was defeated.

But Sauni wasn't old enough to remember life before the Rankan empire had reached north into the mountains. Her eyes sparkled with excitement at every elegantly dressed lady she saw and every exotic treat on the laden Festival board. Only once did her face fall, when she saw Kama in her 3rd Commando dress uniform.

Bashir was quick to tell the priestess that women looked better in soft and flowing robes, and when she said, "Oh, look! There's Crit and Straton! Aren't they handsome in their parade gear! What a pair they make!" Niko offered to take her over there so she could tell the Stepsons personally how well they looked.

And Bashir was glad to let him. Bashir remembered fighting Ranke all too well, for far too long. The two friends knew each other so well that they didn't have to speak about it: shared feelings were exchanged with a touch.

Then Niko guided Sauni through the crowd, thinking that his little priestess was perhaps the prettiest girl there that day, and that somewhere inside her a child was growing that was part his, if officially the god's.

"Crit! Strat! Life to you, brothers. Sauni wants to tell you something." Niko urged her forward.

She stood wordless for a moment before the Stepsons'

task force leader and his huge partner, then brushed her hair off her forehead and said, "Sirs, the two of you look exactly and completely like Stepsons should—better than any men here, more valorous and elegantly brave."

Crit took off his helmet, his sly grin kind and wise. "Thank you, priestess. Does that mean we qualify for the god's blessing? We'll need all the blessings we can get, today." Over Sauni's tawny head, Crit's eyes met Niko's, not questioning what Stealth was doing here, but approving that he'd come.

Straton was trying to return Sauni's compliment. Although Strat had lost in boxing, the pair had won in team chariot-racing, and Tempus (Crit confided as Sauni solemnly blessed Strat's head once he'd knelt down where she could reach it) had relaxed the prohibition on attending when Crit argued that it would look worse if all Stepsons stayed away.

"So I'm glad you're here, Stealth. We may need your sword arm yet." Crit's lips hardly moved as he talked and his eyes roamed the crowd. "I hope your horses and your gear are ready—packed."

"I'm ready," Niko said. "Just tell me where you want me."

"Right up front where the priests can see you. We'll worry them, watching you, since it's you they know about. It'll be a good diversion."

Niko almost told Crit then that he was here against the Riddler's orders, but Crit would find out in good time, and having his task force leader position him thus was a piece of good fortune.

Then Crit had to let Sauni bless him—the lightning bolts she'd commanded against the witch were the talk of the Stepsons' camp.

When she'd done with both of them, she turned to Niko, asking shyly, "And you, my lord, my love—won't you let the god sanctify your battle this portentous day?"

Looking at her, she seemed too wise, too grown up, as if the god were whispering in her ear. "Don't talk that way, not here. But bless me if you will, Sauni."

As she was finishing her ad hoc rite, drums beat and horns blared and Abakithis and his courtiers came in, monkeys and leopards on leashes parading before him.

All the obedient servants of the fat little emperor clapped their hands and whistled as the mismanager of empire came mincing in.

Niko found his fists clenched, all his hatred of Rankans and his worst childhood memories coming to the fore.

He slid away from Sauni and took up a position where Critias had placed him as the emperor ascended his Lion Throne, a priest on either side.

Abakithis raised his jewel-heavy hands. Quiet descended. In a piping voice, the blond-haired monarch said, "Let the Festivities begin, O mighty heroes of the empire. All of you, gathered here to celebrate My Majesty and do homage to our nation, deserve a round of applause."

To one side, a priest began clapping and all the crowd, once prompted, joined in.

Then a cart drawn by two snow-white asses was led inside, piled high with trophies to be given to the winners.

But Niko wasn't paying attention to the prize wagon. He was counting Rankan soldiers, palace pretorians, peltasts, and whomever else stood between him and Abakithis.

By the time the applause had died, Niko had realized that his only chance was to rush Abakithis during a presentation—Sauni's would be the best. He could walk her to the dais and thus be close enough to leap on the emperor before anyone could stop him. He wasn't as nattily dressed as some, but his duty gear was good enough for what he had in mind.

He settled on that plan, locating Sauni in the crowd and smiling at her so she'd come to him and he could lead her up there later. He'd push her out of the way first thing; she wouldn't be hurt if the god truly loved her.

Normally, a Stepson facing certain death disposes of his possessions, his horses and his arms and armor, giving them to this good friend or that. But since Niko's partner was the Riddler, he'd let Tempus have it all—the sable stallion, his sorrel mare, her half-Trôs foal, and the quotidian arms he had left now that Randal had inherited his dream-forged panoply.

He was in a dreamy state, ordering his thoughts for death, when a hand came down hard upon his shoulder.

"Don't move, don't turn around," came a growl from behind him: Tempus had arrived.

"Crit needs me here, Commander."

"So he said. That's no excuse. We'll talk about this later."

Niko wanted to face the Riddler, say something about how honored he'd been to serve with Tempus, no matter how things looked right now, but he held firm, following his orders.

Then another order came. "And if you've got in mind what I think you do, forget it. It's all arranged, and you'll only muck the matter up."

Then the hand was gone and, out of the corner of Niko's eye, he saw a flash of leopardskin as, from behind the dais, the tenting slit and burst into flame, and from the far end of the assembly, a sound like hell heaving drowned out the presentation under way.

Before Niko's eyes, behind the Lion Throne, a warty arm and then an orange shock of hair catapulted through the flaming tenting as priests scattered to save themselves and soldiers, running the other way, toward Abakithis, careened into them and troops and priests went sprawling.

The asses brayed and bolted, scattering prizes everywhere.

The crowd surged back from the flames, then surged the other way, screaming, as from the tent's far end a grating sound like tortured metal drums resolved into a great chariot drawn by sable stallions spitting froth and driven by the fearsome lord of dreams.

Directly for the dais, Askelon's chariot headed, its horses
trampling soldiers with aplomb. Beside Askelon was Cime,
her scale-armor gleaming, a sword that seemed to flame
and smoke in her hand.

Men of the Rankan pretorians attacked the horses and
the chariot, only to fall back under Cime's onslaught and
the pointing finger of the entelechy of dreams.

Niko, sensing something unplanned in this dual diversion, drew his own sword and leaped, catching Sauni
around the waist in his left arm, toward the dais.

Everyone was screaming as the tent became a pavilion
of flames and rushed to hack exits where they could. He
threw Sauni roughly through one, and climbed the dais,
where all was bodies, confusion, and the flash of swords.

He slew where he could, hacking a path through to
Abakithis, and found that serendipity had put him next to
Tempus, on the Riddler's right.

"Under the circumstances," he gritted, "you don't mind,
I trust?" as he jabbed his shortsword up under a Rankan
cuirass, piercing an unprotected bladder for a killing blow.

"Not unless we don't get them all—every soldier who
sees us fighting against and not for them," Tempus remarked as casually as if they were planning a war and not
fighting one.

Someone landed on Niko's back and he knifed forward,
throwing the man over and then slitting his throat as he
landed atop a corpse, face up. "Good. It's nice to be on
your right, Commander, for this."

And then there was no more time for talk, just fighting,
as Rankans tried to defend their emperor.

Tempus led him over bodies and through the melee in
time to see Abakithis himself, not cowering or struggling,
but sitting, knees splayed, in the presentation bathtub,
blinking like an owl.

And before him, beckoning, was Roxane, the Nisibisi
witch. Behind Abakithis's silver tub, the gray-skinned fiend
was munching someone newly dead, gore running from its

jaws as it chuckled to itself. "Murder, murder! I'm so glad I came!"

Niko thought to strike out for the fiend, but Tempus realized what he had in mind and stopped him. "No. They're fighting for us."

"The witch?" Niko was astounded.

"You think you're the only one who can call on hellish aid?" Tempus grunted, his hand lashing out to cover the face of a Rankan soldier who was plainly fleeing unnatural adversaries, and push the man backward toward the fiend, who caught him.

Then, from behind, the chariot horses squealed and thundered so that Niko took a chance and looked around, and above, where the tent was disintegrating into chunks of fiery, falling death and the center pole was beginning to burn.

Nothing Niko had ever seen prepared him for the death that the hell-chariot was dealing among the Rankan host: its horses were covered with human blood and the chariot's wheels sparked fire and rolled over men and women indiscriminately.

From within it came a humming sound as Cime's sword swept to and fro and Askelon looked nothing at all like the kind, compassionate dream lord from Niko's rest-place.

The sight of those two killing stopped Niko in his tracks, so that Tempus had to pull him out of the chariot's way as it thundered toward the dais and the horses climbed it.

Then, with the tent crashing about them in fragments and men screaming "Run! Run! Save yourselves!" Niko saw Askelon vault down from his car and get between Roxane, who seemed to be delirious with ecstasy, toying with her prey, and Abakithis.

The little emperor was senseless, his soul already gone, his eyes all white, as undeads' usually were.

But the dream lord, it seemed, wanted the emperor for himself.

The witch launched herself at Askelon and there was banshee howling that made every man still fighting turn and stare as the two of them, locked in immortal combat, rolled upon the dais, which cracked and smoked and then began to spin and spark and sink down into the earth.

"Come on, Niko—Riddler! Move! This whole tent's going to come down on top of us any minute," bellowed Strat, come from nowhere. Crit grabbed Niko by the cuirass and threw him bodily through a burned-out hole.

He rolled upon the ground, and by the time he'd gained his knees, Tempus, Crit, and Strat came running out as the whole great tent settled, majestically flaming, to the ground.

"Where's Bashir? Sauni?" Niko demanded, yelling over the screams from the unfortunates caught under the burning celebration tent.

"Right here," Sync said laconically from behind him.

And there they were, Sauni sooty but unharmed, Bashir with some superficial wounds that said he'd done his share of fighting, with Kama alongside.

"Where's the chariot?" Kama demanded. The tent was too flat to contain that hell-wheeled chariot, or even standing horses. "And Aunt Cime? And the witch—were they really working with us on this?"

"Don't say that—to anyone, ever," Tempus snapped, cleaning his blade on his leopardskin mantle. "The witch was, yes, since Niko's word was at stake. But Askelon and Cime . . ." Tempus put on his most innocent look and shrugged as if mystified, which made Strat roar with laughter and elbow Crit, who'd taken a wound in his arm and didn't appreciate the gesture.

Then, from behind Niko, Randal said, "If you'll allow a supposition or two from a lowly Stepson, Kama, I'll answer that."

"Go ahead, Randal," Sync said before Kama could reply.

"The Riddler sent me to tell Askelon and the Rankan mageguild not to interfere—which meant, of course, they'd never stay out of it. You know how Hazards are . . ." Randal beamed. "As for where they are now—don't worry. That was just a little hierarchic quarrel between archmages—Roxane overstepped herself, making an undead out of an emperor, no matter how bad an emperor he was."

"How can you be so sure, witchy-ears—that is, how can you be so sure, *Randal*?" Strat amended, rubbing his big face with his hands. "That looked pretty serious to me."

"You'll see," Randal said mysteriously, and turned to Niko. "Stealth, are you sure you don't want this panoply back? I've got my kris; it's all I need. Take the sword, at least . . ."

So Niko took back the dream-forged sword that Randal held out, because one look at Randal's freckled face told him that it was a peacemaking gift between them, and Niko was feeling ready for a little peace, with his dead family at last avenged and his unit safe around him.

"But not the armor, Randal—you keep it. If we ever pair again, you'll need it."

The smile on Randal's face grew even broader, so that it seemed his jaw might crack.

As Niko buckled on the sword with its scabbard of raised demons and its thunderbolts, Bashir nodded approvingly, then said, "Don't look now, but here comes Theron with fresh troops, a clutch of priests, and too innocent an expression. We'd all better get our stories straight—no one expected this much carnage."

"Hrmph," Strat said to the war party generally as Bashir strode forth to greet his fellow priests and the new Lion of Empire. "If Theron didn't expect this sort of thing, he doesn't know the Riddler."

"That may be, but one thing's sure," Crit said, fingering his cynical smile. "The sooner we get the Stepsons and the 3rd together and ride out of here, the better. What say, Sync. Time to form the units up?"

"Time," Sync agreed, and then Niko and the rest were busy following their orders.

Sauni was left with the Riddler, watching Bashir and Theron greet each other like equals.

"Isn't it wonderful?" Sauni sighed. "We'll even have an embassy in Ranke, if things keep up like this. And temples of Enlil."

"Wonderful," Tempus said, as he went to join the man he'd put on Ranke's throne and the warlord of Free Nisibis to make sure that Sauni was right, and things would be as wonderful as now they seemed.

* 9 *

It wasn't as easy to get out of Ranke as Tempus had hoped it might be: affidavits had to be sworn, stories told that agreed in every particular, respects had to be paid to Abakithis's corpse.

But with Bashir and Sauni, priest and priestess of Enlil, Vashanka's brother god, affirming the tale that the witch and the dream lord went to war and Abakithis simply got caught in the middle and perished because his priests weren't holy enough to have protected him or foretold the dire event, it wasn't as difficult as it might have been.

Heads rolled among the Rankan hierarchy, true, but those heads were overdue for rolling, and most of the worst of Abakithis's incompetent brood had died in the combat or fried in the tent.

Theron was as good as his word, and by the time the Band, the 3rd, and Bashir's Successors rode north together, Tempus's two units were special forces in good standing with the Rankan empire once again.

And Bashir was the recognized ruler of Free Nisibis, a man who was welcome at Theron's court and who would soon have a flag of his own and embassies throughout the land. Even a modest trade in pulcis and a transshipping agreement had been worked out between the two monarchs which would enrich both.

The only shadow over all this good fortune, if there was one, was that Free Nisibis and Ranke were sworn to fight each other's battles, which meant fighting Mygdonia this summer, like as not.

But Bashir's men had been fighters so long that a summer of planting crops and listening to women chatter wasn't what any of them did best, so Bashir said that first night they encamped along the general's route, when the fires blazed and men relaxed with drink and drug and tales of individual heroics.

"You're welcome to defect to Free Nisibis, anytime, Riddler, and bring your Stepsons and your Commando with you," Bashir offered magnanimously. "As a matter of fact, since you're landholders of my country, then dual citizenship is surely yours—I'll just have to write a law decreeing it." Bashir stretched out in the firelight and crossed his legs.

"My thanks, Bashir. It's good to have a place to call home that isn't Ranke. But I think I'll rather miss the days when you'd put on your wolf-skin and slink through the night, howling."

"He'll howl again," Niko put in as he came back from escorting Sauni to bed: this kind of talk wasn't for women, except for Kama, who the Stepsons and the 3rd didn't think of as a woman—except for Crit, and perhaps the 3rd's colonel, Sync.

"As will we all," Tempus agreed. "Nothing lasts forever, especially peace and empires." Not when Roxane was abroad in the land with her Nisibisi power globe, Tempus thought but did not say.

Just then Tempus's daughter appeared, flushed in the torchlight, and since neither Crit nor Sync was present, Bashir wagered with Niko under his breath as to which had put the color in her cheeks.

"Tempus," Kama said, "there's a boy out at the perimeter, one we caught sneaking into camp. He says he knows you and he's got an urgent message."

"Does this boy have a name?" Tempus asked, suspicious.

"He wouldn't give it without persuasion, and the sentry thought he'd better ask before starting any of that. He said only that he's from Sanctuary and that the message is, too."

Strat groaned elaborately and got up on his knees. "Oh, please, Commander, please—anything but that! Don't send your poor fighters back to the empire's anus! I'll muck stables, take a wife—anything but that!"

Niko grinned his quick canny grin and teased: "But what about the vampire woman, your one true love, Strat? She's waiting for you down by the White Foal River, I'll bet, in one of Sanctuary's more commodious slums. She's surely never found another to replace you . . ."

"Sanctuary?" Sync quipped. "What's to be afraid of, Strat? Except your reputation—the Stepsons still in Sanctuary are the laughingstock of empire."

That brought Strat up on his feet. "Sync, I've had about enough of your slurs upon our unit's good name. It's time we settled this, man to man, now that the 3rd can do without its leader if it has to, while you're recuperating."

"I didn't mean to offend. Where do you think that we got the idea you Stepsons were all pansies, impotent and vain? From the scuttlebutt, that's where, and what news has come up from Sanctuary, which, I admit, probably isn't true, the way Sanctuary can't possibly be as bad as everybody says."

"Let's hope you don't find out how bad it is," Strat glowered, mollified to some extent but not entirely.

Tempus eyed Niko. "Stay here and stop any trouble from these two before it occurs, Stealth. Kama, take me to this boy."

As Tempus walked with his daughter through the soft cool night of a newborn spring, he broke a lengthy silence:

"You did well in Ranke, daughter. Better than I'd hoped."
He hadn't meant to call her that; he didn't like to think of
her that way, or wonder who her mother was, or what she
thought to gain from following him around.

But the way she said, "Thank you . . . father," he
knew she was deeply pleased and deeply touched.

"Just don't call me that where the men can hear you,"
he warned. Then: "What do you plan to do? Stay on? Isn't
it time you had a husband? Crit is—"

"That's over. Oh, he'd probably marry me if you asked
him to, but I'm making my own way well enough. I want
to be taken at face value, that's all, given the chance you'd
give any manjack among your Stepsons. That's what everyone in the 3rd wants . . . not to be a second-class unit,
loved less than the Stepsons no matter how we try to earn
your respect."

"Is that it? What the 3rd wants?" He'd never thought of
it that way—never really thought about the 3rd, beyond
their history and their reputation as the hardest-fighting
commandos in the empire. "They'll have their chance,
then, and so will you."

"Is Niko going to marry that priestess . . . what's her
name?"

"Sauni? She's wed to the god, Kama. He'll sniff around
her until the child is born, then realize he's not responsible
for it or her, and go on to other girls. Stealth's a Stepson—"

"Right, I know," Kama said bitterly. "To the death
with honor, shoulder to shoulder, and no one gets closer to
a Stepson than his partner."

Since it was Crit she was talking about, not Niko,
Tempus let his silence answer.

And when at last they reached the perimeter station, a
designated rock where a sentry detained a boy, he was
glad to send Kama back to the campfire alone.

Then he said to Gayle, the sentry on duty, "I'll take
care of this, Gayle. Go about your business."

"You're sure, Commander? He's a porking nasty little porker."

"I'm sure I can handle him."

"Yes sir, Commander." And Gayle removed his blade's point from the throat of the youth he was holding against the rock.

In the dark, Tempus didn't recognize the boy until the youngster said, with just a trace of a Nisibisi accent, "Remember me, Tempus? I'm the one that brought your Nikodemos out to the Stepsons' barracks in Sanctuary with his dead partner that day I found them both in the middle of the road."

Then Tempus did remember, though he couldn't recall the slumhawk's name. The boy had been an agent of Niko's, under Crit's control, when Crit had been running covert operations in Sanctuary.

"I paid you for that service at the time. What do you want, boy?"

The moon was waning, but Tempus could see the dark lips twist. "I've got a message from . . . somebody . . . in Sanctuary. They didn't want to be named, figured you'd know who sent it. There's trouble there they need your help with—bad trouble, and that's the truth. The town's in the control of the fish-eyed invaders, the prince is in deep trouble. . . . and those Stepsons that you left there—" the youth cowered, expecting this news to bring a blow "—can't fight their way out of an outhouse."

When the blow didn't come and Tempus didn't answer, the youth, breathing hard, said, "They said you'd give me somethin' for my trouble, but I'd just like to walk out of here, no problem."

"Not so fast," said Tempus, hitching himself up on the flat rock, intrigued and a bit disquieted. "Tell me more."

He interrogated the youth for a while, then said, decided, "If you're going back that way, you can ride along with some men of mine who'll be leaving in the morning."

"Me? Ride with fighters?" The youth spat and said,

"Naw . . . I'll just handle my own troubles and not buy myself anybody else's." Then he seemed to change his mind. "Well, maybe just a little way . . ."

Tempus called Gayle's name and the Stepson's head popped up from cover not ten yards away. "You heard all that, Gayle. Get this fellow a bed and a mount."

"Yes sir, Commander. Come on, porker. Oh, Commander?"

"Yes, Gayle?"

"If you're sending a strike force down to Sanctuary, I'd like to volunteer—I've never been there. I might be useful. And the Stepsons who served there lord it over those of us who haven't."

"Done," Tempus said.

And Gayle, who'd joined the Stepsons in Tyse and was usually the most controlled of men, let out a whoop of pleasure that Tempus found, when he got back to his campfire, had carried all that way

"What's up, Commander?" Crit had come back from checking horse lines. "We heard somebody yell like the god had made him king of heaven."

"Crit, you're just the man I want to see."

Taking Critias aside, Tempus explained the mission and said, "But I can't spare you. You'll have to stay with the Nisibisi, with Niko and me, for a time, at least until I see if Niko is serious about going to Bandara—in which case, I'd like you to come with us to the islands."

"To *Bandara*? Where they teach what Niko knows? I'm honored that you'd— Oh, I see: Strat. And a commander for the strike force . . ." Crit bent down and picked up a stick, a sure sign that soon he'd start scratching a plan in the dirt, even if it was too dark to see it.

"All right, sir, let's see: Strat will be in charge of the mission, of the Stepsons, and we'll send Sync along to act as his rightman—ad hoc, of course. And Gayle, who wants to go." Crit stopped, looked up, peering at Tempus through the dark. "Oh, I know who I'd *like* to send there . . ."

"It's up to you. Anyone you want."

"Randal—they'll need magical assistance in Sanctuary. And—" Crit scratched his head, then said with a grin that flashed in the meager moonlight: "—and Kama, if it's agreeable to you."

When Tempus didn't answer, Crit rushed on. "It's nothing personal, not because of us: she's as good a covert actor as I've ever seen; Strat's used to working with that sort of help. And a woman can do things in Sanctuary that a man never could, especially among the fish-folk, who're ruled by women."

"You don't have to explain yourself to me. It's settled, then. Let's go tell them."

Tempus himself told Strat and Randal, leaving the rest for Crit.

Strat screwed up his face and glared at the wizard. "Well, witchy-ears, what say? Can we do without Niko and Critias, prove ourselves sufficient on our own? There's a chance for adventure here like you've never had, if you've the stomach for it."

"Only if you'll stop calling me 'witchy-ears.'" sniffed the mage.

"Good man, Randal," Tempus said. "Without you I wouldn't chance it—someone has to be there who can keep me informed of what's afoot. Don't hesitate to use the mageguild network or come home by cloud-conveyance: someone at Hidden Valley will always know where I am."

"Yes sir, Commander," Randal said, his chest puffed out, his shoulders straight. "I'd just like to say farewell to Niko—" The Hazard bit his lip.

"We've all got partners to wish life and glory, Randal," said Strat, putting a big hand on Randal's arm. "Come on, I'll walk you over—this sort of thing's never easy on a fighter."

Watching the little mage and the huge Stepson walk

back toward the campfire where Niko and Crit were waiting with the best of his officers, Tempus felt just a little bit wistful, but he had a right-side partner and obligations to the larger force. He couldn't just go flouncing off on a new adventure at the drop of a hat.

* 10 *

When the hell-wheeled chariot drove into camp, decked out like a marriage-wagon, three days before the mixed militia arrived in Tyse, Niko couldn't believe his eyes.

He'd said farewell to Randal with a mixture of melancholy and relief: if Randal proved himself in Sanctuary, perhaps he'd outgrow his hero-worship, which made Nikodemos uncomfortable. And Sanctuary was just the place to make the mage a man.

But he'd thought he'd seen the last of sorcery for a while when he'd seen Randal on his way. He'd even gotten misty-eyed as the slight, long-necked mageling rode off with Strat into the south.

Cime and Askelon were so bedecked in gleaming armor and the hell-forged chariot car shone so brightly that Niko, the first to see them riding across the hilly sward, didn't at once realize that they had others in the chariot with them.

The three-man chariot was a relatively new invention— men argued that what was gained by the extra man aboard was lost in maneuverability and speed.

Niko rubbed his eyes at the spectacle approaching, then called out for the Riddler without moving, mesmerized by the oncoming apparition from the land of dreams.

By the time Tempus had been found and a crowd of Stepsons had gathered, well back from the bloodthirsty Askelonian chariot team of mare and stallion, Niko was sure of the identity of the dream lord's extra passengers: one was the supernal sprite, Jihan, golden-eyed and femi-

nine in an overpowered way; the other was a boy, thirteen
or so, called Shamshi, whose father had been an archmage
and whose mother was a Mygdonian noblewoman.

Askelon raised a hand in greeting and beckoned.

Only then did Niko realize that Tempus was right beside
him. The Riddler said under his breath, "Well, go on,
Niko, it's you he wants to see."

"Me?" Niko glanced at Tempus, who looked positively
nonplussed. "I think it's you, with all respect, Commander."

Tempus sighed rattlingly, his eyes on Jihan, the Froth
Daughter. "We'll go together, then, rightman, and face
this as best we can."

For the first time, Niko wasn't convinced of the honor
of being Tempus's right-side partner.

But go they did, up to that chariot where Cime and
Askelon waited, leaning on its bracers, smiling like a pair
of cats who'd just upset a milk pail.

By then the Froth Daughter and the wizard's son had
scrambled out of the car and Shamshi was racing toward
Niko, calling out, "Niko! Niko! Wait till I tell where I've
been and all the adventures we've had!"

Skidding to a halt, the tow-headed boy hugged Niko like
a long-lost brother. "You've grown, pud," Niko said, not
taking his eyes from the dream lord who watched everything with satisfaction.

And Tempus, beside him, took the chariot horses by
their guide-rein, stroking the stallion's arched crest. "What
is it now, Ash?"

"What, indeed," Askelon said as, from the horses' far
side, Jihan approached the Riddler hesitantly. "We've
come to invite you to our wedding feast, and give gifts to
the only living relative of my new bride."

Niko, hushing the boy who was chattering on about how
glad he was to be back among the living and how Niko
had been the Stepson he'd missed most of all, saw Jihan
touch the Riddler's arm almost pleadingly and stand on
tiptoe to whisper in his ear.

Tempus said, "Cime, is this marriage agreeable to you?"

The Riddler's sister sat sideways on the chariot's rim. "Come now, brother, would I be here if it were not? And who would you recommend for me, if not the lord of dreams? Don't tell me you're not pleased to have your woman-toy back, or that this chariot," she slipped off its side, "isn't to your liking, or that a breeding pair of horses such as these doesn't warm even *your* wizened heart."

Niko heard Tempus whisper "Damn," and then saw Jihan's fingers twine with his: the Froth Daughter loved the Riddler still.

"And what about Jihan's father? What kind of trick is this?" Tempus growled.

Then Jihan spoke aloud. "My father has relented. He's given me leave to come back and be with you, poor lonely, sleepless man—eternally."

Niko thought he heard his left-side leader groan, but it might have been the chariot's axle or the very earth as Askelon dismounted his car and stepped upon it. Jihan was more than mortal, yet possessed of a child's soul. When she'd been among the Stepsons, the Riddler had gone to great lengths to avoid her.

And yet, to reject her might be to consign her once more to languish in the archipelago of dreams. Niko looked at Tempus, his hand on Shamshi's golden head: the boy hugging him tightly knew that his future was at stake, that if Tempus refused these "gifts" he might end up back in Askelon's immaterial domain.

"We could take Shamshi to Bandara, Commander. It's where he belongs. It would be no trouble . . ." Niko offered.

A glare from the Riddler hushed him as Askelon held out the chariot horses' reins.

All the men were gathered now, well back, muttering among themselves. These gifts the dream lord offered—a chariot of fiery magnificence, another pair of sables, a

mare and stud, which would make the breeding program at
Hidden Valley second to none—were rich indeed.

"All this, for doing me a favor and taking my sister off
my hands?" Tempus said so low that only those close by
heard him.

Askelon smirked sheepishly. "We'd hope to rid you of
Death's Queen, the Nisibisi witch. But—" Askelon spread
his hands "—some matters belong to fate and not even I
can change them. She's loose and in possession of the
power globe—although not Datan's. I told you, I come
bearing gifts. Randal's, which I will deliver through his
dreams, is Datan's globe. Roxane has her own—a matter,
you'll remember, over which Death's Queen and I had a
slight altercation. So, though Randal's is benign and a
counterweight, Nisibisi power globes are loose upon this
land. Surely your new god's told you what that means."

"So what? Things aren't any different than they've ever
been, that's all. And what do you expect from a god of
war—not peace, that's sure. I told him I wasn't interested
in chasing after Roxane. I'm telling you the same. Stay out
of things that aren't your business, Ash. I didn't want you
for an enemy; I don't want you for a friend."

"But you've got me for a brother-in-law, notwithstanding
what you want."

Cime had come up close and now she sidled in between
Jihan and Tempus, raised her hand to her brother's cheek,
and stroked it. "Don't be jealous, dear. It could never
have worked with us. Gods know, I tried. Just accept this
with what good grace you can muster. Forever is such a
very long time."

He shook his head and stepped back from her, his
chagrin and fury ill-controlled. "Fine. I'll take the horses,
the chariot—I'll even throw a wedding for you two, if
that's why you've come. But you'll both be on your best
behavior, not disturb *any*—" here he looked significantly
at Niko "—of my men or try to upset what balance
remains among us."

Jihan, huge eyes glowing red, tugged on his arm like a schoolgirl and in her husky voice said, "And the boy and I? Riddler, tell him we can stay. I shall make you happy; we'll spend a thousand sleepless nights seeking infinitely better pleasures than we've ever sought before . . ."

Then Tempus's shoulders slumped and he rubbed his brow. "Jihan . . ." He stopped, stroked the lead horse who was nuzzling his arm, then said, "This time, you'll have to comport yourself like either a woman or a Stepson, not like a spoiled immortal brat."

"I promise," she said passionately, beginning to raise her arms to heaven, about to swear in her father's name. And as she did, the sky began to boil and to darken and, behind, two dozen Stepsons hit the dirt.

Tempus grabbed her wrists and pinned them to her sides. "That's what I mean—no more of that. Life is complex enough without your all-powerful parent's intervention. Just promise, don't swear in the name of anything or anybody. All right?"

Jihan promised softly, her fierce eyes lovesick as a mare's.

Then Ash said, "Fine. It's settled, then."

Cime said, "Finally, brother, you're showing some faint glimmer of intelligence. Accepting the inevitable may make a man of you, yet."

Shamshi said, "Bandara? Really, Niko, you promise? Tell me all about it."

And the sable stallion raised his muzzle to heaven and trumpeted a victory clarion before he turned in his traces and bit his mare upon the neck.

* 11 *

Crit was glad to get home to Tyse, settle back into his Lanes safe haven, and take care of business as usual. He missed Strat, but his guess was that either the strike force would be home soon, or they'd all end up in Sanctuary by and by.

There was, however, one residual matter he felt honor-bound to expedite.

He invited the Riddler and Niko into town one night for dinner at Madame Bomba's to discuss it.

And there, in a back room the Madame reserved for guests who needed privacy, they ate duck and oranges and drank Machadi wine and smoked pulcis, now in good supply thanks to Niko's uncle in Caronne.

"We're in good financial shape," Crit said, though he was running out of small talk, "thanks mostly to Niko's uncle and the profit-sharing arrangement with Madame Bomba, but in part also to the stud at Hidden Valley." This was true—Crit had just finished going over the books; the Stepsons' pension fund had fattened while they were gone.

"But no thanks to Theron?" Word had come up from Ranke that certain priests, led by Brachis, still insisted that the death of Abakithis was the 3rd Commando's fault. Tempus continued: "Theron will do the best he can, both in the matter of hostile-fire pay, when he can safely send it up, retroactive to our arrival at the Festival, and in clearing the 3rd's good name."

"It's not the financial part which bothers me," Crit continued, watching Niko, who'd been very quiet and had hardly touched his wine. "It's a little matter of revenge. Niko, tell the Riddler whose name you heard mentioned when Abakithis's priests interrogated you in Ranke."

Niko tipped his chair back on its legs and gazed ruminatively at his plate. Then he said, "You know, Crit, I really don't remember. Painful things are quickly forgotten."

Tempus said, "Crit has a point, Niko. Don't hesitate on my account. We all know who Crit means."

"Then, for the record," Niko said, his chair coming down on all four legs with a thump, "I did hear Grillo's name. But Grillo's a good friend of yours, Riddler, and of Bashir's. I'm willing to let it go if you are . . ." He looked between the two. "And personally, I've lost my thirst for vengeance."

Before Tempus could agree with Niko, Crit said, "Well, I'm not willing to let it go. And it's not vengeance, it's security: ours. If he's whispering in Rankan ears, he's no friend of ours—or of Bashir's."

"What do you propose, Crit?" The Riddler's gaze was steady, clear.

Though everyone at Hidden Valley talked of his marathon nights with Jihan, Tempus seemed none the worse for wear. Perhaps she was what he needed, an immortal, indestructible sprite for a man somewhat more than human, but Crit had expected to see some sign of dissipation—dark circles around his eyes, hollow cheeks . . . something different. But the Riddler, as always, was unchanging, just the same.

"I'd like to give him," Crit suggested, "just exactly what Niko got from his Rankan cohorts."

Niko said, "I wouldn't wish that on any man."

But Tempus was almost smiling. "If you feel it necessary, Crit, go ahead. But, since we know he's whispering in the empire's ear, and that empire, right now, isn't our enemy, why don't we leave him where he is, so that we can make use of him later if we choose?"

And since this was exactly Critias's sort of solution, the one he'd have put forth himself if Niko hadn't suffered so because of Grillo, Crit agreed: a live double agent was more useful than a dead man, to Crit's way of thinking.

* 12 *

One night soon after, the night that spring's first breeze
blew over the Nisibisi border into Hidden Valley and down
along Peace River where Partha was in mourning for his
slain son, Grippa, Niko paid the bereaved man a call.

Partha's heavy features were drawn with grief; he was
sitting in his great hall, alone, bundled up in a bearskin
robe before a man-high fireplace.

"Hello, son, it's good to see you," Partha said. "Sit,
sit."

Niko sat, not in one of the carved chairs, but on the
raised hearth, facing Partha, with the fire at his back.
When the day had come to break the news to Grippa's
father, Bashir had done most of the talking, couching
everything in religious terms while Sauni and Niko had
supported Partha as he staggered from the blow.

None of what Bashir had said, Niko knew, had brought
this old man the right sort of comfort.

Not even the fact that his daughter was a priestess
elevated above all other priestesses, who would soon bear
the god's child, could do that.

So now Niko said softly, "I'd like to tell you about
Grippa—there are things you ought to know."

The old man squeezed his eyes shut, then, as if bracing
for a blow, said, "Go on."

"Grippa won both heats of his footrace with the best
times of any athlete from any nation."

"He did?" The old man smiled and let the bear rug fall
from one shoulder. "That's good. Good news. He was
always a fast little snipe. Too bad he never grew to
manhood . . ."

"But he did."

"He did?" Partha's voice was thick, armored, yet hopeful.

"He did. And all of my fellow Stepsons acknowledged
him as a young hero. I told you there were things you
don't know." Niko, seeing the pain in Partha's face, told
himself that this had to be done. Then he began twisting
the truth about a dead boy to save a living soul from
unnecessary grief. "Grippa became a Stepson, was accepted into the brotherhood as a rightman."

"Ah," Partha nodded again and the bear rug slipped
from his other shoulder. "That's very good. Good news
indeed."

"So much was Grippa beloved among the Stepsons that
when he died we held special games in his honor, a full
day of games, with wondrous prizes, and Tempus himself
presided over the rites."

Partha sat up straight, the bear rug falling away. He sat
forward. "That's true? The gods are good to an old man."
He leaned forward, and it might have been the firelight,
but Niko thought he saw the old fierce gleam return to
Partha's eyes.

"And why do you think we held a hero's funeral? Why
did I, myself, though I was sorely wounded at the time,
enter the javelin throwing, win it for Grippa's sake, then
break my prize-javelin and dedicate it to young Grippa's
pyre?"

"Why?" Partha's eyes were locked on Niko as if on his
immortal soul's salvation. "Why?" he demanded again in
vigorous, eager voice.

"Because Grippa died a true hero—fighting witchcraft.
Not just any witchcraft, but the Nisibisi witch, Roxane,
Death's Queen. He fought her bravely, he fought her to
the death and with full understanding."

"My son, my son," Partha murmured, healthy tears
streaking down his face: tears of pride, not tears of anguish.

"And there's more," Niko said. He didn't like this sort
of duty, didn't like to draw things out or twist the truth,
but men who take lives must also save them: Sauni was
sure her father was going to grieve himself to death. And

Partha, who'd given Niko shelter when it seemed everyone was against him, deserved better.

"More? There's more?" Partha put his elbows on his knees and his chin in his fists. "My boy—my *man*—son, the hero—did *more* than that?"

"More. That's why we praised him so extensively when he went up to heaven. Grippa gave his life for me— protecting me from the witch when I was wounded and weak in my sickbed. He sat outside my door and when the witch came for me, he tried to drive her off."

Partha jumped to his feet, thrust his fist high in the air, and gave a whoop that shook the rafters. "Grippa, wher-ever you are, I love you!" Then, to Niko, he said in his old, commanding way, "Well, boy, get up. What are you sitting there for like a whipped pup? This is no time for mourning, but a time for joy! We've a celebration to arrange, a commemorative day for my son, Grippa the Witchfighter, the hero!"

Niko had to bite his lip to keep from smiling as Partha dragged him by the arm through his halls, waking servants from their lethargy to arrange for "Grippa's Day."

He hoped the witch would forgive him for misrepresenting the facts to Partha, but compassion was something he alone knew that Roxane understood.

That night, in Niko's dreams, she came to him from beyond the veil—not to lie with him or ensorcel him, but to smile on him and touch his face and tell him, "Niko, I will always love you, but I will not haunt you. When you're ready, come to me in Sanctuary and we'll have a reunion which will offend neither god nor man."

And there was something in the witch, some sense of poignancy, sacrifice—of a pure and nearly human sort— which made Niko know that he had nothing to fear from her, now or ever.

He woke up smiling, glad that she was safe.

* **13** *

Tempus had to make an appearance at the Grippa's Day fete, the first of what was to be an annual event.

And as he escorted Jihan, in her tri-colored scale armor, onto Partha's grounds, he heard a rumbling in his head and told her, "Go find Niko and young Shamshi. Keep an eye on the boy, keep him out of witch—out of mischief."

She kissed him passionately, saying, "Yes, of course. But don't worry: Shamshi's had his fill of mages after his time with Askelon. He wants to be a secular adept, like Niko, not a wizard like his father."

And off she went, her high rump gleaming in the sunlight. He didn't really mind having the Froth Daughter around, except when she wrestled him to a draw or took it in her head to rape him, which wasn't often. She was on her best behavior, trying to act like a woman, aware that she was a Stepson—or Stepdaughter—on probation, as far as he was concerned.

Tempus was still watching her when Niko emerged from a crowd of soldiers, in full dress helmet and long mantle, to greet her, with Shamshi beside him and the sorrel mare's foal on a tether. The foal was to be the Stepsons' gift to Partha for fathering such a hero as Niko had made Grippa out to be.

It was all coming out very nicely, or at least as well as Tempus had expected, he told himself as he climbed a hillock and sat down there, waiting for the god to speak.

Overhead, the clouds were fluffy, white horseshapes drawing chariots across an endless field of sky. Spring was upon the high peaks, and they gleamed in the distance, proud and snow-capped as if they knew that they were free.

Soon enough he'd venture west, with Niko and the

Mygdonian-born Shamshi, to make the boy an apprentice in the islands where the elder gods still held sway and men studied the old ways and older mysteries.

Tempus had taken Abarsis there, when the Slaughter Priest was just a child. Perhaps if someone had consigned the Riddler to the secular adepts, when he was young and foolish, things would have turned out better—he might have a purer sort of soul, not be the avatar of chaos he'd become.

Niko was sure that the masters of Bandara could help Shamshi overcome his blood and become an initiate of spiritual significance: Niko had the right to demand that they accept the child, despite his wizard's blood. Tempus was sure only that it was worth a try. Shamshi didn't want to go back to Mygdonia and he couldn't stay with the Stepsons, not until he'd been purified from the taint of magic and become a man.

Sitting on a carpet of old dead grass and new green grass, Tempus ran his hands through it, thinking about nature's habit of cycling struggle into rebirth. Springtime always made him feel reborn. Once, in another world and another life, when nature itself was young, he'd been a philosopher and then he'd said: This world order, the same for all, neither god nor men have made, but it always was and is and shall be an everliving fire, with measures of it kindling, and measures going out.

Some day he'd like to slip his bonds and slide back across that border in eternities over which a god had long ago thrust him, back to that world and those simpler men, and see what alterations time's everliving fire had made.

But for now he was content with the upcoming trip to Bandara and even with the news coming back from Sanctuary, though he might ride down to the empire's anus and see for himself, if the war with Mygdonia didn't demand his personal supervision.

He lay back on the hilltop and stared at the clouds, at one cloud in particular which looked like a mighty warrior

in a chariot even more splendid than the one Askelon had
given him on Cime's wedding day, a cloud-chariot drawn
by silver-gray horses whose manes stroked the heavens
and whose mighty hooves seemed about to strike the top of
Wizardwall's highest peaks.

He hadn't had much time for this sort of luxury lately,
for lying under the heavens and letting the magnificence of
the world renew his spirit.

The curse had darkened his sight for eons; now that he
was free of it, he knew that the loneliness and bitterness
with which he'd lived so long weren't necessary, but
optional: life is such a gift, and men so unheedful of it,
that too often they forget.

Remembering, now, he was sure that those thoughts he
thought and those deeds he'd done were right enough, in
the greater order of the universe, and that the legacy he'd
bequeathed his Stepsons was the rightest thing of all.

Life and everlasting glory was the potential of every
soul, if only each one held the thought and lived with
honor. The rest, as Niko said, was lend-lease, borrowed for
the moment, meaningless in the end.

So as he waited for Father Enlil to come and grumble in
his ear about Nisibisi power globes and wars to come and
blood to spill, he didn't mind: it was his lot.

He was content.

JANET MORRIS

BESTSELLING AUTHOR OF INTRIGUING FANTASY

THIEVES' WORLD NOVELS

__BEYOND SANCTUARY #1 0-441-05636-9 $3.50
__BEYOND THE VEIL #2   0-441-05512-5 $2.95
__BEYOND WIZARDWALL #3 0-441-05722-5 $2.95

THE KERRION EMPIRE TRILOGY

__DREAM DANCER 0-425-07688-1 $2.95
__CRUISER DREAMS 0-425-07983-X $2.95
__EARTH DREAMS   0-425-07985-6 $2.95

Available at your local bookstore or return this form to:

THE BERKLEY PUBLISHING GROUP
Berkley • Jove • Charter • Ace
THE BERKLEY PUBLISHING GROUP, Dept. B
390 Murray Hill Parkway, East Rutherford, NJ 07073

Please send me the titles checked above. I enclose _____. Include $1.00 for postage
and handling if one book is ordered; add 25¢ per book for two or more not to exceed
$1.75. CA, IL, NJ, NY, PA, and TN residents please add sales tax. Prices subject to change
without notice and may be higher in Canada. Do not send cash.

NAME_____

ADDRESS_____

CITY_____STATE/ZIP_____

(Allow six weeks for delivery.)

MURDER, MAYHEM, SKULDUGGERY...
AND A CAST OF CHARACTERS YOU'LL NEVER FORGET!

THIEVES' WORLD™

EDITED BY
ROBERT LYNN ASPRIN and LYNN ABBEY

· ·

FANTASTICAL ADVENTURES

One Thumb, the crooked bartender at the Vulgar Unicorn...
Enas Yorl, magician and shape changer...*Jubal*, ex-gladiator and
crime lord...*Lythande the Star-browed*, master swordsman
and would-be wizard...these are just a few of the players you will
meet in a mystical place called Sanctuary™. This is *Thieves' World*.
Enter with care.

__	80591-4 THIEVES' WORLD	**$3.50**
__	80590-6 TALES FROM THE VULGAR UNICORN	**$3.50**
__	80586-8 SHADOWS OF SANCTUARY	**$2.95**
__	78713-4 STORM SEASON	**$3.50**
__	80587-6 THE FACE OF CHAOS	**$2.95**
__	80596-0 WINGS OF OMEN	**$3.50**
__	14089-0 THE DEAD OF WINTER	**$2.95**
__	77581-0 SOUL OF THE CITY	**$2.95**
__	80598-1 BLOOD TIES	**$3.50**

Available at your local bookstore or return this form to:

ACE
THE BERKLEY PUBLISHING GROUP, Dept. B
390 Murray Hill Parkway, East Rutherford, NJ 07073

Please send me the titles checked above. I enclose _____. Include $1.00 for postage
and handling if one book is ordered; add 25¢ per book for two or more not to exceed
$1.75. CA, IL, NJ, NY, PA, and TN residents please add sales tax. Prices subject to change
without notice and may be higher in Canada. Do not send cash.

NAME _____

ADDRESS _____

CITY _____ STATE/ZIP _____

(Allow six weeks for delivery.)   **SF 2**